# FORGOTTEN
# GIRLS

# BOOKS BY D.K. HOOD

# D.K. HOOD
# FORGOTTEN
# GIRLS

bookouture

Published by Bookouture in 2024

An imprint of Storyfire Ltd.
Carmelite House
50 Victoria Embankment
London EC4Y 0DZ

www.bookouture.com

ISBN: 978-1-83525-729-6
eBook ISBN: 978-1-83525-728-9

*To Jake and Zack Smith. I'm so proud of you guys.*

# PROLOGUE

## THEN

Ginny Styles figured it couldn't get any worse—and then it did.

Sunday started off as normal, a boring hour not listening to the pastor in church, and instead watching dust motes dance in the sunlight pouring through the stained-glass windows. Her brother Dax sat beside her, tugging at her braids and undoing the ribbons just to annoy her. She pushed him away and then her mom glared at her to sit still. She couldn't wait to get home but the moment she stepped inside the house, her mom told her to change clothes and take Dax down to the river. He wanted to fish. It was always about Dax. She liked to read and he ran through the house playing soldier, shooting at everyone and rolling on the ground to crawl through the house on his belly.

The walk to the river was nice. Dax strolled beside her, fishing pole over one shoulder, looking at the three hooks and lures her dad had stuck into his hat, deciding which one to use. At eight years old, he could already shoot and fish well enough to feed himself. Dax was the favorite. An all-American boy, baseball crazy and big for his age, he excelled at everything he did. Her dad told her not to worry too much that she wasn't like him and that a pretty girl had an advantage.

They walked along the dusty trail, winding through the trees. The shadows formed leopard spots across the dry ground and the scent of wildflowers filled the air. She loved summer and couldn't wait to kick off her shoes and dip her toes into the cool flowing river. A rustle came close by and she gripped Dax's shoulder and looked all around for wildlife. A shadow moved and then blended into the trees. Under her palm, Dax shrugged her away and dashed for the river's edge. She kicked off her flip-flops and ran after him but lost him on the winding path. "Dax, stop. You know what Mom said about running away. Come back now or I'll tell her."

As usual, he didn't reply. She reached the river's edge. His fishing pole was lying on the bank, but Dax was nowhere to be seen. Panic gripped her, and turning a full circle, she searched the bushes, and seeing a movement run through the trees, she stopped dead at the sight of a man with his back to her. As she stared at him, he turned around slowly and smiled at her. She swallowed the fear. Not a stranger but a cop. She could trust cops. Couldn't she? Mom said if ever she needed help, she should call the cops. Taking a deep breath but keeping her distance, she lifted her chin and waved absently toward the forest. "Have you seen my brother?"

When the cop ran his gaze over her, the sudden need to run gripped her. Heart pounding, her legs refused to move as the cop came closer. "My brother? He's eight and ran away from me."

"What's your name?" The cop took her by the arm and his lips formed a thin line.

"Ginny Styles." She looked up at him. "My brother is Dax. Did you see him?"

"My partner has him. He's safe." The policeman looked down at her and his mouth turned down. "I was looking for you, Ginny. I have some bad news. Your parents are dead. Before your mom died, she said you'd gone into the forest. So we came looking for you. Come with me now. I'll keep you safe."

Shocked, Ginny burst into tears. She'd only seen them less than an hour ago. "What happened?"

"You don't need to worry about that now, but you're not safe. Come with me and I'll look after you." The policeman handed her a bunch of tissues but didn't release his hold on her arm. "Be a good girl now and don't make a fuss."

Indecision crossed her mind. The need to run away and search for Dax gripped her and she tried to step from his grasp. His hand tightened on her arm, and she couldn't escape him. This man was a stranger, and she shouldn't go with him, should she? She looked at his uniform. He had a badge on the sleeve of his blue shirt. A cop was safe, wasn't he? Reluctantly, she went with him, looking all around for Dax. "Where is my brother?"

"He's been taken somewhere safe. Hurry now, the men who killed your parents might be close by. My truck is just through there." He led the way to his vehicle and opened the back door.

Trembling, Ginny peered inside. It wasn't a police cruiser; it was a pickup. Terrified, she pulled hard against him. "I'm not going with you. This isn't a cop car."

"That's because we had to sneak into the forest after your mom called 911." He lifted her up and tossed her onto the back seat. "You need to keep down or the bad men might see you and come after us."

Shaking, Ginny looked at him. "Why would they want to kill me?"

"Because of your dad." The cop stared at her. "Would you rather I left you here? They'll kill you for sure. I heard them calling your name just before I found you."

Very afraid, Ginny brushed tears from her face. "No, I'll come with you." On the back seat was a pillow and blanket. "It's too hot for a blanket."

"We have a long way to go and you might get sleepy." He

took a juice box from the front seat and handed it to her. "Have a drink. It will be dark before we get there."

Frightened, Ginny gripped the juice box and stared at him uncomprehending. "Where are we going?"

"To your new home." The policeman smiled at her and cupped her chin. "I'm your new dad."

# ONE

## NOW – MONDAY

Special Agent Dax Styles swallowed the lump in his throat. He'd never imagined in his wildest dreams that his partner and expert in cybercrime, Special Agent Beth Katz, could have found his sister. He'd spent his entire life in law enforcement. Before joining the FBI, he'd attained a high rank in the military police and finding AWOL soldiers came with the territory. In his time with the bureau, he'd worked on a wide variety of criminal cases, and yet with all his experience, after hunting for his sister for ten years, he'd assumed she was dead and given up. The guilt never left him. He'd carried all his life the soul-destroying knowledge that the blame for her being kidnapped was his. If he hadn't run away and played the fool, she would be alive and well. Emotion overwhelmed him as he stared at Beth in disbelief. He blinked away unshed tears, unable to believe his ears. "You found Ginny?" He sprang to his feet and went to her desk. "Is she alive? Where is she?"

"Hold your horses, cowboy." Beth smiled at him. "I'm not one hundred percent sure but I figure I'm close."

The pain around Styles' heart tightened and then dissipated like a popped balloon. "Have you found a lead on her whereabouts or not, Beth? You're torturing me here."

"Yeah, I've found a lead but it's old." Beth searched his face. "I'm sorry to build up your hopes but let me explain." She indicated to the screen. "I used a few AI tricks to age the photograph you gave me and fed them through the facial-recognition program. I used driver's license images, newspapers, yearbooks, and other ambiguous publications just in case I got a hit. Well, I got more than one hit and they all come back with the same name, except one—and that's the image the newspaper ran when she went missing."

Deflated, Styles dropped down in a spare chair next to her and stared at her computer screen. "Okay, that's all I found as well. Everything led back to the old image. So what's new? Show me what you've got."

Styles had respect for Beth and valued her opinion. She'd joined the field office at Rattlesnake Creek under a cloud of uncertainty. She'd failed a psych test after the bloody murder of a kid killer she'd been following. The notorious and almost mystical Tarot Killer had gotten to the killer and cut his throat before he raped and murdered his last victim. Beth had come along moments later and tried to save the perp's life. Personally, he wouldn't have bothered but he tended to do things his way, most of the time. With Beth around he had to pull his head in and act as an example. He'd found her blunt, very professional, although unconventional in her approach to law enforcement. She went in boots and all, as if lacking any fear, to catch a criminal. In fact, she was much like him.

Although Beth was like a chameleon. She'd been working undercover for a time and excelled in disguises, was proficient in many occupations, including pole dancing, and had passed as a young prostitute at one time. Her slim build and blonde hair made her look much younger than her late twenties, and with the application of makeup, wigs, and contacts, she'd fooled him more than once. Yeah, Beth was an asset, but a slightly eccentric one. In fact, one day he admired her and other days she scared the heck out of him.

"Look at these images." Beth opened a file with images lined up to show the progression of age of a young girl to a woman in her late thirties. "These have a ninety-nine percent chance of being Ginny, but this woman's name is Rene Shoebridge. She lives out of Louan. It says here she is married to a security guard. That's about all I have apart from her high school and college records. Seems she stays at home, no jobs, zip." She opened another image. "This is all I could find on him, although it looks like he's wearing some type of disguise, unless men wear their hair like that in Louan. He looks way older than her and I discovered she has a child by the name of Billy."

Excitement and trepidation gripped Styles in equal measure. He stared at the images, zooming in to look closer. His heart raced. The woman could be Ginny. She looked like his mom. Emotion gripped him in an uncontrollable wave. He swallowed hard. Could this be true? Was this really Ginny? He noticed Beth's concerned stare and pinched the bridge of his nose to stay a headache and leaned back in the chair. "Ninety-nine percent chance of it being her? That's incredible." Beside him his dog, Bear, a Belgian Malinois, whined and rested his large head on his knee as if sensing his anxiety. "I gave up too soon. I should have kept on searching."

Concern gripped him. Maybe after all this time, Ginny didn't want to be found. He gave Beth a long look. "Why didn't she try and contact the family?" He gestured to the images. "She attended high school. It's plain she wasn't being held against her will."

"Hmm." Beth leaned back in her chair and clicked the top of a ballpoint pen on and off while eyeing him with annoyance. "You're not looking at this logically, and blaming yourself is crazy. Someone obviously abducted her. The case before I came here: A young girl had been groomed by a cleaner at the school to trust him. When he told her that her parents had been in a car wreck, she went with him willingly." She eyed him critically. "Do you recall anyone coming by often or anyone at school hanging around Ginny?"

Absently stroking Bear's ears, Styles allowed his mind to drift back twenty-five years. Not many people visited his home. His dad wasn't sociable, apart from chatting to the other fathers at the Little League baseball games. He didn't recall anyone hanging around or talking to Ginny at all. He shook his head. "Nope. I can't remember anyone at all. The cops asked me the same question at the time, and thinking back, I really don't believe Ginny would allow any man to get close to her. Mom was always warning her about men."

"It could have been an opportunistic abduction." Beth placed the pen on the table and met his gaze. "The perp was driving by and saw you walk into the woods. He decided to see if he could grab Ginny. Most would murder or rape them right away but when you ran away and left her alone, maybe he told her he'd seen you somewhere and offered to help look for you. She could have gone with him voluntarily. What you don't understand is these men have so many aces up their sleeves and kids are vulnerable. They know how to charm a kid and convince them to go with them. They've lost a puppy, they have candy in their vehicle, so many ways to make the kid go with them."

Shaking his head, Styles stared at her. She didn't know Ginny. "There is no way she went voluntarily. She knew about stranger danger."

"So where were you?" Beth wrapped one hand around her coffee cup and then brought it to her mouth for a sip and eyed him over the rim. "If she didn't go willingly, how come you didn't hear a scream? You didn't see anything either, did you?"

Standing and dashing a hand through his hair, he spun to

face her. "I was hiding. It was a joke and, no, I didn't see or hear anything. I was down alongside the river hiding in the rocks. The rush of the water would have covered any noise."

"So why are you blaming yourself constantly?" Beth raised both eyebrows. "You were a young kid, pranking your sister. That's normal behavior for an eight-year-old. You'd played at the same place many times previously and nothing bad happened. You believed it was a safe place to play and so did your parents, so why do you blame yourself for something that was out of your control?"

Styles recalled the beating his father had given him when he returned home without Ginny. His mother's accusations about being irresponsible and blaming him for her disappearance. The arguments that followed and his father leaving home and later taking his own life. He blamed himself for everything that had happened. It was his fault and he should not have left her alone. He lifted his gaze to Beth. "My parents blamed me. The following two years after her disappearance, my parents' marriage fell to bits. My father left home and later took an overdose of prescription drugs. My mom told me that it was my fault. If I hadn't left Ginny alone that day, we would all be happy."

"That is one heck of a burden to put on a small child." Beth's expression turned sympathetic. "It's just as well you haven't got psychopathic tendencies or maybe you would have ended up a serial killer." Her mouth curled up in the corners. "Take it from an expert, you were not to blame. When we find the man who took her, you can take out your frustrations on him and I'll watch." She snorted and held up one finger. "No, wait a moment. I'll definitely help."

This was typical Beth. Her wonderful dark sense of humor took some getting used to, but after a year working with her, he'd started to see her in a different light. Beth hated abusers with a passion, and he understood that every joke she made carried an underlying truth with it. If she found a pedophile, in truth, she'd like to mess them up real bad, but her badge prevented her from acting. Luckily, she'd be satisfied with bringing them to justice. He smiled at her. "Well, I guess we can hope that he comes at me and I have to defend myself."

"I have to admit that using a weapon is counterproductive if you want to get revenge." Beth picked up her pen and twirled it in her fingers. "A good old street fight is much more satisfying. Like you said, in a street brawl there are no rules." She chuckled. "We've been in a few of those and didn't kill anyone. I've come to the conclusion that no one takes any notice of an FBI badge around these parts. Every time we run into a group of angry men, it's game on. Do you figure it's the same out at Louan?"

Styles thought for a beat and then shrugged. "I'm not sure. Louan is a wealthy town. They mine sapphires, so there will be miners the same as here. One family seems to run the town. The law enforcement is the sheriff and his four sons. I heard lately that they had taken on a couple of extra deputies, so maybe they keep the miners under control."

"How do you want to do this? I have a current address and it's not far in the chopper." Beth spun in her chair to look at him. "The problem is, without DNA we don't have any proof this is Ginny and we can't really go by her house unannounced and start demanding answers."

Styles nodded. "Yeah, we can. It's a cold case and you have new evidence." He smiled. "I'll run it past the director to ensure my involvement in the case doesn't create a conflict of interest." He went to his desk to make the call.

After explaining the situation, the director wanted to speak to Beth as well, and Styles put his phone on speaker.

*"Have you looked into the background of Rene Shoebridge?"*

"Yeah, I can't find anything before high school." Beth brought up a screen of information on her computer. "The records at the high school state that she was homeschooled. Her maiden name is listed as Rene Blackstone. Everything looks legit. Whoever faked her documents is very good. This type of coverup would be expensive and not what I'd expect from a pedophile. He's gone the extra mile to keep her for himself, and it's very unusual for them not to tire of them once they get older."

The hairs on the back of Styles' neck stood to attention. "Blackstone was the name of the town we lived in when she disappeared."

"Okay, that's good enough for me. Notify the local sheriff that you are in the area and investigating a missing persons case. I don't believe that your involvement constitutes a conflict of interest in your sister's case. Her case is outside the statute of limitations. However, if this person is still abducting children, I would expect you and Agent Katz to bring them in. Good luck, Styles. I hope you find your sister."

Styles disconnected and smiled at Beth. "Pack a bag. I'm planning on staying until we get answers." He glanced at his watch. "Wheels up at eleven."

# TWO

Ice crunched under Beth's boots as she crossed the blacktop to Tommy Joe's Bar and Grill. It surprised her that she'd finally slipped into life in Rattlesnake Creek. The small mining town was totally different to her time in DC. A city girl at heart, she at first found it difficult to fit in with the laid-back local culture. Harder still to keep her dark side from emerging in front of Styles. Her need to remove unstoppable monsters permanently didn't come under the FBI's code of conduct. Constantly under Styles' supervision, she needed a place to escape his scrutiny and had purchased a cabin in the woods. As far as Styles was concerned, she spent her downtime painting pictures of the local landscape or visiting antique stores. In fact, she did do the latter as a cover to allow her to slip away in the guise of the Tarot Killer to hunt down predators who had slipped through the net of justice.

She'd grown to like Styles. He was as honest as the day was long, strong and dependable. In fact, he was a good friend and she hated deceiving him, but he'd never understand the psychopath lurking below her FBI agent persona. Heck, she didn't understand why she had the urge to kill monsters, but she figured her abusive time in foster care had fueled the fire. Her father was in prison for life. Known as Cutthroat Jack, he'd murdered her mother in front of her. The need to get vengeance had burned inside her for many years, like an out-of-control rabid dog, but since joining the FBI, she'd gained control of her urge to kill and diverted it toward violent criminals who had eluded the law. These people continued to rape, murder, kill, or enslave because of the protection around them. She'd seen many criminals set free because of friends in high places during her time in law enforcement. These elite unstoppables became her targets. It was never a case of taking the law into her own hands. She followed rules, and one was to witness the crime. If there was no legal way to stop the monsters, she'd stop them even if it meant becoming a victim.

Beth's research into the disappearance of Ginny had opened doors that she hadn't expected. Snippets of information had emerged on the dark web, leading her to suspect that Styles' sister was only the tip of the iceberg. Finding her and discovering a few scraps of evidence might lead them to a pedophile ring that encompassed the entire country. Many cases of missing children remained unsolved. In one of their recent cases, the perpetrator always abducted two girls. He'd murdered one and sold the second into slavery. Try as they may, the FBI had not been able to locate the second girls who went missing, although they knew their fate as one of them was found dumped in San Francisco Bay dressed as a sex worker.

In Black Rock Falls, a group of men had purchased young girls from foster parents as sex slaves. The resulting babies, it was assumed, they'd sold to an adoption agency, the name of which remained a mystery. The web of secrecy surrounding this group of people was unbreakable. They covered their tracks so well even the most proficient of cybercrime experts had not been able to discover their whereabouts. The key that would unlock the information that Beth needed to proceed was hidden in the memories of Ginny Styles.

Pulling her woolen cap over her ears against a blast of freezing wind, Beth considered the consequences of opening up a can of worms of this magnitude. Moving into a high-stakes world of darkness and danger would take careful planning. With so much money involved, and children used as a commodity, they would risk being murdered at every turn. It would be like negotiating a tripwire of crisscrossing laser beams, but if they destroyed the biggest pedophile ring in the country, it would be worth it. Now all she had to do was convince Styles it was the right thing to do.

She walked into Tommy Joe's and went to the counter. TJ gave her a warm smile and she returned it. She liked TJ, an ex-military man who'd retired and opened up a superb bar and grill in Rattlesnake Creek five years previously. He always had a smile, was a good listener and was prepared to help in a crisis, but right now she needed some takeout for their trip to Louan. She'd learned over the past year that men needed to eat all the time. She got by on little food but had found Styles became like a bear with a sore head if he missed meals. "We're heading out on a case. Can you make me a survival pack for Styles? I'm happy with an egg salad sandwich."

"You want a couple of flasks of coffee as well?" TJ made a few notes on a pad and looked up at her.

Beth nodded. "Yeah, that would be good. He'll need to eat and fly, so nothing complicated."

"Wez made some savory turnovers." TJ smiled. "He usually makes fruit ones but decided to experiment with a few different flavors. I'll toss them in. They're easy to eat. Leave it with me." He handed the note to Wez, the chef, and then turned back to her and poured a cup of coffee. "Do you mind if I ask for your opinion on something?"

Slipping onto a stool, Beth nodded. "Sure."

"Wez has a feel-good, cold-weather, savory warm-up menu at the moment." He wiggled his eyebrows at her. "He made quiche. Can you try it and tell me what the heck it is? I'm a barbecue and steak guy. This fancy food is foreign to me."

Laughing, Beth nodded. "Sure, but you know it's just fancy scrambled eggs in pastry?"

When TJ came out from the back carrying a plate as if it would explode, she inhaled. "That smells delicious." She took the fork he offered her and ate a mouthful. Her tastebuds salivated at the delicious creamy cheese and bacon flavor dancing across her tongue. She closed her eyes and moaned. "This is wonderful. You need to try it." She pushed the plate toward him.

"So it's for breakfast?" TJ picked up a fork and took a small piece. He placed it on his tongue and blinked. "That does taste good."

"Told you so." Wez came out of the kitchen with a paper sack in one hand and juggling two Thermoses. "The savory turnovers are good hot or cold. I've added your sandwiches and a mess of donuts. That should keep him going for a time."

Beth finished the quiche and smiled. "Thanks. Put it on our tab. We might be out of town for a couple of days, if Cash is looking for us."

"In this weather, the sheriff only comes out of his office if someone calls 911." TJ indicated toward the kitchen. "Unless we have a special on ribs, then Ryder is first at the door ordering dinner."

Beth collected the takeout and smiled. "I'll see you in a couple of days." She headed back out into the cold. *If we survive.*

# THREE

*Louan*

Beth loved traveling in the chopper and seeing all that Montana had to offer. The landscapes were diverse, from lowlands to mountains and vast areas of forests. She expected the towns to be all the same, but they were not, each having their own little peculiarities. Scattered across the state, old and new mining towns, industrial areas, cattle and horse ranches, and then the Native American reservations appeared to her. Most of all, she loved the forests, mountains, lakes, and rivers. The views from the air were spectacular. It gave her a peculiar jolt, as if she'd been thrown back in time, when she watched herds of bison moving across the open plains. The variety of wildlife was breathtaking and seeing eagles circling in wondrous freedom made her heart sing.

She understood that her appreciation of animals and nature was unusual for a psychopath. Of late, her friendships with Styles, TJ, Wez, Dr. Nate Mace, and Sheriff Cash Ryder had surprised her. She'd never been able to form a close relationship with anyone, and becoming part of a group of friends astonished her. It made her heart sink at the thought of them discovering that the Tarot Killer lurked inside her. If she could stop killing, she would in an instant, but there was no cure apart from incarceration. Being physically restrained from killing was the only thing that worked, but then a psychopath would be like a tripwire on a bomb. Give them the chance and they'd kill everyone in sight. Not many people understood that the need to kill grew like a festering wound. She would follow her rules, and if she died in the process, she died. The thought of being locked up and drugged for the rest of her life wasn't an option.

"We're coming into Louan now." Styles flicked her a glance. "The firehouse has a helipad, so we're looking for a red $X$ on top of a redbrick in town." He glanced at the instrument panel. "It's close by."

Beth searched all around and found it. "There on the left, about halfway down Main." She turned to him. "Do they know we're coming?"

"Yeah." Styles chuckled. "I called them earlier. I don't figure anyone would be happy to have the FBI land on their roof without notice."

The chopper dropped onto the helipad and Beth looked all around. "I hope the sheriff's office isn't too far. I called them to tell them we'd be dropping by and to ask where we could hire a truck. They're giving us one of their vehicles. We'll be staying at the local motel. It's on the outskirts of town and I'm afraid more of a truck stop. I'm not expecting anything nice, but it does have a greasy spoon right next door."

"As long as the beds are clean, it will be fine." Styles shut down the chopper and stretched. "Sheriff's office first and then we'll drop by the motel to check in." He finished his cup of coffee and pushed the cup back onto the top of the Thermos. "I'll grab our bags."

Beth hurried from the chopper and went to his side as Bear jumped down and ran around sniffing the ground. "The small bag has my laptop, spare phones, satellite sleeves, and spare weapons and ammo." She grasped it as Styles lowered the chopper to the ground. "I packed a first aid kit as well."

"We're going to see if Rene Shoebridge is my sister." Styles gave her a long look. "Do you have some reason to expect trouble?"

Rolling her eyes, Beth took her suitcase from him and pulled up the handle. "You're assuming that the man who is her husband is legitimate. At this time, we don't know if he is the man who abducted her in the first place."

"If he is, give me five minutes alone with him before we take him in. I'm owed that at least." Styles lips flattened.

Not believing Styles would risk his job for revenge, Beth touched his arm. Under her palm, Styles shook with emotion. "Hey, we don't know for sure it's her yet. I know you're angry—"

"Angry doesn't come close to how I feel about this man. He ruined Ginny's life and destroyed my family. He deserves to pay and I'll make sure he spends a long time in prison." He lifted down his suitcase. "I've been tossing around a few options. Not knowing is driving me insane. Maybe she got away from him years ago. I'm clinging to the hope a family took her in and she's been living a pretty normal life." He snorted. "I can't even imagine why she'd want to live with the man who abused her."

Concerned, Beth moved into his line of vision. "Look Styles, if she's with him willingly, it might not be her fault. Have you ever heard of Stockholm syndrome?"

"Yeah, I know. The thought she might actually care for him makes me sick to my stomach." Styles picked up the bag containing the laptop and weapons and placed it on top of his suitcase.

Beth glared at him. She couldn't allow him to beat up the guy. "You'll need to show compassion for her, not anger. We'll need to bring him in, not beat him to death, no matter how we feel."

"Really?" He started rolling it toward the door on the other side of the helipad. "Don't look at me like that, Beth. We can both read people, and if the situation isn't playing out right, we'll take it from there." He pulled open the door and waved her through. "I need to know if it's her. If it is and she's living with him, nothing is going to stop me taking down that pervert."

They took the small elevator and the doors opened up on the ground floor of the firehouse. The local fire chief was waiting for them outside the door. Beth smiled at him and held out her hand. "Special Agent Beth Katz and this is Special Agent Dax Styles. Thank you for allowing us to use your helipad."

"It's not often we get the FBI in town." The fire chief shook their hands and looked at Styles. "Are you chasing down a criminal?"

"Nope." Styles shook his head. "It's a missing persons case at the moment. Which way to the sheriff's department?"

"Twenty yards along Main on the left." The fire chief pointed out of the door. "It's a large redbrick. You can't miss it."

"Thanks." Styles headed out into the watery sunshine with Bear on his heels.

Nodding to the fire chief, Beth followed. Louan was a clean town and its variety of different stores surprising for a small town. Prosperity oozed from every brick. As she walked past the locals, she couldn't help noticing the way they were dressed. Most were wearing expensive winter gear and really good-quality boots. She slowed her step outside a shoe store and peered into the window. "Styles, wait one second. Look at the winter boots. We can't get anything like this in Rattlesnake

Creek." She gave him a determined look. "I need new boots and so do you."

"We're not shopping now." Styles stared at the sky as if seeking intervention. He lowered his gaze to her. "When we're through here, we'll stop by on the way home, okay?"

Shaking her head, Beth stared at him. "Okay, I've already picked out the ones I want."

"Let's go." Styles pulled down his hat to cover his eyes and continued along the sidewalk, his suitcases' wheels squeaking as he went. "I guess I could do with new boots too."

They wasted no time at the sheriff's office and, keys in hand, picked up their ride from the parking lot out back. The vehicle was a sheriff's department SUV and still had the new smell inside. Beth raised her eyebrows at Styles. "Wow, I wasn't expecting this. It's brand new." She asked the GPS for directions to the motel, and they were soon on their way.

The motel was larger than she'd expected and more for drivers and miners staying the weekend in town. The double bed in Beth's room was clean, but the carpet and furnishings were at least twenty years old. The room had a lingering odor of tobacco, and she flung open the door to air out the smell. She unpacked her bag but stared at the suitcase carrying her laptop and the weapons. The room would be easy to break into and she couldn't risk anyone stealing her laptop or the weapons. She heard a noise and spun around to see Styles leaning against the doorframe.

"Sorry to spook you." Styles frowned and glanced at the unopened suitcase. He wiggled the doorknob on her door and met her gaze. "This isn't the safest place in town. I figure we leave the valuables in the SUV and bring them inside when we get back."

Breathing out a long sigh, Beth nodded. "I was thinking the same thing. That door might as well be paper, it's so thin. I could push through the lock using my shoulder. I can't risk anyone taking my laptop. It's encrypted, but criminals are smart these days."

"Okay." Styles took the suitcase and propelled it outside to the vehicle. "Are you ready to go? I can't wait to see if this woman is Ginny."

# FOUR

The drive to the Shoebridge ranch house took about ten minutes. The home sat on a decent block of land. A chicken coop was at one end, and a garden bed dug over for planting sat ready beside a garden shed. Beth glanced at Styles. "You okay?"

"I'm a little apprehensive." Styles climbed from the vehicle and straightened. "If it is her, I have a ton of questions."

Dogs barked and Bear's hackles raised as he took a position in front of them. The front door flew open, and a woman stopped in the doorway gaping at them. They'd decided to wear their FBI jackets as visiting properties uninvited could be dangerous. Beth raised her voice over the dogs. "FBI, ma'am. Could you control your dogs, please? We need a word with you."

The woman yelled at the dogs, and they slunk off around the back of the house. Beth glanced at Styles. He was wearing his shades and had his hat pulled down over his eyes. He looked intimidating but Beth could feel his anxiety. "Thank you." She moved forward. "Rene Shoebridge?"

"Yes, that's me." The woman looked from one to the other, her expression startled. "Is there something wrong?"

"Is your husband at home?" Styles moved forward.

"No, his shift started at one." Rene's brow wrinkled. "What do you need to speak to me about?"

"Can we come inside?" Styles lifted his chin. "We need to talk to you and it's freezing out here."

"I want to see some ID." Rene looked at Beth. "Just because you're wearing an FBI jacket means nothing."

Surprised by her diligence, Beth pulled out her cred pack and held it up for her to see. "Agent Beth Katz, and this is my partner." She avoided mentioning Styles' name in case it spooked her.

Beside her, Styles flicked open his cred pack displaying the FBI badge. The woman nodded and stood to one side. "Not the dog. I don't allow dogs inside the house."

"Sure." Styles walked back to the SUV and opened the back door and waved Bear inside.

Stepping inside the home, Beth took in the polished floors, kids toys everywhere, and the face of a young boy peeking out from behind a door. "Is that your son? How old is he?"

"Yeah. He's four." Rene waved a hand at the boy. "Go upstairs and play in your room while I'm talking to these folk." She waited for the boy to slowly climb the steps and then led the way into a warm kitchen. She sat down at the table. "Take a seat and tell me what this is all about."

Inside the bright kitchen, Beth got a good look at Rene Shoebridge. She appeared to be the right age and had the same coloring as Styles, light brown wavy hair, and cornflower-blue eyes. She sat at the table, leaving Styles in the doorway. She looked at the woman. "It's a delicate subject. We've been hunting down missing persons using facial recognition and you came up as a match for a girl who went missing over twenty years ago by the name of Ginny Styles." Beth noticed a flicker of recognition in the woman's eyes and placed a photo of Ginny and Dax on the table and pushed it toward her. "Ginny was out fishing with her brother, Dax, when she went missing. We assume she was abducted by a person or persons unknown." She met the woman's startled expression and pushed on. "Ginny's family and her brother have been searching for her since she went missing. We need to put their minds at rest one way or another. Are you Ginny Styles?" Seeing her resistance to talk, she leaned forward. "You've seen our credentials. You can trust us. Nothing bad will happen. We just need to know what happened to Ginny."

Beth watched as indecision crossed the woman's face. She was fighting an internal battle. Beth tried another angle to break through the resistance. "I can tell you about Dax. I just happen to know him very well." Her gaze moved over the woman's face. "You're safe. We already got the bad men. Now it's time to set Ginny free. Are you Ginny Styles?"

"Okay, yes, my name was Ginny Styles, but I didn't go missing." Ginny took the picture in her trembling hands and stared at it. "A cop in the forest told me he'd come to get me because my parents were dead. He told me his partner had got Dax." A confused expression crossed her face. "How could my parents look for me? They were all dead. All my family, every last one murdered."

Beth nodded. "I understand there was some confusion at the time. So why did you change your name?"

"The cop told me bad men wanted us dead and they'd already killed Dax." Ginny frowned. "The cop took me a long way away and cared for me. He has ever since. If you tell anyone my name, more bad men will come and kill me and my son."

Surprised by her naivety Beth tread carefully. "Nothing can happen to you. We'll protect you and your son. You have my word." She took a chance and smiled at Ginny. "There's someone here I'd like you to meet."

Behind her Styles walked into the kitchen and removed his

sunglasses and hat. Beth inhaled, smelling furniture polish and cleaner. Apprehension gripped her stomach as she waited for him to speak.

"Ginny?" Styles looked at her. "It's me, Dax."

"Dax?" Rene stared at him, and her mouth hung open in disbelief. "It is you. You haven't changed a bit. I thought I'd never see you again. What happened to you?" Her gaze moved over him. "I can't believe it's you." She burst into tears.

"It's me." Styles sat down and took both her hands and stared into her eyes. "What we want to know is what happened to you. I went home, and Mom and Dad had search parties out for a week looking for you. I've been searching for you for years, and Beth found you this morning."

"Mom and Dad are alive?" Ginny dropped his hand to pull tissues from her pocket and wiped her nose.

"Dad died a year or so after you went missing, but Mom is still alive and living in the same place." Styles frowned. "Can you recall exactly what happened in the forest that day?"

"It was like I told Agent Katz. I searched for you and then I saw a cop." Ginny's mouth turned down. "He told me Mom and Dad had died and he would look after me. He said his partner had you safe, so I went with him. He wasn't a cop. Ethan is a security guard."

"Why didn't you run away and tell the cops what was happening to you?" Styles' gaze was intent on her face, but he still held her hand.

"I couldn't." Ginny dropped her eyes to the table. "Ethan kept me locked up for years because the bad men were after me too. He told me if they found us, they'd kill us both. He told me they'd killed you too."

"You went to school. We've seen the yearbook. That's how we found you." Styles examined her face frowning. "Why didn't you tell someone then what Ethan was doing to you?"

"Why? Everyone in my family was dead. I had nowhere

else to go, and Ethan told me he loved me. He didn't beat me. I don't understand what he did wrong. He was protecting me from the bad men." Ginny looked confused. "When I went to school, he told me we don't discuss our private lives with anyone, and if the cops found me, they'd take me to jail. He said the cops blamed me for Mom and Dad's deaths."

"So why marry the guy?" Styles wiped a hand down his face. "He took you to his bed, Ginny. That's not acceptable behavior and it's against the law. Can't you understand he's been abusing you for years."

"No, he protected me and cared for me. You're wrong about him. He loves me." Ginny met his gaze. "I love him, Dax. He'd never hurt me."

Beth gave Styles a side-eye to pull back with the interrogation. She smiled at Ginny. "He seems to be a caring man. So what happened after the forest? Did you move around or were you here the entire time?"

"We moved around all the time, but when I left high school he told me I would be safe if I agreed to move here and tell everyone we were married. We didn't have a wedding, but I didn't mind because that was when I had Billy." She mopped at her eyes. "When he came along, Ethan said we were a real family now. Billy was a sign we were meant to be together. You see, he wasn't my first baby."

Beth stood and went to the sink and filled a glass with water and handed it to Ginny. "How many babies did you have?"

"Five." Ginny's face paled. "They died but it wasn't my fault."

"No, it wasn't. You were very young. Did Ethan tell you what happened to the babies?" Styles gripped her hand. "You can tell me, Sis."

"Okay. When the pains started, a doctor came to the cabin where we lived." Tears streamed down Ginny's cheeks. "He took my babies away and told me they'd died, but I heard them crying." She sobbed into her tissue. "Ethan said I was too young to keep a baby. He said we could move to another town and I could go to school, but I got pregnant again. We left that town and moved back to the cabin and the same thing happened."

This was Stockholm syndrome, and Beth glanced at Styles' sheet-white face. His hands trembled with anger. She looked at Ginny. "Then what happened? Did you come back here after the baby was born?"

"Not here. The doctor said I needed a break from having babies and gave me pills. I finished high school, but Ethan didn't want me to get a job. He told me we could move here if I agreed to say we were married. That's when I became Rene Shoe-bridge. The doctor told Ethan we needed to look like a family to keep the bad men away. Ethan told me to stop taking the pills and we had Billy. This time the doctor told me Billy was healthy. Ethan was happy, and the doctor sent a woman to show me how to care for Billy. Her name was Rose and I didn't like her." Rene rubbed at her puffy red eyes. "She only came by the one time and then I didn't see her again."

Beth nodded. "So Rose was only there to give you advice on caring for Billy?"

"Yeah, how to feed him, change his diaper, bathe him. That sort of thing. She said she visits many first mothers who have home births." Ginny frowned. "The doctor insisted she drop by to make sure I could care for Billy. I cared for him just fine. I wasn't stupid."

"The doctor sounds like a nice man." Styles' voice dropped to just above a whisper. "What's his name? I'd like to meet him."

"Dr. Paul Benson." Ginny frowned. "He doesn't live in town. I think he's out at Blackwater."

Beth nodded. "What's he like? Is he young and handsome? I've always wanted a doctor like that."

"He's about fifty, fat and bald. He's nice to me, always gentle, and sometimes lets me call him Paul." She went to a drawer and pulled out a book. "I have his number. If Ethan is at work and anything happens, or someone comes by the house, I call him. He takes care of me and the others."

"I'm sure he does." Styles rubbed the bridge of his nose and looked away as if unable to meet her gaze.

Concerned, Beth had never spoken to a woman so completely oblivious to the outside world. She leaned forward and kept her voice low. "You mentioned others? Did Ethan bring home other girls?"

"Yes. Ethan likes to help kids in trouble. He's brought home girls since I turned sixteen." Ginny's eyes flashed with anger at Styles' sharp intake of breath. "He doesn't hurt them. He loves them and cares for them. They stay for maybe six months or so and then the doctor comes by and takes them away to their new homes. I don't get to speak to them. He keeps them in the root cellar in the barn out back. He leaves food for them and takes a hot meal to them when he comes home. I always cook them a nice supper."

"What time does he finish work?" Styles glanced at his watch.

"Around nine." Ginny met his gaze. "Will you come by and meet him?"

"I sure will." Styles nodded. "Where does he work?"

"The Broken Hill Mine." Ginny smiled. "It's an important job. He guards the gemstones."

"I bet he has a ton of friends there too." Styles flicked a knowing glance at Beth. He looked back at Ginny. "I need to go check on my dog. Can you give me a hand, Beth?"

Beth stood and laid a hand on Ginny's shoulder. "We'll be right back." She hurried after Styles and had to run to catch up to him. "Hey, slow down. Getting angry won't help."

"We need to get her and Billy out of here right now." Styles was heading out of earshot. "Who is the priest who runs the Her Broken Wings Foundation in Black Rock Falls?"

Beth pulled out her phone and scrolled through the contacts. "Father Derry." She turned to Styles. "I'm so sorry."

"It's Ginny, but I don't know this version of her. She was so responsible, and my mom drummed into her the right and wrong of things. She'd know better than to cover for this pedophile. She'll go to jail for standing by and allowing him to abuse kids. I can't believe she can't see that it's wrong." Styles shook his head. "I'll call the priest and make the arrangements. The local sheriff here will need to take them to the shelter, and we'll need him to take charge of the prisoners when we find them. As soon as the sheriff arrives, we'll locate Shoebridge and that darn doctor. He is in this up to his neck." Styles pulled out his phone.

Beth swallowed the bile creeping up her throat. "I'll go and see what I can discover about the other girls she mentioned." She hurried back inside.

"Is Dax staying for a while?" Ginny looked toward the door. "I'd like to assure him we're safe here with Ethan."

Beth nodded. "He is very concerned about you. What can you tell me about the other girls? How often did he bring them home?"

"One would go and another would arrive soon after." Ginny shrugged. "Ethan brought Ava here a couple of weeks ago. I saw her but she was asleep when he took her out to the barn. He's been spending all his time with her because she needs him." She looked at Beth and smiled. "Isn't he just the kindest person?"

Alarmed, Beth tried to keep calm. This woman was so far gone, saving her would take years of counseling. She'd attended high school and yet was so under Ethan's control she appeared to have no concept of right and wrong. "Where is Ava now?"

"In the root cellar." Ginny picked at her nails.

# FIVE

Scanning the barn, Beth was finding it hard to believe a woman who went to high school was so naive she didn't understand that the man she was living with was openly abusing kids. The only excuse was that, as she suspected, Ginny displayed the classic symptoms of Stockholm syndrome. The unusual psychological phenomenon became established in abuse victims. They would develop a positive bond with their abusers. As more lost kids had surfaced years since their abductions, the condition had become frighteningly prominent. She'd never witnessed the behavior firsthand and seeing it troubled her. For someone to have so much power over another person seemed unimaginable. She'd read reports about abused kids becoming attached and actually caring and protecting their abusers from law enforcement. This seemed the case here. Ginny had apparently been so brainwashed by the man who'd abducted her that not only had she agreed to tell people they were married but turned a blind eye to the abuse of other kids, believing it to be normal behavior.

She found the trapdoor to the root cellar and pulled it up, surprised to see how easily it opened. Steps led down into darkness, but even in the dim light, she made out a metal door at the bottom. Using the flashlight on her phone, she walked down the steps. The door was old, dark brown, and rusted. It reminded her of something she might see in a castle. It had bands across it attached by large bolts, and the lock on the door was way past her expertise to open and she could open just about anything. Scanning all around with the flashlight, her attention settled on a small metal object pushed between a gap in the bricks. She reached up and discovered a small metal box, half the length of her hand. Inside, she found two keys on a ring. The larger of the two keys slid into the lock and the deadbolt turned over with a click. The door opened to a small storage area, the shelves filled with various items and a closet set into the wall.

At the back of the room, Beth came to another door, slipped the key in the lock, and pushed it open. To her surprise, the door led to a brightly lit modern one-bedroom apartment. Warm air rushed out to greet her, with a quite pleasant floral fragrance. A TV played in one corner, and in front of it sitting on a sofa was a young girl of no more than twelve years old. The girl turned to look at her, eyes wide with fear. Trying to turn her astonished expression into a friendly one, Beth moved forward. "You must be Ava. My name is Beth."

The girl looked at her with distrust, stood and backed away. "I want my mom. I don't like it in here. I don't like that man."

Beth ran her gaze over her. Ava wore a dress and socks. She would freeze if she went out into the cold wind. "I'll find your mom, but first we need to get you out of here. I'm an FBI agent, a cop. You can trust me. Do you have any warm clothes?

"No." Ava chewed on her nails. "Ethan took them. He said he'd keep them safe." She stared at the open door, trembling. "I want to go home. I want my mom."

Beth nodded. "That's the plan, but you can't go out in the cold like that. I'll find your clothes. Wait there while I look in the closet." She backed out of the room into the small storage area and opened the closet. Inside she found a coat, jeans, and a sweater. On the floor sat a pair of boots. She collected the things and took them inside, leaving the door wide open. "Can you put these on? It's cold outside."

"Okay." Ava pulled on the sweater. "The man said the bad people are out there and they want to kill me."

Shaking her head, Beth handed her the pair of jeans. "Not any longer. My partner and I got rid of them. It's time for you to leave here now and come and meet some other kids. We have a safe place for you while we wait for your mom to come get you."

"Okay." Ava pushed her feet into boots and looked at her. "Can we go now?"

Glad she was cooperating, Beth nodded. "Yeah, we have a police cruiser outside. Is there anything here you need to bring with you? A toy perhaps?"

"I don't play with toys." Ava pulled on her coat. "I'm almost eleven and all grown up."

Trying to control the anger welling up inside, Beth took the girl's arm. "Okay, let's go."

When Beth got to the SUV, Styles was missing but Bear was still in his harness. She opened the door and waved Ava inside. "I won't be long."

As there were no door handles inside the back of the sheriff's SUV, Ava wouldn't be going anywhere. Beth scanned the area and, not seeing Styles, headed up the front stoop. The door was open and she could hear voices coming from inside. Hurrying into the kitchen, she stopped at the sight of Styles holding a little boy. Her gaze moved over to Ginny, wild-eyed and brandishing a carving knife. "Put the knife down, Ginny. Violence will only get you a jail cell for the night and I'm sure you don't want that."

"He wants to take my son away from me." Ginny poked at Styles with the knife.

"I don't. I want to take both of you to somewhere safe." Styles stepped back, keeping the boy well out of Ginny's reach.

"Look at you, Ginny, trying to hurt your son and your brother. Tell me that's an okay thing to do."

As Styles kept her talking, Beth moved slowly, step by step, behind Ginny, and then pounced. She closed one hand around Ginny's wrist and, pushing her off balance, slammed her onto the kitchen table. The knife spun from her hand and clattered onto the floor. The woman was stronger than Beth imagined, and it took effort to drag her hands behind her and cuff her. The scream from Billy almost burst her eardrums and she lifted her head to see the little boy's terrified expression. She gave Ginny a little shake. "Stop cursing. You're frightening Billy. Come along quietly." She held the woman's arm. "I'll pack a bag for you. Is there anything special you need for Billy?"

"Yeah, he has an elephant on his bed. He can't sleep without it." Ginny slumped against Beth. "I haven't done anything wrong." She burst into tears again and her son wailed.

"Once you've stopped being violent, we'll remove the cuffs." Styles bounced the boy on his hip. "Do you figure I enjoy seeing you so upset? I want what's best for you and that's getting you as far away from Ethan as possible. He's the bad man you need to be afraid of, Ginny. It's always been him."

"I don't believe you." Ginny sucked in a deep breath. "I'm not violent. I was just protecting my son. You say you're Dax, but what proof do I have?"

"Look, do you believe the FBI?" Styles pulled out his cred pack and showed it to her.

"Okay." Ginny indicated to her son. "What about Billy?"

"No one is going to take him away from you, Ginny. I won't allow it." Styles removed the cuffs. "You can't go attacking people with knives. If you do, I can't help you. Do you understand? All I want to do is make sure you and Billy are safe."

"By taking me away from my home and the man I love?" Ginny stared at him.

"It's only until we can speak to Ethan. If he's not involved in child trafficking, you're welcome to him." Styles shook his head. "Right now, if you care about Billy, then you need to listen to me and do as I say." He squeezed her arm. "Please, Ginny. Don't make this any harder than it is."

Seeing Styles' deep concern, Beth tugged at her arm. "Come along. I'll put you in the truck."

"I'll never forgive you for this, Dax, not ever." Ginny turned and glared at him. "Mom will take my side. You're dead to me, just like before."

# SIX

Styles' experience with kids was zip. He liked kids just fine but had no idea what to do with the crying child. He took him into the kitchen and sat him on a chair. "Hello, Billy. I'm your uncle, your mom's brother. My name is Dax. What's your favorite food? Can I get you something?"

"Cookies." Billy hiccupped and wiped his eyes on the back of his hand. "Why is Mommy angry?"

Pulling out a few wipes from a packet on the counter, Styles gently wiped his nephew's tear-streaked face. "You don't have to worry. She's not angry with you. It's my fault. When I was a little boy, I ran away from her in the forest and got lost. She couldn't find me. It was a long time ago."

Styles looked around the kitchen and found a jar of cookies, homecooked by the look of them." He held up the cookie jar. "These cookies?" He opened the jar and placed it in front of the boy.

"And milk." Billy took two handfuls of cookies and stuffed one in his mouth.

Breathing out a sigh of relief at seeing a small cup with the name BILLY on one side, Styles opened the refrigerator and poured a glass of milk. Whatever he was doing, it was working. His nephew was settling down and let out a sob only occasionally. Maybe kids took a while to run out of steam, like an old engine. "Nothing is happening to Mommy. We're taking you to a nice place for a few days, so you can play with other kids." He looked at the child, so much like his mother, and smiled. "I'm very happy to meet you at last, Billy."

The boy sipped milk and ate cookies but didn't make any further conversation. Styles heaved a sigh of relief when Beth came back into the kitchen. "Ah, what now?"

"I'll pack a bag for Ginny and Billy." Beth removed her gloves and pulled her long blonde hair back into a ponytail and secured it with a band from around her wrist. "The sheriff will be here soon. I guess then we go and hunt down Ethan Shoebridge and the doctor." She stood hands on hips looking at him. "Ava will need treatment. There's a good chance they'll place Billy into care. Ginny is naive and has no idea about what's happening here."

Styles looked at Billy devouring the cookies and shook his head. "I can't allow that to happen. You of all people know what can happen to kids in care."

"Not in Black Rock Falls." Beth met his gaze. "You know how diligent Sheriff Alton is about the system in her county. You can't possibly care for a four-year-old. We're never home and, going on the amount of cookies you've given him, you have no idea how to care for a child."

Styles shook his head. "Okay, fine. I figure Ginny was doing just fine raising him. I don't believe it will be an issue, but I'll step up if needs be." He stared at her. "Anyhow, we have other things to deal with right now."

Not wanting to discuss Billy any longer, Styles waved a hand toward the stairs. "You mentioned something about packing a bag?" He glanced at the boy and took the jar of cookies from him. "Do you want to watch some TV?"

"Yes." Billy ran into the family room and climbed on a chair.

Following close behind, Styles found a kids' channel and walked back to the passageway. "You asked permission to pack their bags, didn't you?"

"Yeah." Beth smiled at him. "It will give us the chance to look around, although I don't believe we'll have a problem getting a search warrant. We can't take anything incriminating but I'll photograph anything I see. Then we'll come back when we've got the paperwork."

Styles headed along the passageway and into the den. He found a man cave with a big-screen TV and games. In one cabinet a stack of DVDs in numerical order, none of them with more than a number on each one. Pornography was left out as if on display. A bar along one side, large comfortable leather sofas, and the smell of cigars tainted the air. The house looked modest but this room held expensive equipment. He pulled on examination gloves and opened a few drawers. Video equipment, cameras of the highest quality, and on a table beside the sofa, he found a laptop. He opened it but it was password protected. He shook his head. Beth could crack it, but right now he couldn't touch a darn thing. He pulled out his phone and took photographs of the room and everything he'd seen. Not for court but as a record to see if anything mysteriously went missing when they left the premises. With young girls coming and going on a regular basis, it didn't take too much imagination to realize Ethan Shoebridge was running a halfway house for the supply of minors to pedophiles. If they'd stumbled on the tip of the iceberg, just how deep did it go?

# SEVEN

After pulling on examination gloves and looking through the house, Beth located two large suitcases in a closet under the stairs. She went into the bedrooms and packed as many clothes for both of them as she could find. There weren't many clothes at all for Ginny and nothing new. She added all the toiletries from the bathroom and went through the cabinet and found a number of pill bottles. Having a wide knowledge of prescription drugs and herbs, Beth was able to distinguish the different medications. Ginny's behavior became clear when she read the labels. If Ginny had been highly medicated over a long period of time, it would explain why she didn't understand what was happening to the girls her husband brought home. From a young age, she would have been groomed to accept certain behavior. The drugs kept her under control and likely had been used for a number of years. She made a mental note to make sure that a full tox screen was completed on Ginny and Ava. There were many drugs on the market that could alter brain chemistry, and if used in an illegal way, an unscrupulous person could bend someone to their will. If this proved to be the case, it might save Ginny from a long jail sentence. She would need rehabilitation until all the drugs had left her body, plus therapy to ensure she could function in society and care for her son. Although, looking at the boy, he appeared to be healthy and well adjusted.

She went to the top of the stairs. "Styles."

"Yeah." Styles came out from the family room.

Beth dragged a suitcase from the bedroom and hauled it into the passageway. "Help me with the bags." She turned and went to retrieve Billy's. "I have just about everything they own. Billy doesn't have much, only the basics. Shoebridge didn't overindulge either of them."

"Hmm, from the man cave, I figure he spent all the money on himself." Styles glanced at his watch. "We'll need to get moving. The sheriff is waiting outside. He's leaving two deputies on duty here at all times until we can obtain a search warrant." He gave her a long look and concern shadowed his eyes. "He has a social worker with him from Her Broken Wings. I explained the situation to her. She appears to be competent. I believe she has their best interests at heart."

Beth ducked inside the bathroom. "Just a minute." She grabbed the evidence bag filled with drugs and smiled at him. "This is probably the reason your sister is so strange. She wouldn't know what day it was if she'd been taking these meds. We'll go to the local pharmacy and find out where we can locate Dr. Paul Benson."

"I handed Billy over to the care of the social worker." Styles met her gaze. "I didn't want to leave him with her, but she insisted he'd be kept with Ginny until they made an assessment. The child is in no danger from his mother as far as I could ascertain. When you explain to her about the drugs, they'll take that into consideration and take the necessary steps to help Ginny. I'll be notified of the outcome either way and made sure my name was down as next of kin."

Noticing the strain on Styles' face, Beth smiled at him. "I'm sure he'll be okay. He looks well looked after and is a normal little boy. The best-case scenario is to keep kids with their moms. Don't worry too much. They're in safe hands in Black Rock Falls. I've heard only good things about Her Broken Wings."

Beth went to pick up the suitcase, but Styles grabbed it as if it weighed nothing and headed downstairs. They went out the front door and she stopped and walked back inside, seeing a purse on a small table. She opened it and looked inside. It held a few bills, a phone, a few personal items, and a house key. She pocketed the house key, secured the front door, and followed Styles to the waiting cruisers. Ginny and Ava were already inside the sheriff's vehicle. Billy was in the other cruiser. "Styles, wait up. There's an elephant in the smaller bag. Give it to Billy. He'll need it with him for comfort."

"Good idea." Styles handed the larger suitcase to a deputy and bent to open the smaller one. He snagged the elephant and tucked it under one arm, zipped up the suitcase, and straightened. He handed the bag to the deputy. "This one belongs to Billy." He opened the back of the cruiser and handed Billy the toy. "I'll see you soon."

Beth went to the social worker and explained about the drugs and handed her the bag. "Will you make a note of the drugs and dosage before these are logged into evidence? You'll need to get medical assistance for Ginny ASAP. Coming off this concoction will need medical supervision and advice. She can't go cold turkey. These are powerful drugs."

"Yes, not a problem. I have a doctor standing by to examine all of them." The social worker smiled. "Please don't worry. Her Broken Wings deals with this kind of thing all the time. We have private funding, and the clients receive the very best care. You have my word they are in the safest of hands." She pulled a notebook from her purse and wrote down the names of the drugs. When she replaced the notebook, she handed Beth a card. "Any questions or updates, don't hesitate to call me. Agent Styles gave me his contact info, so we're good to go."

Beth remembered Ginny's purse and handed it to her. "Ginny's purse. It has a few personal things in it, no weapons."

"I'll see that she gets it." The woman headed toward the cruisers.

Beth liked the woman's efficiency, and she sure wasn't like any social worker she'd ever met before. Maybe Sheriff Alton out of Black Rock Falls was as good as everyone claimed. If she stood up for the abused men, women, and children, they were of like minds, but no doubt the sheriff stayed on her side of the law. She had no choice or excuse to take out the bad apples. Beth watched as the vehicles drove away. "Maybe that's why I'm here. I have a place in this madness. I'm here to clean up what she misses."

"What did you say?" Styles walked up to her, his boots crunching on the gravel driveway.

Beth shook her head. "Nothing, just talking to myself."

"They say that's the first sign of madness." Styles grinned at her. "But you going the extra mile to make sure Billy and Ginny were okay was a nice touch. I figured your compassion only stretched as far as animals."

Beth pulled open the door of the SUV. "I don't know, Styles. Twelve months or more working together and you still don't understand me, do you?"

"I just don't dig too deep." Styles slid behind the wheel. "I'm not sure what lies beneath your mysterious exterior. You're like a chameleon. I never know which Beth is coming to work each day."

Snorting, Beth clicked in her seatbelt. "Really? Do you figure I have multiple personalities? That's a serious disorder, you know?" She frowned at his serious expression. "Although I don't believe so because most with that disorder do know about the other personalities or the main one usually has missing time, when the others take over. I don't have either of those symptoms, so you'll just have to accept I'm a little eccentric."

"You can say that again." Styles added an address to the GPS. "I got the details of the mine where Shoebridge works. I can't wait to see his face when we drop by to see him."

Beth thought for a beat and then looked at him as they drove through town. "I'll write up a warrant request and email it to the local judge's office. I want to get inside Shoebridge's computer. He must have a list of contacts."

"Good idea." Styles headed out of town as the GPS issued instructions. "The doctor might be the key. Ginny said she heard her babies crying and he said they were stillborn. He's the middleman for sure. There is money all along the line. I wonder how many men like Shoebridge are dealing in kids."

Beth worked swiftly on her tablet. She could multitask with ease and glanced up at him. "There, that's sent. I kept it basic: Abducted child found in root cellar. We need to search the home for evidence of a suspected pedophile ring." She pushed her tablet back into her backpack and dropped it at her feet. "I'm wondering if Shoebridge has feelings for Ginny as he kept her. Usually when girls reach their best-by date, as in get too old, they move them on, but she mentioned he brought home girls since she was sixteen. He keeps them for about six months."

"That sounds like a baby farm to me." Styles gave her a sideways glance. "Do you figure we'll find out what happened to Ginny's kids?"

Considering his question was like a double-edged sword. "There are two outcomes. One would be the babies were adopted by loving parents. This is the best option. If this was happening, because desperate people will spend any amount of money to get a baby, then there will be a judge involved as well. Think about the chain of events: Shoebridge abducts the girls, gets them pregnant, hands them and the babies to the doctor.

The girl would be moved on to another predator; the baby handed to an adoption agency that deals with a crooked judge who signs the babies over to the adopting parents. It would look legit from the outside. Some of the parents would have no idea it was part of a pedophile ring."

"What's the second option?" Styles pulled onto a road with signs on either side.

Beth swallowed the bile in her throat. "Slavery, or worse. The options are endless. We can only hope the babies went to people desperate for a family and they are loved. When we break this ring, those children might be removed from their parents' care as they were illegal adoptions. It will be a mess if a judge, or more than one judge, is involved. Shoebridge is one man, and we know about a recent case in Black Rock Falls similar to this one but on a smaller scale. I would bet a dollar to a dime they belonged to the same outfit. Someone, a kingpin, is organizing these people and they have billions behind them. It is going to be a bumpy ride. Once they know we're hunting them down, all hell will break loose."

# EIGHT

Out at the Broken Hill Mine, Ethan Shoebridge's phone buzzed in his pocket. He frowned. No one called him at work. Not that his job entailed much physical work. He checked the miners as they left the mine to ensure they hadn't stolen any of the uncut gemstones. He didn't need to work. His involvement with the Company had made him a rich man. The security job was a coverup, a front to hide behind. In his business, every attempt to appear normal was imperative. No one would suspect a man with a wife and young kid of having his particularly lucrative and pleasurable pastime. He pulled out the phone. It was a burner. He'd never owned a regular phone that could be traced and every call recorded. It must be the Company, but they'd never given him two girls at the same time. "Yeah."

*"It's Rene. I know you said never to call you at work, but the FBI came to the house and I'm in the back of the sheriff's cruiser with Ava."*

Alarm bells sounded in Shoebridge's head and he started to move. "Don't tell them anything. Play dumb—you'll be good at that—and don't tell them about the doctor. Got it? If you do, they'll throw you in jail and you'll never see Billy again. I gotta go."

*"Ethan, wait. I did tell them about Dr. Benson. I'm sorry, I didn't know it was a secret."*

Panic welled up inside him. "That's okay, just don't tell them anything else." He disconnected and called Dr. Benson. As he waited to be put through, he went to the locker in his office, spun the combination lock, and pulled out his to-go bag. It had the items he needed to get away: emergency cash, a driver's license in a different name, and the keys to a storage locker close by that held everything he needed for a fresh start. He started for his truck with the phone pressed to his ear. "It's over. Head for the hills. The FBI showed at my house. I'm leaving now. I'll meet you at the next location."

*"Don't worry. We've done this before. You know what to do."* Benson sounded as calm as always.

Throwing open the door of his truck, Shoebridge climbed inside. "I know. I haven't called in yet. Get the heck out of town. They'll know your name by now, but Rene's not at the sheriff's office yet. She called me from the back of the cruiser. Rene spilled her guts about everything. I'll call in and give the Company my new number, they'll give it to you when you call. Dump your phone as usual. Catch you later." He disconnected and tossed the phone out of the window.

He took the backroad out of the mine that looped around and came out past the front entrance. He slowed at the security gates and used his remote to open them. Ahead was another short, wide road and he accelerated. The road came out right before the access ramp to the highway. It was a short drive to his storage locker from there and inside he had a well-maintained vehicle and cans of gas. Suitcases, packed and ready to go, would give him a whole new identity and a ton of cash to make him disappear. He'd swap vehicles, change clothes, and then call the Company. He arrived at the locker, made haste to fill the vehicle with gas, moved it outside, and replaced it with his truck. He changed clothes swiftly, pulled on a pair of worn Levi's, a warm winter jacket, and pushed on a Stetson, a pair of sunglasses, and his appearance was like a hundred or so men around town. He unwrapped a new burner phone and pressed in a memorized number. When the man answered, he explained his situation. He waited a few long minutes before the voice came back with the name of a town he'd never heard of. "Where?"

"It's a mining town by the name of Rainbow. There are miners' cottages all over. We'll have one ready for you by the time you arrive. Along the way, we'll find you another girl. I'll see if I can arrange a second one to cook and clean. One of our people died recently and had one really well trained. She won't try to run. I hear she's a rare beauty. Her last owner refused to sell her."

Relieved, Shoebridge chuckled. "Rare beauty, huh? As long as she can cook and clean, I'll take her. It would save raising another one and I'm fifty now. I'm not sure I could be bothered."

"I'll send her along. Your new identity will be set by the time you arrive. I'll start the backup files right away. I'll send the coordinates of the cabins. We have renovated a few in that area. Same as your last place, with a soundproof barn. It's nice and quiet in Rainbow and there are mines all over. I'll make sure you get a part-time job to make you look legit." The man at the other end of the line paused a beat. "This time, it's a fast turnover, three months max. I don't want you getting the urge to send another one to school. That's probably how they found Rene. I'll check with our cyber-specialists and see what the FBI discovered. We'll take out the agents involved if necessary. Right now, all they have is a drugged psychotic. Nothing she says will stand up in court, but Ava might be able to give them descriptions. Did you leave any photographs in the home?"

Carrying out the suitcases to the truck, Shoebridge dumped one in the back and then shook his head. "Nope. I kept it just as you recommended. No photographs of anyone. There are the master tapes of the videos I took of the girls in my den but no one can be identified by them."

*"Don't worry about them, we have copies here. It's a long drive to Rainbow. I would advise that you don't stop to eat until you buy gas. You know the drill. Use cash and we'll have a new card sent to you soon. You'd better be on your way. You'll need to be well away from Louan before they know you're missing."*

Shoebridge disconnected, pocketed the phone, and pulled down the door to the storage locker and locked it. Everything inside would be dealt with by the Company. That's why he allowed himself to be recruited by them. After a sexual assault charge when he turned nineteen, a man had approached him and offered to get him off the charges. He went on to tell him he could have all the girls he wanted and be paid a fortune. All he had to do was be the middleman. Alone in the world with jail time hanging over his head, he jumped at the chance and had been with the Company ever since. They paid well and protected him from the law. He loved his work. He figured he could describe himself as a girl whisperer. They came to him wild and spitting and left placid. Over the years he had gotten the concoction of drugs he gave them down to a fine art. He pushed the phone into his pocket, climbed into his new truck, and headed out of town. He wouldn't give the town, Rene, or Ava a second thought. Excitement tingled through him at the thought of a new girl and the housekeeper sounded nice too. His future was all planned out and he didn't have a care in the world. *I guess I was born lucky.*

# NINE

Icy patches on the road glistened as Styles drove toward the mine entrance. The security around the mine surprised him. In Rattlesnake Creek they had security, but nothing like this sapphire mine. Metal gates spanned the entrance and on one side a small building housed a security guard. He flicked a glance at Beth. "I wonder if we'll hit pay dirt twice in one day and that's where Shoebridge is working."

"I guess we're going to find out soon enough." Beth pulled her cred pack from her pocket and held it up as they approached the building.

A man in his late twenties strolled out to greet them. Styles pulled out his cred pack and held it up as he buzzed down the window. "We're looking for Ethan Shoebridge. Can you point us in the right direction?"

"Just a minute." The security guard turned away. "I'll call the office and see where he's at."

Styles drummed his fingers on the steering wheel as they waited. "I wonder why the hold-up."

"Beats me." Beth yawned. "I need coffee."

Hunger gnawed at Styles' belly and the thought of eating

made him salivate, but he wanted Shoebridge more. He planned to wring every ounce of information out of the pathetic excuse for a man and then go and find the doctor. "Yeah, me too."

The time ticked by and at least ten minutes later the man came out rubbing the back of his neck. "I couldn't locate him. He must be around here somewhere. He's not answering his radio."

"You'd have seen him if he left the premises, right?" Beth leaned toward the security guard.

"Yeah, usually." The security guard frowned. "Unless he took the backroad. I'm not sure if he has a remote for the back gate. It's for emergencies, like fires or a cave-in."

Exasperated, Styles let out a long sigh. "Where does he park his vehicle? I know you'll have a list of vehicles in your office. We need to know right away if he's left the mine."

"Okay." The security guard ducked back inside the office, emerging a few minutes later with a clipboard. He flipped through the pages and looked at Styles. "I figured I knew his truck by sight, but I was just checking to make sure of the license number." He read the details from his list. "The parking lot is straight ahead and to the right. The security guard parking is in the first row as you enter the parking lot. If he's not there, he's left the premises by the back gate." He turned and walked back into his office.

The huge iron gate ground open like a squeaky wheel that needed oil. Styles drove through and followed the road to the parking lot. He crawled the SUV along the line of parked vehicles, scanning the makes and the license plates as they went by. When they got to the end of the first parking bay, he drove from one end of the parking lot to the other, slowly scanning each of the vehicles. He looked on one side and Beth on the other, but the truck in question was nowhere to be seen. He turned to Beth. "He's not here. Somehow he's been warned we were coming. Don't tell me we have another crooked cop in this town."

"Oh, no. I believe this is my fault." Beth stared at him and one hand went to her mouth. "The purse I gave Ginny, it had a phone inside. I didn't think she'd call him, Styles. I'm sorry." She stared at him with round eyes. "I didn't think of her as a suspect as she is a victim. I gave her the purse as it contained personal items I thought she might need."

Wiping a hand down his face, Styles stared at her. Beth never made mistakes like this. He shook his head slowly, not knowing what to say. "Did you miss the part when she said she loved him? Of course she called him and warned him we were coming. Call the local sheriff and get an APB out on him and his truck." He sucked in a deep breath. "Although it's probably pointless. He'll be in the wind by now."

As Beth made the call, Styles scanned on his phone for the address of Dr. Benson out of Blackwater. He got the number and made the call. "This is FBI Agent Styles. I'm trying to locate Dr. Benson. Is he in today?"

"*I'm sorry, Agent Styles, Dr. Benson left due to a personal emergency about twenty minutes ago. He was heading out of town and said he won't be back for the rest of the week and to cancel his appointments.*"

Styles rolled his eyes. "Okay, thanks."

He used the mobile data terminal to run the doctor's name to discover what vehicle he was driving and the license plate. He found the information quickly and indicated to the screen. "While you have the sheriff on the line, give him this information. We want an APB out on Dr. Benson as well. Seems like the grapevine moves like lightning in these parts." He turned the SUV around and headed for town. "We might as well find a place to grab a bite to eat. By the time we're done, the judge should have issued a search warrant. If we can't catch the players in this tragedy, then I'm wasting no time going through the house. No doubt, Shoebridge's den is filled with evidence. Man, he had Ginny so confused she didn't even think to question him, did she?"

"From the concoction of drugs he was feeding her, I'm surprised she knew what day it was, Styles." Beth squeezed his arm. "Don't blame her for calling him. She did what she thought was best. For many years he's been the person who has cared for her. Brainwashed her, yes, but she didn't understand what was happening did she? She was ten years old, Styles. Ten. She lost her childhood. She witnessed what had happened to her repeatedly, and all the time Shoebridge told her he was helping the girls just like he did her. Now she believes what happened to her is normal."

Incredulous, Styles shook his head. "She went to high school and could have told her teacher. They have counselors there and she could have confided in one of them. Why didn't she? It makes no sense whatsoever."

"Going to high school didn't make any difference because the damage was already done." Beth's forehead creased into a deep frown. "I know how she felt. I went to high school and never told a soul that I was being abused. I was embarrassed but I knew it was wrong and ran away many times. I had street smarts, but she was a little girl who spent most of her time in shock, believing everyone she loved was dead. Pedophiles are so convincing, and at ten she didn't understand anything was wrong. He offered her comfort, at least at first. I understand why she never said a word when he told her not to tell anyone." She chewed on her bottom lip. "You know this has happened before to many kids. It's not the first time you've seen this, is it?"

Shaking his head, Styles looked at her and allowed the anger to slide away. "Nope. I've seen it many times. Abducted kids get attached to the monsters that took them. I just didn't believe it would happen to Ginny. My mother told her that men weren't allowed to touch her. She said it so often, like on a daily basis. It's as if she had a premonition this would happen." He pulled into a parking spot outside a diner and gave her a long look, searching her face. For once, he could see deep regret in her expression. Beth rarely showed emotion. In fact, he couldn't recall when he'd last seen her worried about anything apart from his dog. "It's not your fault. You showed compassion to a victim, is all. Let's go and eat, because once you get your hands on Shoebridge's laptop, we won't be leaving the motel until you're done."

# TEN

The diner was a little more upmarket than Beth had expected. Glass-topped tables surrounded by wooden chairs gave the small diner the feel of a more expensive restaurant. They waited for Styles to explain that Bear was a patrol dog and allowed inside before entering the dining area. Moments after they'd sat at a table, a server brought them a bottle of water and two glasses and then handed them menus. Beth perused the menu and then looked at her. "I'll have the chili followed by peach pie with ice cream—and keep the coffee coming."

"I'll have the same." Styles folded the menu and handed it back to the server. "The coffee is a priority. Can you bring it out now?"

Beth watched the woman walk back to the kitchen and looked at Styles. "That would be about the first time in my life that a server hasn't filled a cup of coffee in front of me the minute I sat down."

"The prices look normal enough, but the place looks classy for a diner in the middle of town." Styles removed his jacket and hung it on the back of the chair. "I hope the food is as good as the decor."

While they were waiting for their food to arrive, Beth pulled out the tablet from her backpack and placed it on the table. "I'll request a search warrant for the doctor's premises as well. I'm sure you'll want to go through his home, and I can't wait to see what he's got on his computer, although there may be a problem because of the confidentiality of his patients. I'll have to specify that I don't want to look at his patients' records, I just want to look at his private computer inside his home. I need to know if he's been using the dark web."

"From their fast getaway, I would imagine they're very well organized." Styles leaned forward, clasping his hands on the table. "This might be the breakthrough we've been searching for since San Francisco. If we can find a link between what's happening in this town and what was happening there, we'll get closer to the kingpin who is running this organization." He smiled at her. "I have faith in your skills at searching the dark web. If they've left any kind of trail behind, I'm sure you will find it."

Beth pressed send and the search warrant request was flying through cyberspace and on its way to the judge. Now all they had to do was wait. Since meeting Styles, the one thing she'd noticed about him was his confidence in any situation. He rarely drew his weapon, preferring to take down a perpetrator with his bare hands. She wondered if he realized just how much danger they would put themselves in by digging deep into this syndicate's pedophile ring. She gave him a long look as the server returned to pour the coffee and left a pot with the fixings on the table. "I have two ways of dealing with these people and we need to discuss the ramifications."

"How so?" Styles slowly added the fixings to his coffee and stirred.

Beth eyed him over the rim of the cup. "I can dig into their files and they'll never know I've been there. In that case we can try and find the players, but one mistake and the same thing will happen. They'll vanish without a trace. In my experience these criminal rings are so well organized, each player has a backdoor plan. One hint of suspicion and it's activated. They just move on with a new identity and set up in another county or state."

"I'm aware of the setup." Styles' mouth flattened into a thin line. "We might catch a few of them but the kingpin remains untouched. So what's your second choice?"

The next step made the hairs on the back of her neck rise in a warning, or was it excitement? She needed to get close to the kingpin and this time she needed Styles' help. "If you want to flush them out, I can leave a few telltale signs behind and they'll trace me back to the bureau. They'll have my IP address and know where I am at all times. It will be putting our necks on the line, but we might catch guys who work closer to the kingpin."

"I've been involved with these big syndicates before and they're extremely dangerous. They wouldn't think twice about taking us out just to destroy the evidence we might have collected." Styles examined her face. "We do have a few aces up our sleeve. They don't understand the way the FBI works and how we update our files on the server for the director to keep track of our progress." He placed his cup back onto the table as the server returned with their chili and crackers. "The second is they won't know we'll be expecting them."

Sucking in a deep breath, Beth took in his confident stance. He never avoided a fight, but this time he might be the underdog. She nodded. "You have a point and I'd agree with the second choice once I've checked them out and discovered just how deep and widespread this goes. Drawing them out will mean that we'll be able to arrest some of the lesser players, but we really need to get to the kingpin and destroy the empire."

"We might be heading into a war?" Styles cracked his knuckles and smiled at her. "I say bring it on."

# ELEVEN

*Bison Ridge, Montana*

Shiloh Weeks waved goodbye to her friends and turned the corner that led to her house. It was a short walk along the dirt road and one she did every day. Her mommy worked until five and left the key under a flowerpot beside the front door. Since her daddy died in the mine, Mommy had to work. She didn't mind. It wasn't long before she came home, and Shiloh liked the milk and snacks her mommy left for her in the refrigerator. She understood her mommy didn't have much time and she liked to help. She kept her room tidy and cleared the table after meals to help out. The bumpy dirt road had dried out after the snow but had deep ruts from her mommy's truck. Daddy used to smooth out the road, but Mommy didn't know how to use the big machinery in the barn. They'd have to wait until her Uncle Bob came by to fix it.

She picked her way along the uneven ground, jumping over the larger holes and singing. She liked to sing, and it kept her company as she walked home. She heard a noise and looked up to see a vehicle coming toward her from the direction of the house. Shiloh moved to the side of the road and stared at the truck. No one ever visited apart from her uncle. A shiver of fear went through her and she looked around for a place to hide. The wheatgrass on each side of the track grew tall and anything could be lurking in there. She swallowed hard as the truck slowed and a man in a blue shirt buzzed down his window and looked at her. Not knowing what to do, she stared at him.

"You Shiloh?" The man's expression was serious.

Shiloh nodded and, noticing the badge on the man's shirt sleeve, wondered what she'd done wrong. She'd never seen a real police officer before, but she'd seen one on TV. Around these parts the sheriff and his deputies were the same as a police officer, or so her mom had told her. She stood up straight and looked at him. "Have I done something wrong?"

The man climbed down from his truck and crouched in front of her. Shiloh took a step back and he closed one large hand around her arm.

"Not so fast, little lady." The man smiled and pulled a candy bar out of his pocket and handed it to her. "Your mom is in the hospital. She sent me to come and get you. I'll be looking after you for a few days. Get into my truck."

Shocked, Shiloh stared at the house and then back to him. She could trust a police officer. He wasn't like a regular stranger. "What happened to her?"

"She was in a car wreck and asked me to take care of you." The man straightened but kept his hand on her arm. "I can't take you to see her. She's in surgery."

Unable to think, Shiloh stumbled toward the truck. Being small for her age, she took time climbing up, and the police officer picked her up and tossed her into the seat. She scrambled across the console and into the passenger seat. "Was she hurt bad?"

"Bad enough." The police officer climbed back behind the wheel, leaned toward her to remove her backpack, and secured the seatbelt. He handed her an open bottle of soda. "You must be thirsty after your long walk." He drove along the bumpy road and within a few minutes they were heading along a highway.

Sipping the drink, Shiloh pushed down the need to cry. Only babies cried and she peered ahead at the endless strip of blacktop wondering where they were heading. The police officer drove really fast and the fields and forests alongside the highway became streaks of color. She looked at him. He'd put on sunglasses and turned up the tunes on the radio. "Where did they take Mommy and where are we going?"

"We're going to a place called Rainbow." He turned and smiled at her. "You'll have a room all to yourself and you don't have to go back to school." He laid a large hand on her knee and squeezed. "I figure you're all grown up now. I hear you help clean and keep your room as neat as a pin."

She moved away and his hand fell from her knee. "Did Mommy tell you?"

"Yeah, she said you might be small but you're very smart. She said to tell you to do everything I say." He rubbed the tip of his nose. "You'd better be a good girl like she said, or I'll have to put you into the system."

Frowning and feeling sleepy, Shiloh yawned. "What's that?"

"It's a bad place for naughty kids." The man glanced at her. "They beat them with long sticks and lock them in closets. You don't want that, do you, Shiloh?"

Horrified, she shook her head. "I'll be very good. I promise." Sleep tugged at her. She leaned against the truck door and closed her eyes. "When can I see Mommy?"

She didn't hear his reply.

# TWELVE

*Louan*

Styles disconnected the call and walked slowly back to Beth's motel room. He knocked on the door and pushed it open. Beth was sitting at the small table in the room staring at the screen of her laptop. He walked inside and closed the door behind him. "The call was from Sheriff Griffin."

"Trouble?" Beth spun around in her chair and looked at him.

He leaned against the wall and grimaced. "I'm not sure. Ginny didn't ask for a lawyer or anything, but one showed at the sheriff's office demanding to see her. The sheriff mentioned that he wasn't holding her as a suspect in anything. He said she was in the lunchroom drinking coffee when the lawyer arrived out of the blue."

"If she called Shoebridge, she could easily have called a lawyer as well. Did the sheriff think to check her phone?" Beth frowned. "Although I guess he wouldn't have got anywhere near to her once the lawyer arrived."

Styles pushed away from the wall and started pacing the

small motel room. "The thing is, Beth, the sheriff said that the lawyer was with her for at least thirty minutes and then he left without saying a word to the sheriff. When Griffin spoke to her, she refused to say anything at all. A short time after that, the bus with Father Derry and a Black Rock Falls deputy arrived and took the three of them to the Her Broken Wings safe house."

"Did the sheriff say anything else about the lawyer? Did he ask him any questions?" Beth twirled a pen in her fingers and leaned back in her chair, observing him with interest as he paced up and down.

Nodding, Styles stopped pacing and turned to face her. "Yeah, he asked about the search warrants that we'd requested. He insisted that the sheriff give him photocopies."

"Oh, they came through, then? When is the sheriff going to drop them by?" Beth stood and peered out of the window. "Don't worry, that's not an unusual request from a lawyer."

Mind reeling, Styles waited for her to turn back from the window. "No, it's not an unusual request but how did he know we'd requested search warrants in the first place? The only person we mentioned it to was the sheriff, as the warrants would be delivered to his office."

"I can see where you are heading with this." Beth turned away from the window and sat down at the table. "You figure the lawyer wanted to know who applied for the search warrants. Now he has our names. It wouldn't take too much brainpower to put two and two together and know we're staying in one of the motels or hotels in the immediate area. Hmm."

Styles sat on the edge of the bed and ran a hand down his face. "What do you mean, 'Hmm'? Come on, spill it."

"The lawyer must be part of all this. Did the sheriff get a name? It will be phony for sure." Beth waved a hand toward her laptop screen. "A doctor and now a lawyer. The latter no doubt wanted to know exactly what Ginny and Ava have told us. If she'd spilled her guts, there's a good chance they might try and take her out." She stared into space for a beat. "They know our names and approximately where we are staying. I would say they'll try and nip the information leak in the bud by taking us out as well, before we discover anything else about their organization." She shrugged. "Ginny and Ava could be in danger. They have information, but I doubt Shoebridge would have divulged very much to her. The organization would have strict rules to protect themselves against prosecution."

Unconcerned about Ginny and Ava, Styles leaned back on his hands. "The sheriff of Black Rock Falls was made aware of the situation, and Ginny and Ava are on their way to a safe house. I actually spoke to Sheriff Alton about the foundation the last time we met. They will be initially taken to the Her Broken Wings shelter and then they'll be whisked away to a safe house known only by a very few people in the sheriff's department. She informed me they had many houses in the area they use to protect the vulnerable. This means, of course, that I won't be able to see Ginny until the danger to her has passed." He sighed. "In the meantime, it's Sheriff Alton and her team that have taken over hunting down Ava's next of kin. She has a skilled forensic team at her disposal, as we well know, to get as much evidence from the victims as possible."

"How long ago did the search warrants arrive?" Beth chewed on the end of her pen. "We've been sitting here all afternoon waiting for them."

Styles indicated with his chin toward the door. "They should be on their way now. The sheriff said they'd just arrived at the office when the lawyer showed. It was as if he knew that they were there."

"Understand now why I'm so concerned, Styles?" Beth shook her head slowly. "Do you fully realize how deep and dangerous these pedophile rings can be? We'll never be able to discover who we can trust and who we can't. If the lawyer was tipped off by the judge or someone in his office, it will be difficult to prove." She wagged the pen at him. "I've been investigating pedophile rings for years, and you will be surprised at the different walks of life of the members. Some years ago we pulled down a ring that included judges, law enforcement, teachers, and preachers. It seems to me that no one can be excluded if we're making up a list of suspects. Right now, the only person you can trust in this town is me."

Styles gave her a long look and pushed down the need to roll his eyes. "Yeah, I know all about the members of pedophile rings, Beth, and I agree, no one can be trusted."

The sound of car tires on gravel outside the motel room had Styles jumping to his feet. He went to the door and pulled it open as a deputy stepped out of a cruiser. He relaxed and moved forward to take the paperwork from him. "Thanks, we'll get through the searches as quickly as possible, but we're going to need deputies to secure the scene for the next twenty-four hours at least. We can't get a forensic team out until first thing in the morning."

"That's fine, we can call out deputies from Blackwater if necessary." The deputy touched his hat and climbed back into the cruiser.

"Here, grab the forensics kit." Beth handed him a case and reached for her coat. "I figure we're going to need a ton of evidence bags." She bent to rub Bear on the head. "We'd better take him with us. I'd like an early warning system watching our backs. Like I said before, right now we can't trust anyone."

Styles nodded. "I'll go and grab my coat. What about backup?"

"We have two deputies guarding each place." Beth shook her head and raised both eyebrows at him. "It won't take me too long to gather computer hard drives and other incriminating evidence. The rest we'll leave to Dr. Wolfe and his team. I'm sure glad the Black Rock Falls medical examiner and his team are available to sweep Shoebridge's place for evidence. It will save us time to move on with the case. Wolfe, I figure we can trust."

Styles opened the back door of the SUV to allow Bear to jump inside. He gave the dog an affectionate pat and clipped in his harness. When he slid behind the wheel, he caught sight of a shadow moving through the trees opposite their rooms. He kept his gaze ahead. "Don't look now, but I figure we're being watched. Left at two o'clock."

"Got him." Beth moved around in her seat. "This is too open for a hit. There are people in the office and greasy spoon. If they plan to take us out, my bet is that they'll try tonight, when we have gathered all the evidence."

Styles backed out and swung the SUV around, scanning the trees. The person had blended into the lengthening shadows. He shrugged. "If they've sent one person to take us out, they sure are underestimating us."

"You can say that again." Beth chuckled. "I'm not too worried unless they come in guns blazing. After seeing what they did to your sister and Ava, I'm ready to work off some steam."

# THIRTEEN

They stopped by the greasy spoon beside the motel to collect four cups of coffee. When they arrived at Shoebridge's house, Beth took two to-go cups to the deputies on stakeout. As they buzzed down their windows, she gave them a bright smile. "Anything unusual happen while you've been on duty?"

"It's been as quiet as a mouse." The deputy sipped the coffee and sighed. "Thanks for bringing the coffee. It's been very cold today. I assume you've done your share of stakeouts?"

Beth nodded. "Too many to count." She gave them a wave and headed into the house.

In the kitchen she found Styles wearing examination gloves and spreading out the evidence bags across the kitchen table in piles of various sizes. Beth collected a pile of medium-sized bags and looked at him. "I figure we leave all the forensic stuff to Wolfe's team and rip this place apart looking for video or image files. Any evidence we find will give us an idea of the number of girls that Shoebridge abducted and sold. We might have a chance of tracing the girls now we know the doctor was involved, or at least their babies, if they were part of the scheme, and from what Ginny told you, I figure he didn't stop with Ginny."

"You've searched the dark web. What kind of money are we talking about when it comes to buying a child?" Styles removed his Stetson and dropped it on the table and pushed a hand through his light brown hair. "Thousands?"

Holding the evidence bags to her chest, Beth breathed in between her teeth. "It depends on the quality. From what I can ascertain, it can be hundreds of thousands. Not just little girls, they sell little boys as well, so if you figure they kept Billy because he was male, you'd be mistaken."

"I'm fully aware of pedophiles' preferences, Beth." Styles pushed his hands into the front pockets of his jeans and inclined his head to look at her. "If you want my opinion, I think Shoebridge kept Billy to appear like a normal family man to the neighbors and his workmates. I figure someone would have noticed that Ginny was pregnant at the time. I'm sure she went to the stores and he didn't keep her locked in the house all the time. Like you said, by the time she went to high school she was well and truly brainwashed. She had lost her identity and believed every word that came from that assclown's mouth." He straightened, slapped his hands together, and turned toward the passageway. "Let's get at it." He headed toward the den, switching on lights as he went. "That's strange." Styles ran the scanner over a desk. "No prints. The place has been wiped down. Hang on, I'll check the other rooms."

Beth pulled on gloves and headed after him. She pulled out her scanner. "I have one set of prints that must be Billy's." She stared at him. "He wiped the place down before he left or made Ginny do it."

The den had a distinct smell of cigar smoke and an ashtray sat beside the computer. A half-smoked stogie lay in a pile of gray ash. She wrinkled her nose. Wanting to push the ashtray to one side but thinking better of it, she took out her phone and captured an image. She lifted the ashtray, holding it away from her and looked at Styles. "Here, I photographed this. You can deal with it. I can't stand the smell of cigars."

"Me either, but that's perfect for a DNA sample. Why did he leave a cigar and wipe his prints?" Styles opened an evidence bag and Beth dropped the ashtray inside.

A prickle of uncertainty ran across Beth's neck, and she stared at the cigar. "Unless it's not his and he's directing us toward someone else?"

"It's possible." Styles raised both eyebrows. "Ingenious, if he's that smart. I'll make sure the ME Dr. Wolfe gets it. If he made a mistake and left it here, we'll have a chance of tracing Shoebridge with his DNA. Security guards are required to take drug tests. If he happens to take another position, anywhere in the next month or so, we can get a warrant to obtain all the samples collected and run them against the result from this to get a match."

Beth sat down at the computer desk and powered it up. "I hope it's his. I guess they could use Billy's DNA to confirm it?"

"He wouldn't be a reliable source." Styles frowned. "We have no idea how many men Ginny was exposed to over the time she lived with Shoebridge. From what we've discovered in the past and from the cases that I've dealt with in my time in the FBI, I know that pedophiles share."

Beth grimaced. "Point taken." She made a few keystrokes and smiled. "I'm in." Taking a thumb drive from her pocket, she pushed it into the USB port on the computer. "I'll download the hard drive files onto a thumb drive and place the computer into evidence." She smiled at him. "For an organization of this size, their encryption codes were weak. If this is the standard of protection they're using on their hardware, we'll be able to track them down with ease."

"I've found a pile of DVDs. Can you look at these and download the hard drive at the same time?" Styles handed her a stack of plain white DVDs with just a number written on them in pen.

Nodding, Beth took them. "This might be a general collection. These monsters usually have a private collection secreted away somewhere. It will be in a place he can come back to if he needs to leave in a hurry." She played the first DVD, and distaste crawled over her like a swarm of angry ants. "Okay, that's enough. They have people in the FBI who can cope with this, but I'm not one of them. I didn't notice any of the men visible, so whoever filmed them was taking precautions not to be seen on film. The fact he didn't take these with him proves my point."

"The numbers on each disk should correlate with a record somewhere. Can you search the hard drive and see if you can find it?" Styles went back to collecting the disks and placing them into evidence bags. "I figure these were like a sales catalog."

Beth's fingers flashed over the keyboard. "I'll search for any recent uploads and see if I can locate the server they are using. It's likely protected to the max." She bent her head and went to work.

She appreciated the fact that when she was working on the computer and delving into the dark web Styles remained silent. After about fifteen minutes had passed by as if in an instant, Beth looked at him and shook her head. "I found it, but I can't break into it. It's going to take a lot longer than we have time for tonight. Now, I have the contents of the hard drive I can work on it from my motel room."

"I believe I've collected every piece of evidence from this room." Styles turned a full circle. "I've checked for a safe but found nothing. There are no secret panels I can find, and I've looked all over. Where next? The bedroom?"

Beth often thought like a criminal. Putting herself in their position often yielded amazing results when hunting down a perpetrator. She shook her head. "That's too obvious. We'll go and look around outside because if he needed to sneak back here without anyone seeing him, he would have hidden his trophies in a location he could easily access."

"Okay." Styles smiled at her and brushed the tip of his nose with the back of his hand. "You think like them, don't you?"

Beth looked at him aghast. "Pedophiles? I sure hope not. If I did, I figure I'd eat a bullet."

"Criminals." Styles gave her an apologetic look. "It's as if you have the ability to see through their eyes sometimes. It's an investigating tool I've been trying to perfect over the last ten years or so, but it seems to come naturally to you and so fast. It's as if you don't even have to think about it."

Unsure if this was a compliment or not, Beth stood from the desk and pushed the thumb drive into her jacket pocket. She went about opening the computer and removing the hard drive. She handed it to Styles. "Keep an eye out for a laptop or tablet. It doesn't make sense that he only uses an office computer. If he was using photographic gear in the root cellar, where it seems most of these videos have been taken, he would have been viewing the footage on a laptop for sure."

"That would have been easy enough to take with him." Styles headed to the front door. "There's a chance he has all his trophies on there as well and we're looking for something that doesn't exist."

Beth shook her head as she followed him into the kitchen and they dumped the bagged evidence onto the table. "He wouldn't risk losing the data. He'd have a backup hidden somewhere close by for sure."

"If it's here, we'll find it." Styles pushed his hat on his head and headed for the door. He whistled to Bear, who was rolling in the last remnants of fall leaves, and turned to Beth. "We'll leave the root cellar to Wolfe and concentrate on anything that looks out of place."

Beth scanned the yard, taking note of anything easily accessible from the road. They walked back and forth, searching hollowed-out trees, and then she noticed a small pile of leaves. She kicked them to one side with her foot and stared at the maintenance hole cover. Made of cast iron, it had obviously been stolen from a town somewhere. She waved at Styles. "I believe I've found something."

"That looks interesting." Styles crouched down and took hold of the ring in the maintenance hole cover and pulled. It opened with a whine and bumped on the ground as he tossed it to one side. "What do we have here?"

It wasn't a set of steps leading away to the sewers but a plastic box. Inside they found a second plastic box. Thrilled to have found something, Beth waited impatiently for Styles to open the boxes. The second box, as she had suspected, carried a number of thumb drives. "I think we've just hit gold." She grinned at him. "Although I hate looking at what's on them, they might give us positive proof of who was involved." She opened an evidence bag for him to drop the thumb drives into and turned toward the SUV. "We can look at these on my laptop. If they're not what we're looking for, we'll have to continue the search."

"Time is getting away from us, Beth." Styles followed her to the SUV with Bear on his heels. "I want to get to the doctor's house today. If we clear his house, we can get back home first thing in the morning and start investigating the case using your equipment."

Beth gave him a long look. "I agree that finding these kids is a priority, but we can pass most of this onto another team that deals with child abuse. They will have the most up-to-date listings of missing kids. Giving them that part of the investigation will speed things up for us immensely. Our goal is to bring down the kingpin of this organization. Don't you agree?"

"Yeah." Styles gave her a sideways glance as he opened the

back door for Bear to jump inside. "So how would you suggest we proceed?"

Surprised that Styles had dropped back and literally given her the lead in the investigation, she nodded. "By the morning, most of the drugs will be out of Ginny's and Ava's systems. I would suggest we go and have another word with them. I know Ginny has lawyered up, but Ava is only being supported by the social worker at Her Broken Wings. What we need to do is convince Sheriff Alton to bring the girl from the safe house to the sheriff's office so we can speak to her." She slipped inside the SUV and reached for her laptop. "You know her. Can you give her a call and set something up for first thing in the morning? While you're doing that, I'll take a look at these thumb drives."

"That sounds like a plan." Styles smiled at her and pulled out his phone.

# FOURTEEN

Styles soon discovered that dealing with Sheriff Jenna Alton wasn't as easy as he had anticipated. She couldn't understand the reason to remove a girl in potential danger from a safe house just to be interviewed by them and refused absolutely to give them the details of her whereabouts. He glanced at the images on Beth's laptop screen, took in her blank ashen expression, and cleared his throat. "Beth is going to send you a small portion of the media files we found on Shoebridge's property. It's his private collection. It's sickening. Take a look and call me back if you change your mind." He disconnected and looked at Beth. "Can you send the sheriff a small excerpt of that footage. I believe it's self-explanatory."

"I've scanned the first three files and they're all the same." Beth ran a hand down her face and then looked at him. "It's times like this, I wish I weren't an FBI agent."

Horrified at what he'd seen on the screen, he nodded. "Agreed, but we need proof he's abducting kids and involved in selling babies and children into slavery. Likely he's involved in murder as well." He ran a hand down his face trying to block out the images stamped in his brain. "The people involved were careful to keep their faces off camera. These movies wouldn't be enough to convict the men we believe are involved. Ginny and Ava aren't talking. Making even abduction and deprivation of liberty charges stick will be a problem."

In truth, all they had on Shoebridge was possession and maybe distribution of child pornography. He had no absolute proof that Shoebridge abducted Ginny. He'd never seen the man, and Ginny was so twisted in her mind that whatever she said in court would go in Shoebridge's favor. He chewed on the inside of his cheek. He understood Beth's inner struggle to take down monsters like this and then trust the legal system to do the right thing. Agreed he'd see many such men walk in his time. He looked at her. "I know this stirs memories you'd rather forget, and I know deep down inside you want to do the right thing. What you feel now, I feel too. Trust me, if it were legal, I'd break both their necks in a heartbeat."

"You would?" Beth looked at him, her expression softening. "That's good to know. I figured it was just me who wanted to exterminate every last one of them."

Styles nodded. "Yeah, but not doing it and taking them in is the difference between us and a psychopath. We might want to kill them, but we don't act on it... Well, I admit, sometimes I let my disgust with the men who abuse kids sway my judgment, and my takedowns of them are never gentle if they resist arrest." He shrugged. "It's my way of getting even for the kids, but I never take it too far. I just let them know they're dealing with a man and not a helpless kid, is all."

"You could just shoot them if they make a break for it." Beth shrugged. "Many city cops wouldn't think twice about taking down men like Shoebridge and Benson with a bullet. It's only fools like us who run after them and bring them in alive." She looked away from him, her shoulders dropping in defeat. "This evidence will get them five years if we're lucky. It's not enough. If we catch them, they'll be out hurting kids in three years.

That's not acceptable." She turned slowly to look at him. "We must build a convincing case."

He started the engine, and after waving to the deputies, they headed along the driveway. "I agree. If you enter the doctor's address into the GPS, we'll go and search his house. Although, I believe we've stumbled on a team. This cache of thumb drives might be their entire private collection. You could be right about Billy's paternal father. I noticed he has brown eyes, unlike me and Ginny. Shoebridge, according to his driver's license, has blue eyes, and guess what? Benson has brown."

"That poor girl. She went through hell and yet she's sticking by him. It's hard to believe she figured Shoebridge was protecting her." She shuddered. "The doctor gives *monster* a whole new meaning. The man disgusts me. They both do, but he swore an oath to do no harm." Beth pushed both hands through her hair, removed the band around her ponytail, and slid it onto her wrist. She pulled a comb from her pocket and slowly combed her hair staring into space.

Styles glanced at her. "I can see the wheels turning in your mind. What are you thinking?"

"Trust me, you don't want to know." Beth put the comb away and retied her ponytail.

# FIFTEEN

*Blackwater*

After driving for forty minutes, they discovered Dr. Benson's residence. A rustic log cabin on the outskirts of Blackwater set on the edge of the forest and shielded from the road by a line of trees. Beth climbed out of the SUV and scanned the area, noting it was five miles from town without any neighbors to worry about. In fact, a perfect place to hide a child. She followed Styles to the front door and stood to one side as he picked the lock. The door opened and the stink of cigar smoke drifted out in a miasma of nasty. This man didn't just enjoy cigars, he bathed in the smoke. She looked at Styles and pulled a face mask from a pocket. "I think that stink is as disgusting as the smell of dead bodies." She pushed the face mask over her nose and then pulled on examination gloves before stepping inside the house.

They found a family room, a kitchen, and bathroom. Two bedrooms. One room was used as the main bedroom and the other smaller room held office equipment but had a cot in one corner. A closet held a few empty hangers. Beth walked into the office and stared at the desk. The room was unkept and dusty. On the desk in the dust she found the outline of a laptop. All the drawers in the desk hung open. "It looks to me like he made a fast getaway and took everything with him."

"Not so fast. It's the same as Shoebridge's house." Styles moved his scanner over the surfaces. "No prints. The place has been wiped down."

Dismayed Beth stared at the room. "Go and search the rest of the house." She checked the bed. It was too neat and the bedding smelled musty. No one had slept there for a time.

"Come and look in here." Styles' voice came from the other room.

Beth walked into the bedroom. The first thing she noticed was the unmade bed, the second was the clothes that Styles was holding up. "He had a kid here? I've checked him out and he had no children of his own. He's a doctor, which makes it so much worse."

"I found these on the bed." He tossed a pair of PJs to her. "Look at the size. How old do you figure? Twelve?"

Hands trembling, Beth examined the clothing, fingered the pink teddy bears, and nodded. "Yeah, or younger." She pushed the clothes into an evidence bag and sealed it and then took a pen and wrote on the outside. She looked at Styles and shook her head. "We have to catch this guy before he hurts anyone else."

"It's my top priority." Styles scanned the room. "They've left most of their things behind. I'd say they had a bag packed and ready to go." He looked at her. "I know this case is cutting deep, Beth, but stay focused. Right now, you're the only weapon we have to put these animals away and take down the entire organization."

Unsettled, Beth led the way out of the bedroom and stood in the hallway leaning against the wall. Memories of her time in foster care after her father murdered her mother came into her mind in a torrential rush. The years of sexual abuse she'd suffered had triggered her need to rid the world of monsters. She looked at Styles, trying to gain her composure. "I know. The problem is when I walk into a bedroom and see things like that, it brings back too many bad memories." She searched Styles' face. How could he ever understand what she went through in foster care? "I don't have flashbacks, so you don't have to worry about PTSD. I've lived through many of the things these girls are suffering right now, and I need to stop it. All that's on my mind at the moment is an all-consuming need to bring these people to justice."

"Mine too." Styles scratched his cheek and took a tentative step toward her. "You're trembling." He slipped one arm around her shoulder and pulled her against him. "I wish I could have been there to protect you. It breaks my heart to know what you went through. I look at you and think, how did that small woman survive?" He pressed a kiss to the top of her head. "You did survive, Beth. I'm here now and together we will stop this happening to other kids if it's the last darn thing I do."

Usually when men put their hands on her, Beth's skin crawled and her reaction was usually violent. To her surprise, she leaned into him and rested her head on his shoulder finding comfort in his warm embrace. Without realizing it, her hand snaked around his waist, and she gave him a squeeze. "Thank you. That means so much to me."

"That's okay." Styles straightened and smiled at her. "I couldn't find a root cellar, but I'll check the loft and then we can head back to the motel. I hope Sheriff Alton changes her mind about allowing us to speak to Ava. If she doesn't, we'll head back to Rattlesnake Creek. I want to get copies of all the media files we discovered to the violent crimes against children division ASAP. They have the resources needed to identify the victims in the files."

The need to do something burned in Beth and she nodded.

"I can start uploading them to the server via my laptop. I'll create an encrypted folder with eyes-only protocol to ensure the files aren't leaked or hacked by anyone." She waited in the passageway for him to pull down the loft steps and climb up to look inside the small dark area.

"There's nothing here." Styles pushed the steps back into place. "Wolfe will do a forensic sweep when he gets here in the morning. We'll hand over to him and head on home."

As her mind planned the next steps in the investigation, Beth followed him out to the SUV and then walked up to the deputies watching the place. "The medical examiner will be here in the morning with his team. We're heading back to Louan. Thanks for your assistance."

"Not a problem, ma'am." The deputy behind the wheel smiled at her and tipped his hat.

She headed back to the SUV as Bear came bounding back, tail wagging. He had cobwebs and twigs stuck in his coat. "What have you been doing?" She bent to wipe his head clean.

"On his downtime, he likes to explore new areas." Styles opened the back door and waved Bear inside. "I figure he searches for some poor creature he can protect."

Beth smiled and climbed into the passenger seat. "As long as it's not a chicken, right?"

"No, his fear of chickens is absolute." Styles started the engine. "He busted a feather pillow once and it was like Armageddon. I honestly believed he'd have a heart attack. He wouldn't stop shaking. I ended up calling Nate to give him a sedative."

Taken aback, Beth stared at him. "Nate's not a vet. He's a mighty fine doctor."

"It might say DR. NATE NACE on his shingle, but when the chips are down, and an animal is in trouble, many townsfolk call Nate. He has completed a course or whatever to handle sick animals."

Chuckling, Beth stared out the window at the multicolored scenery. After a long white winter, everything looked fresh and clean and so green. She recalled a time when Nate had given her a drug to take down a dangerous criminal. "He's a man of many talents."

Nate was a man she could trust, but the person she trusted the most, apart from Styles, was Dr. Shane Wolfe. She recognized something in him akin to herself. Not the psychopath side but the part of him that would die before giving up a secret, and she guessed he held many people's lives in his hands. If ever she told anyone about her dark side, it would be him. Maybe he could help her? She swallowed hard. The images on the thumb drive rose up like hot lava in her brain. Her fingers closed into fists and anger trembled through her. While predators roamed the earth and she still drew breath, she'd make them pay.

# SIXTEEN

*Louan*

The wind whined and buffeted the motel as Beth worked late into the night, uploading countless videos and images to a special encrypted file on the FBI server. Cold crept into the room. Even with the heat turned up as high as it would go, a chill crept across the floor from under the door and through the cracks on each side of the windows. Although exhausted, she'd consumed so many cups of coffee that she couldn't sleep and decided to follow a couple of leads she discovered on Shoebridge's hard drive. It always made her smile when people believed that when they deleted information from their computer that it vanished into thin air. What they didn't know is someone like her could usually find threads of data in places they would never think of looking. Little clues to where the person had been were all she needed to do a full-scale search of certain areas of the dark web.

She almost missed a clue as she went through strings of data and then it popped out at her, like a beacon for a lost ship on a dark night at sea. She'd found a highly disguised password and punched the air in excitement. Whoever had manipulated the data surrounding this syndicate showed a cunningness close to her own. She ran the password again and waited for the data stream to fill the page. She copied the page and saved it to a thumb drive. She had gained a very small piece of information so far, but with the password she'd be able to follow communications between Shoebridge and whoever was pulling his strings. She cleaned up all traces of her hack and closed the laptop.

Suddenly exhausted, she staggered into the shower. The hot water poured over her and by the time she'd dried her hair, exhaustion had claimed her. She didn't care that the bed smelled damp or the blankets were rough. She crawled into the freezing bed and had fallen asleep in seconds. Sure only minutes had passed since she'd closed her eyes, she woke to a noise. The smell of stale sweat crawled up her nostrils. Someone was in her room. Lying very still, she listened and heard a sharp intake of breath. Opening her eyes a slit as a shadow passed across the window, she tensed her muscles ready to fight. The next second, an almighty crash came from next door. From the noise, Styles had woken to the sound of a visitor as well.

Instead of sitting up in bed as most people would do, Beth rolled away from the sound and dropped on the floor beside the bed, crouching ready to attack. She would need all her wits to take down this intruder. Instinctively her hand went for her Glock, but her weapon was in her shoulder holster hanging on the back of the chair in front of the table. It was only two or three paces away from her but it might as well have been a mile. Crashing and the sounds of furniture breaking came from the next room. It didn't take a genius to know that Styles was fighting for his life. The next second a dark shadow lunged toward her and a fist landed hard against her shoulder. She rolled away, aiming a kick at the man's legs, missing and hitting air. On her back on the floor, she aimed again and this time struck him hard on the hip. He staggered away from her cursing and she saw the glint of metal in the moonlight coming through the drapes.

"I'm going to cut you real bad." He waved the knife around trying to slash at her.

Glad she'd chosen to sleep in black sweats, and was able to blend into the shadows, Beth rolled away, getting behind him. Her head hit the leg of the chair in front of the desk and she reached up and grabbed her Glock from the shoulder holster. She backed toward the door and fumbled for the light switch. The room flooded with light and the intruder lunged at her, swinging the knife. "FBI, drop your weapon." She raised the gun and racked the slide.

The man kept coming, Beth lunged sideways to avoid the slashing blade and cold poured over her arm as the fabric split open. Fully awake, anger trembled through her, heightening her senses. She rolled across the floor, avoiding the blade, and lifted her gun. Aiming center mass, she fired a double tap. The intruder's startled expression as he grabbed his chest and staggered back surprised her. Hadn't he seen her gun? The noise next door sounded like a herd of rampaging elephants as she jumped to her feet. She needed to help Styles and kicked the knife away from the intruder's open hand as the life left his body.

Beth stepped over him and ran to Styles' room as a man crashed through the window, landing at her feet. His head hit the ground and his neck twisted in an unnatural angle. He wasn't moving and the fight was still raging in Styles' room. *Two down.*

Adrenaline pumped through Beth's veins as she moved to the door and, keeping her back to the wall, snaked a hand around the doorframe and switched on the light. Rolling through broken furniture, Styles, from what she could make out, was giving plenty, but these men were trained assassins, not drunken miners. From the blows and kicks, the three men were skilled in martial arts. Heart thumping and fingers tingling with anticipation, she stepped inside the room, Glock raised in both hands. "FBI, get on your knees, hands on your heads, or I'll shoot."

Everyone ignored her and the melee was a tangle of bodies. She couldn't fire for risk of killing Styles. She ran up behind one of the men and swiped her gun across his head, hitting him in the ear. The man howled and turned to face her, his eyes wild. She backed away, holding her Glock in both hands. She wouldn't miss at this range. "FBI. Move one step closer and I'll shoot."

"You just couldn't leave well alone, could you?" The man staggered but pulled a knife. "The penalty for interfering in our business is death."

The man lunged at her, and without hesitation she squeezed the trigger. The bullet passed through his neck and thumped into the wall. Arterial spatter sprayed the room. The man grabbed at his throat and staggered around before collapsing. The room had suddenly gone quiet. She looked up and took in the impossible situation at a glance. Styles was bent over a man, his muscles bulging as he held him in a headlock. One twist and he'd break his neck. A second man stood behind them holding a long sharp blade to Styles' throat. That man smiled at her, and a low chuckle rolled from his mouth. By underestimating her, he'd just made the biggest mistake of his life. Beth allowed her psychopath calm to rise up and her finger dropped to the trigger.

Her gaze slipped to Styles and he mouthed the words. *"Do it."*

Staring into the grinning man's face, Beth took careful aim. "Put down the knife."

"You won't risk killing your partner." The man holding the knife chuckled. "Drop the gun like a good little girl, or I'll give him a permanent smile."

She pulled the trigger.

# SEVENTEEN
## TUESDAY

Head filled with cotton and mouth so dry her tongue stuck to the roof, Shiloh blinked into the darkness. Disoriented, she shook her head trying to remember what had happened but had no memory of anything after climbing into the truck with the cop. The sudden realization that her mom was hurt and in the hospital frightened her. Fear crawled up her spine. What if Mom had died? What would happen to her? At the thought of losing her mom, tears stung her eyes and fell down her cheeks. She tried to search for a memory of what happened and could only recall drinking the soda the cop had given her. How did she get here and where was she? A tiny light glowed on a table that held a bottle of water, but darkness closed in around her.

A sob escaped her lips as she pushed one hand over the sheet beneath her. The bed was huge and seemed to stretch out around her. It held a musty smell that reminded her of old socks left in the bottom of her laundry hamper. She ran a hand over the silky material covering her. She didn't recall getting undressed or wearing anything so thin when ice was still on the ground, although the air inside the room was warm. She tried to sit up and her head swam, the room moved in and out of focus.

Gritting her teeth, she crawled to the edge of the bed. Every muscle in her body ached. Her back hurt bad, but she needed to reach the water. Had she fallen and banged her head?

Crying wouldn't help, and her mom always told her she was sensible for her age. She needed to drink and survive. Struggling, she dropped her legs onto the floor. No carpet but cool tiles pressed against her bare feet. She stood for a few moments, getting her balance, and then headed slowly toward the light. Gripping the table, she reached for the bottle of water, removed the top, and allowed the cool water to moisten her parched throat. The light was a lantern and the same as her mom's. It had a dial on one side to make it brighter. She turned the dial and held it up to peer around the room. On the wall she noticed a light switch, and using the wall for support, she moved her wobbly legs toward it and switched it on. Light flooded the space and she blinked at the brightness. When her eyes adjusted to the light, she scanned the room.

The area was bigger than she'd imagined. The bed sat at one end of the room alongside a closet and nightstand. The other end of the room had been split into two. One part held a large sofa and two chairs opposite a fireplace with a large flat-screen TV above the mantel. The other half was a small kitchen, complete with a refrigerator, microwave, and sink. An L-shaped countertop led to an island in the center with chairs all around. Above these, a line of kitchen cabinets and a pantry set in one corner. She noticed two doors, one leading from the sitting room, the other located at the bedroom end of the room.

Shiloh took a few deep breaths and moved to the first door at the end of the sitting room. She closed her hand around the doorknob and turned. A wave of panic shot through her. The door was locked, and she shook it hard but couldn't move it. She pressed her ear to the crack in the door and peered out into daylight but couldn't see anything but a few green patches that could be trees or grass. At least it was daytime. She looked around the room again and realized to her horror that there were no windows anywhere. Moving back the way she'd come using the wall for support, she headed toward the door near the bedroom. This time the door opened and inside she found a bathroom. An old iron bath on ornate feet looked strange next to a modern shower with gleaming white tiles. She used the toilet and then washed her hands and splashed water on her face at the bathroom sink. Maybe the cop had locked her in to protect her?

She dried her face and went back to the bedroom and opened the closet doors and found more nighties and a robe. Where were her clothes? She pulled on the robe, but it was too long and dragged along the floor as she headed back to the kitchen. Hunger gnawed at her belly. She'd cared for herself many times during vacations when her mom was at work and could cook a few meals. She opened the refrigerator and found milk and juice. Each shelf was packed with food of one description or another. She turned and went to the pantry, pulling it open to find a variety of different packages and cans. One thing for sure, she wouldn't be going hungry. She selected her favorite breakfast cereal and placed it on the kitchen table and then went in search of a bowl and spoon. She'd just finished eating when she heard a key in the lock and turned to see a girl coming inside.

"Hey." The girl walked into the room and closed the door behind her. "I'm Luna and your name is Shiloh, is that right?" She unbuttoned her coat and tossed it over the back of a chair. "They sent me to talk to you to explain things." She gave her a long look. "Don't make a fuss, but your mom is dead. Mine is too."

Unable to control the flood of tears, Shiloh sobbed into her hands. Her heart ached and she trembled all over. "What's going to happen to me?"

"That depends"—Luna's eyes held a faraway look—"on if

you're good or if you make a fuss and cry all the time. I've seen the girls who do that, and they are sent away to the bad place."

Sobbing, Shiloh peered at her between her fingers. "Bad place?"

"Doc said those girls are locked into a closet with spiders and snakes. They starve them until they behave." Luna shuddered. "I don't want to go there, do you?"

Shaking her head, Shiloh went to the countertop and pulled a strip of paper towel from a roll. She blew her nose and wiped her eyes. "No." She sat down and looked at Luna. "How did you come to be here?"

"Doc took me in two years ago and I care for him. We just came to this town, like you, but it's different for me. I did as I was told and now I get to live in the cabin. Before I was in a room like this for a long time."

Stomach knotting, Shiloh stared at her, uncomprehending. "I can be good and not make a fuss."

"There's something you need to know." Luna went to her and bent to whisper in her ear. She straightened. "And they take a ton of pictures and movies."

Shocked beyond belief, Shiloh shook her head. "I can't do that."

"You already have. You just don't remember." Luna let out a long sigh. "The fruit juice they gave you makes you forget things. They give me pills all the time as well. They make me sleepy."

Trembling, Shiloh looked at her hands and then lifted her head. "Can you help me escape?"

"We are many miles from anywhere and you wouldn't survive a day without shoes and dressed like that in the cold." Luna shook her head. "I tried to escape once and I was punished for three days and locked in the root cellar for a month. If you want to have good food, a TV, and a warm place to sleep, you'll need to do everything they say without making a fuss."

Unconvinced, Shiloh shook her head. "How come you're allowed to walk around?"

"I'm not." Luna shrugged, defeated. "I talk to the other girls when they arrive to make it easier for them, is all." She pointed to the ceiling. "Before you try and break down the door just remember there are cameras all around the room. They can hear and see everything."

Suddenly very alone, Shiloh grabbed her arm. "Will you come and see me again?"

"No." Luna shook her head. "You might see other girls from time to time, and you might be given to someone else. I met a girl who had been moved six times and she was only twelve." She leaned closer. "I figure she was crazy. She tried to bite me." She turned, grabbed her coat, and headed for the door and then looked back at Shiloh. "Good luck."

The door closed behind her and a few minutes later it opened again and in a rush of cold air the cop walked in and smiled at her. She stood up and swallowed hard. Fear gripped her belly and she wanted to pee. "Luna told me what you did to me."

"Did she now." The cop slowly removed his coat and hung it on a peg beside the door. "You don't believe her, do you?"

Shiloh shook her head. "No, I'd remember something like that."

"You will from now on." He chuckled and switched on the TV. "Come sit with me and watch. It's all on tape."

Backing away, horrified, Shiloh shook her head. "No!"

She gasped when in two strides he had her by the arms. Zip-ties cut deep into her flesh and then he tossed her onto the lounger. She glared at him. "Leave me alone. You're never going to touch me."

"I can do whatever I like with you. Get used to it." The cop sat down beside her. "I'll ignore this outburst one time only. Step out of line again and you'll suffer the consequences." A smile curled his lips. "I met your grandma this morning. Shame she's too sick to take care of you. You be good or I'll go and burn down her house with her inside."

Shiloh shook her head and tried to move away from him. "Cops don't do that to people."

When he grasped her face and squeezed hard, pain shot into her eyes. His face was an inch away from hers and terror shivered through her at the hate in his eyes.

"Here's the problem, Shiloh. I'm not a cop." His mouth twisted into a smile. "I'm the big bad wolf."

# EIGHTEEN

Locked inside an interrogation room, Styles held his pounding head in his hands. His muscles ached from the fight. The intruders had known exactly how to do the most damage with the least effort. Who were they and why were they attacking him and Beth? He needed desperately to speak to the man that they had arrested on scene. He wanted answers and couldn't do anything while they had him locked in this room as a suspect in a multiple homicide. The men had all been dressed similarly in black and carried knives rather than guns, which led him to the conclusion that they had intended to get in and out of the motel rooms as fast as possible without being seen or heard. Why had someone sent five trained assassins to the motel to kill them?

His thoughts went to Beth and he slammed the table with his fist. The case had been a mental torment for her from the start and now this. Right now she needed his support. She had taken down four armed intruders and each time, he'd heard her clearly calling out that she was an FBI agent and intended to shoot. She had saved his life and now she was somewhere in this building alone and in shock. He had given his statement to the local sheriff and was informed that they had contacted the FBI to inform them of the incident in their town. That had been hours ago and he'd been sitting here cooling his heels without any idea of what was happening. It had been a righteous kill and the local law enforcement had no right to be holding them. The worst part of all of it is that they'd taken Bear. His dog would be beside himself.

A key turned in the lock and the door swung open to reveal Agent Ty Carter and Agent Jo Wells, a behavioral analyst from Snakeskin Gully. Behind them came Zorro, Carter's dog, and then Bear rushed into the room, almost knocking him from the chair. To his surprise, Carter carried a four-pack of to-go coffee and a takeout bag of sandwiches. Styles looked from one to the other and smiled. "I'm sure glad to see you. I've been unlawfully stuck in this room for the last six hours. Thanks for finding Bear." He rubbed the dog's head.

"Here. Clean up a bit." Jo handed him a packet of wipes. "You've blood on your face and arms. Then I suggest you eat something. You look like shit."

Taking the wipes, Styles nodded. "Thank you, I appreciate it. They allowed me to go to the bathroom, but I wasn't allowed to clean off the blood."

Once he'd cleaned up, he reached for the coffee. "Have you seen Beth?"

"Yeah, we've spoken to her, and we've been out to the crime scene and run through your statements. We wouldn't allow anyone to touch the bodies or anything else until Wolfe had processed the crime scene. Hence the delay." Carter pulled out a chair and sat down. "The director called us at about four this morning and we've been on the case ever since."

Styles bit into an egg salad sandwich and washed it down with a mouthful of coffee. "Is Beth okay?"

"We've determined it was a righteous shoot. Beth seems a little distant, but I believe she's okay to continue working on the case." Jo took a cup of coffee out of the cardboard carrier and took a sip. "I consider it to be a natural reaction after killing four men. Wolfe has examined her as well and she doesn't seem to be carrying any substantial injuries. He'll be dropping by to see you very shortly."

Styles frowned. "Beth didn't kill four men. She shot three as far as I know. I threw one of them out of the window and he broke his neck when he hit the ground. If she hadn't come into the room when she did, I would be lying on the floor of that motel room with my throat slit. She saved my life. In my opinion, it took incredible mental strength and guts to pull the trigger. It was a split-second decision that required absolute accuracy and she pulled it off. She should get a medal."

"That's not the problem." Carter moved a toothpick across his lips and leaned back in the chair with a sigh. "The director wants to know how going to find your missing sister has escalated into a case of epic proportions. Last night, Beth forwarded the images and media files that you discovered and switchboards have lit up all over town. It's all hands on deck to discover who these kids are and where they're keeping them."

Styles finished a second pack of sandwiches and reached for another cup of coffee. "That was the intention. I hope he didn't expect us to hunt down all those children ourselves."

"Nope, he is more interested in the five men who tried to kill you last night." Carter met his gaze. "You see, according to all the records that we have at our disposal, those men don't exist. The intruder we took into custody isn't saying a word. He was taken to County about an hour ago and is on suicide watch. We figure the moment he's left alone he'll try and take his own life."

"We're hoping he'll try and deal his way out of trouble." Jo crossed her legs and leaned back in her chair. "He's refused a lawyer. In fact, he's saying nothing at all. We don't even know if he speaks English."

Surprised, Styles viewed her over the rim of his to-go cup.

"They were speaking English well enough when they were threatening to cut my throat. You do know why they're after us, don't you?"

"Do tell." Carter spread his hands wide. "That's why we're here."

Running both hands through his hair, Styles leaned back in his chair and yawned explosively. "The guy who took Ginny and the local doctor are involved in a pedophile ring that spreads at least across the state, more likely the entire country. Beth believes that if we get involved it will stir up an ant's nest. The last thing they want is for the FBI to be aware of them. What Beth wanted to do was to hack into their files and leave a subtle trace behind so that they could track her down." He shrugged. "Although, last night's attack was a complete surprise."

"What? You planned for them to murder you in your sleep?" Carter raised both eyebrows. "That sounds a little extreme."

Lack of sleep dragged at Styles and slowed down his mental acuity. The coffee helped some, but in truth, arguing with Carter wasn't on the top of his list. "No. As far as I'm aware, Beth hasn't got into their files yet, so that part of the plan hasn't been executed. It seems to me that just finding Ginny and Ava was enough for them to send in the goons. They sure as heck got the main players out of town fast. We were hunting them down from the moment we found Ginny. They obviously had an escape plan set up well in advance, which makes us believe that they are a very small part of a huge organization. Now you tell me that the men attacked us don't exist. Makes the entire case all the more intriguing."

"Yeah." Carter stared at him. "You've stumbled into a pedophile ring with assassins who are expendable. I'd say, we might be talking about a worldwide organization. And if it is, they won't stop until they've killed you."

Styles took another long gulp of coffee and let out a sigh. "Their knowledge of the FBI is seriously lacking if they believe this all stops with us, and that's going to be their downfall. It seems to me they have no idea that we've already dispersed all the information and that killing us will get them nowhere." He ran a hand down his face and looked at Carter. "What information did you get from the director? Does he want us to continue with the case, or do I have to contact him and get new orders?"

"He is aware that Beth was a little unstable after the homicide she was involved in in DC." Jo gave him a direct stare. "He wants to know if she is capable of continuing. Wolfe and I both gave her the equivalent of a psych test, and as it was only hours after the event and she was very stressed from lack of sleep, she passed it with ease. When I asked her what was troubling her about the case, she continually asked me how you were doing. When I pushed her to concentrate on the case, she told me she was wasting time sitting in an interrogation room rather than being out on the streets preventing pedophiles from molesting children."

Styles smiled and rolled his shoulders. "That's Beth. Her mind is on the job twenty-four/seven. I've seen her work most of the night digging into files to discover perps. You have absolutely no idea how dedicated she is to her job. Sitting on her hands now, while kids are in danger, must be driving her insane."

"Like I said before, she's fine to get back to work." Jo smiled. "In my opinion, so are you, as long as Wolfe passes you as fit. You look a little banged up to me."

"That's nothing to worry about. It's all in a day's work for guys like us, right, Styles?" Carter grinned around his toothpick. "Like us, they both need a solid eight hours and we'll all be good to go." He stood. "I'll speak to the director and sign the necessary paperwork to get you out of here as soon as possible."

Nodding, Styles ran the case through his mind. "Any trace of Shoebridge or the doctor? He has a child living with him."

"No sign of either of them. It seems they vanished into thin air. We looked into the girl you mentioned, and apparently he adopted a young girl a year ago." Carter frowned. "Do you figure he's abusing her as well?"

Anger welling, Styles stared at him. "This doctor organizes illegal adoptions. No one checks on the kids. He could be swapping them out regularly, for all we know. He has a judge in his pocket for sure to push through the adoptions. We have reason to believe he's the doctor involved in a baby-selling racket. From what Ginny told me, he's taken four of her babies at birth. He told her they'd died." He punched the palm of his hand.

"Okay, calm down." Carter frowned. "We're working on it."

Not happy with the situation, Styles stood. "I want to see Beth."

"Sure, grab your coffee and sandwiches and we'll take you to her." Carter banged on the door and a deputy opened it. "We've booked you rooms at the same hotel as us. It's just across the road. Get some rest. We've taken your things there and returned the SUV. I'll drop you by the fire station first thing so you can get back to Rattlesnake Creek. We'll be staying to clean up the mess, but if you need any help, just call."

"You don't need to worry about the case involving your sister." Jo smiled at him. "I was able to speak to Ava and she is doing fine. Wolfe has collected blood samples from her and Ginny to determine what concoction of drugs they had been fed over what period of time. Your sister, unfortunately, will not roll over on Shoebridge. She has compartmentalized the abuse and now is living outside of the box. What she sees is 'normal,' although it hasn't affected her caring for Billy. Her lawyer allowed her to speak to a social worker about keeping her son and she made all the normal responses of a loving mother but refused to speak about anything else whatsoever. Ava, on the other hand, gave us some information but not enough to use against him. One time after Shoebridge argued with Ginny, Ava was taken to the house for a week or so while Ginny cooled her heels in the root cellar. It was his normal punishment for her if she complained. Ava was left alone in the house for hours when Shoebridge was at work and did a great deal of snooping. She discovered Shoebridge's go bag hidden under the floorboards in the main bedroom. Although she is young, she's astute enough to understand that people do not have driver's licenses and other documentation in a number of names."

Interested, Styles stopped in the passageway and stared at her. "Did she recall any names?"

"She said they all began with E." Jo smiled at him. "The one on the top of the pile was Evan something."

"I guess that's in case he makes a mistake signing something." Carter followed behind them. "It's easier to cover up a slip if the name is similar." He indicated to the door on the left. "Beth's inside. We'll go and spring you from this joint. We won't be long."

Styles handed the coffee and sandwiches to Carter, turned, and picked up a chair outside the room. He pushed open the door and wedged it open with the chair. He looked at him. "I don't appreciate being locked in a room." He took the coffee and sandwiches. "Thanks, I appreciate it."

"My pleasure." Carter followed Jo along the passageway. "Don't kill anyone while I'm gone."

# NINETEEN

Exhausted, Beth had long given up fighting the thirst and hunger. She pushed the pain to another part of her mind and rested her head on her arms and then tried to sleep. At the sound of voices, Beth lifted her head. Relief flooded through her at the sight of Styles coming through the door with Bear at his heels. The dog went straight to her and rested his big head on her lap. She peered through the door to see Carter and Jo standing in the passageway. Sticky with blood, stinking, and dying for a cup of coffee, she stood, waving slightly from exhaustion. "Styles, what's happening?"

"Sit down before you fall down." Styles placed a bag on the table and a to-go cup of coffee. He fished in his pocket and handed her a packet of wipes. "That's just for now. I'm not shutting the door, and once you've had something to eat and drunk the coffee, you can go down to the bathroom and clean up. They had no right to treat us like this. In case you didn't know, I've been right next door and interrogated worse than a criminal. I'm assuming the same thing happened to you?"

Beth took a long pull on the coffee and then used the wipes to clean her face and hands. "They didn't even offer me a glass

of water. I had to ask Wolfe to get me one and then he and Jo
ran me through a series of questions. They were nice, not like
the sheriff. He didn't even read me my rights." She shook her
head. "We were the victims. This is just the same as what
happened to me in DC. Honestly, what choice did I have? The
guy in my room came at me with a knife, he cut through my
sweater, and then you saw what happened in your room."

What was happening to her? She'd never experienced
vulnerability before and now she couldn't control the trembling.
She looked at him. "Is it inappropriate if I ask you for a hug?"

"No and I figure I need one too. It's been a nightmare. The
adrenaline letdown gives me the shakes too." Styles moved his
chair closer to her and placed one arm around her shoulders.
"Four people died and the sheriff was just following procedure.
I convinced him to call the director as it was an FBI matter. It
was the director who ordered Jo to do an on-the-spot evaluation
along with Wolfe. The director values his opinion. The director
wants us back on the case ASAP and you're his best cybercrime
expert."

Unfamiliar to being hugged, Beth stared at her bloodstained
hands. "Did you get any feedback from Carter?"

"Yeah, they cleared me without a problem." Styles pulled
her closer. "Did you figure they'd suspend you, because Jo said
she'd inform the director you're shaken but okay." He bent to
look at her. "That's normal... being shaken after what
happened. You know that, right?"

Nodding, Beth tried to control her mixed emotions. "Yeah, I
admit that five guys attacking us was a little intense. They were
skilled mercenaries and nothing like the drunken miners we're
used to handling."

Trying to understand why she appreciated Styles holding
her, she gave up and rested her head on his shoulder. Maybe
this was a normal response to his caring nature. She'd never
experienced a feeling of safety before and allowing anyone to

touch her was out of the question. She swallowed the bite of the sandwich and leaned against him. "Jo would know a lie in a heartbeat. Wolfe, I like. I told him a time ago about what happened to me in foster care and he offered me his confidence if I ever wanted to talk. I trust him."

"Do you trust me?" Styles gave her a squeeze. "I don't have a Hippocratic oath to back me up, but you have my word as your friend. What we discuss will never go any further. That's a solemn promise I'll take to my grave."

Beth thought for a beat. She wanted to be honest with him. "I've already trusted you with most of my secrets." She finished the coffee and looked at him. "There are just some that if I told you, they would break me apart. I'd rather keep them locked up where they can't hurt anyone."

"I figure we all have secrets like that, especially soldiers." Styles rubbed her back and then stood. "Some things are best forgotten." He indicated with his chin toward the door. "The bathroom is just across the hall. You go and clean up and I'll wait outside and keep watch. I don't want the sheriff to believe we've escaped custody." He pulled a comb from his back pocket and handed it to her. "This might be useful."

Beth smiled at him. "Thanks." She thought for a beat with one hand pressed against the door. "What about our things at the motel?"

"They'll be at the hotel; Carter took them over for us." Styles smiled. "It's just across the road. We'll be staying there tonight and heading home first thing in the morning."

It took some time to wash the blood from her hands and face. She used paper towels to dab at the red spots in her hair. She needed a shower and a change of clothes. She'd started to smell of blood hours ago, and everyone's refusal of her basic human needs disgusted her. Once done, she went out to find Styles and Bear waiting for her. Styles had dark circles under his eyes and a bruise on one cheek. One side of his hair was matted with blood. The spatter of a head shot at close range had covered both of them. In a few minutes she'd killed three men. She remembered the scene almost clinically as if through different eyes. She could see herself pulling the trigger, there was no emotion only survival. Did she care she killed them? No. Would that be the correct answer in a psych test? Or would the truth bring her down? Maybe she'd test her newfound closeness to Styles and ask him. Somehow, she'd need to understand how to interpret the correct emotions and react accordingly. Going forward it was the only way to survive.

Beth combed her hair and tied it into a ponytail. She looked a little better, although her clothes were covered in blood. She wondered what the clerk on the hotel desk would say to them when they walked inside. Her boots were ruined. Maybe she'd have time to by a new pair before returning home. She stepped into the passageway and pointed to her boots. "I'll never get the blood out of them. Do you mind if we stop by the store I mentioned yesterday? I want to buy a pair."

"Sure, once we've cleaned up and changed clothes, but I really need a couple of hours' sleep." Styles glanced at his watch. "It's still early. How about we go to the hotel, grab some shuteye, and go shopping around three? We can have dinner and get a good night's sleep and head home first thing in the morning."

Beth nodded and sat on a chair outside the interrogation room. "Mind if we wait out here? I hate being locked up."

"Me too." Styles pulled up a chair and sat beside her. "Anything else worrying you?"

Nodding, Beth stared at her blood-spattered boots. "I need to get into Shoebridge's files. I found a tiny link to data I can follow. The longer I wait, the easier it is for him to cover his tracks." She frowned. "I hope they didn't take my laptop into evidence. I'd like to work on it ASAP."

"I don't believe they'd take the laptop. It's FBI property."

Styles touched her arm. "Why aren't you looking at me? Is it the blood in my hair?"

Avoiding his gaze meant he couldn't read her thoughts, and as he was so perceptive, often she couldn't risk it. Maybe this time she should. Covering the awkward moment with a laugh, Beth turned to face him. "No, sorry. I was miles away thinking about the events last night and how they played out. It's kind of hard trying to push them out of my mind. The killing and all." She took a deep breath. It was now or never. "I don't feel any remorse for killing them, Styles. I'd do it again in a heartbeat. Does that make me crazy like my dad?"

"Nope, that makes you a good agent." Styles frowned and shook his head slowly. "I can't imagine how it feels to have the burden of a psychopathic killer as a father hanging around your neck. I guess it's normal for you to worry you might become like him, especially in a job like ours where killing people is a reality. If it makes you feel any better, I meant to hurt the guy I threw out of the window. He came at me with a knife with the intent to kill. I didn't think twice about breaking the other one's neck and would have before the third guy cut my throat if you hadn't arrived on scene." He shrugged. "When it's me or them on the streets, I rarely think of them after the fact. I know in my heart it was a just kill. I don't lose sleep over people who make the mistake of trying to kill me. You shouldn't either."

Breathing out a sigh of relief, Beth nodded. "The thing is, if I weren't an FBI agent when what happened last night went down, I'd be locked up and viewed as a criminal." She poked at her temple. "It would have played out the same. In here, I can't understand how carrying a badge makes it okay." She blew out a long breath and took her life in her hands. "For example, look at the Tarot Killer. Put him in my place and he'd go for murder one. He'd have killed the bad guys same as I did but ended up in jail."

"Maybe not." Styles rubbed his chin. "Five men breaking

into a motel room with the intent to murder makes it self-defense." His concerned gaze moved over her. "You're exhausted and not thinking straight. Promise me when you get to the hotel, you'll get some sleep. Fine if you want to work later, but right now, we both need some rest or we'll be no good to anyone."

Beth nodded slowly. "Okay. What are you going to do about Ginny?"

"Nothing right now." Styles stared at the ceiling. "I'll wait until we've wrapped up the investigation into Shoebridge and the doctor and then I'll give her time to get her life back together. The Her Broken Wings Foundation will care for her and Billy. Later they'll find her a place to stay and work. Once I know she's stable, I'll contact my mom and tell her I've found her. I really don't want her to know the circumstances of what happened, but that will be up to Ginny." He glanced at her. "I figure she'll blame me for Shoebridge leaving—and she'll be right. I guess it's debatable if she'll ever accept the truth."

Footsteps came from the passageway and Beth watched the sheriff walk toward them. She pushed to her feet and glared at him. "Are we free to go?"

"Yeah." The sheriff nodded and looked at Styles. "The director wants you to call him when you get back to your office. The exit is through the door and to the left." He opened a door with his keys and allowed them to pass.

Beth shot him a stare she hoped conveyed everything she thought of the treatment she'd received by him and his men. "Thank you, Sheriff. I'll be sure my report includes every aspect of our stay with you. If you're real lucky, you might get someone from the Justice Department dropping by to give you a lesson on duty of care."

# TWENTY

## WEDNESDAY

*Rattlesnake Creek*

A blue sky dotted with cotton clouds spread out across the mountains but an icy wind bit into Styles' cheeks as he walked across Main and into Sheriff Cash Ryder's office. He pushed open the door and held it to allow Bear to walk in behind him. The girl at the counter smiled at him and he nodded to her. "I'm Agent Styles. Is Cash in his office?"

"I'll see if he's in." The girl pressed an old-style intercom and announced him. "Yeah, go straight through." The girl smoothed a strand of hair over one shoulder and smiled at him. "I'm the new sheriff's assistant."

She looked straight out of college and Styles nodded. "Nice to meet you." He hurried past the desk and to Cash's office door, pushed it open, and walked inside.

"So you're back." Cash took his boots off the desk and straightened his chair. He held up one finger and pressed the intercom. "Bring in a fresh pot of coffee and two clean cups." He waited for the girl to come in and replace the coffee pot in the machine and then get two cups. "Thanks, Amber, that will be all for now." His gaze followed her out the door and when it shut behind her, he looked at Styles and grinned. "Recall when I put in a request for a deputy? Well, the mayor sent *her*. I'm not exactly sure what I'm meant to do with her as it seems the only thing she can do efficiently is answer the phone and make coffee." He stood and went to the coffee machine and poured two cups. He added the fixings and walked back to his desk.

Scratching his cheek, Styles stared at him. "I figure, as she's straight out of college, she'll have some experience in typing, at least, and computer skills they all have at that age. All those reports you're expected to write? You can just dictate them to her, and she'll type them for you and then upload them onto the server."

"You think?" Cash leaned back in his chair, making it creak. "I can't imagine describing some of the crime scenes that we've investigated over the last couple of years to that young girl out there. I figured she'd either go running down the street screaming her lungs out or be traumatized for life."

Styles removed his hat and dropped it on the desk. He picked up his cup of coffee and sipped the rich aromatic brew. "So I gather you didn't have the chance to interview her and ask her if she was interested in law enforcement?"

"Nope." Cash leaned forward, resting his elbows on the table and stared at him. "The mayor called me and told me she'd be arriving this morning." He shook his head slowly. "I don't know a darn thing about the girl."

Frowning, Styles thought for a beat. "Maybe she is more experienced than you're giving her credit for? Do you mind if I speak to her?"

"Nope, I'll call her in." Cash pressed the button on the intercom and made the request.

The door opened and the girl walked inside carrying a notepad and pen. She looked expectantly at Cash. Styles turned to her. "We have an ongoing investigation and we'll be needing your assistance. I want you to check all the databases for any missing children, particularly girls, over the last week or so in this state. I also want you to contact all the employment agencies in the state and ask them to send you the names of any men in their fifties who have applied for a position of security guard in the last twenty-four hours. If you're able to obtain any information, make sure everything is forwarded to my office." He waited for her to finish writing and looked up at him. "Is what I asked within your job description?"

"Yes, of course." The girl looked slightly confused. "Office management is only a small part of what I can do. I could also be a legal secretary or a court clerk. I'm very interested in all aspects of law." She flicked a glance at Cash. "The mayor asked me specifically if I was squeamish when it came to taking down information about crime scenes, including violent homicides."

"And what was your reply?" Cash was looking at her with an interested expression on his face.

"I'm not squeamish and I'm very good at what I do." She straightened and gave him a tight smile. "Reading about forensic science and crime scenes is a passion of mine. I don't figure there's anything you can tell me that will give me nightmares."

Biting back the need to smile, Styles nodded. "Good. That's great. We'll leave you to it."

Once she had left the room, closing the door behind her, he looked at Cash. "There you go. She might be more help than you imagine, and looking at her more closely, I'd say she's in her early twenties. Next time you get the chance, ask her what experience she had prior to taking this job. You might be surprised."

"Sure, but now I'm intrigued." Cash sipped his brew. "What investigation is behind the questions you asked her?"

Styles explained what had happened in Louan over the last few days. "I would like you to extend the all-points bulletin out on both men, across the state. The doctor has a young girl with him we assume is around twelve. He has an adopted daughter on paper. We're not sure if she's ever been seen. Beth will follow that part of the investigation today. We believe, if the doctor is as entrenched in the pedophile ring as we assume, he could be changing the girls at will. We believe there's a judge or judges involved and the paperwork to cover his predilection would be issued to his needs. It would be his cover story for having a young girl in the house."

"So I'm guessing he's telling everyone she's homeschooled?" Cash's mouth turned down at the corners in disgust. "No one actually gets to see her and she would never come in contact with anyone to ask for help."

Nodding, Styles placed one booted foot on his knee and leaned back in the chair. "The other guy, Shoebridge, will be under an assumed name, but most of these people moving from place to place still retain the same employment. We have a good chance of tracking him down if he takes another job in the next couple of weeks. The other thing with Shoebridge is that, according to my sister, he had a different girl frequently."

"So you want me to be on the lookout for any reports of missing children over the next couple of weeks?" Cash placed his cup on the table and let out a long sigh. "What's your take on the attack in the motel room? Do you figure it's all tied up with this pedophile ring?"

Images flashed across Styles' mind in vibrant color and he nodded. "Oh, yeah, they intended to kill us quickly and silently. It showed a complete lack of knowledge of the FBI. I guess they figured that we didn't have the chance to put in a report about Shoebridge and the doctor. They wanted to take us out before we had the chance to complete an investigation." He rubbed the scar on his chin. "What actually surprised me more than anything was the way the suspects vanished without a trace. This tells me these people have done this a hundred times before. Both Shoebridge and the doctor are two of the main players or very valued players."

"It would seem so." Cash thought for a beat, drumming his fingers on the desk. "Do you figure this is tied into the Pied Piper case?"

Recalling the hideous waste of life taken by the man they'd dubbed the Pied Piper, Styles nodded. "Yeah, he would have been a supplier. This is why he took two girls, one for himself and one for the organization. It was how he financed his life. To him it was a business arrangement." He finished his coffee. "We don't know just how wide this spreads, but I'm inclined to believe it will include a case handled by Sheriff Alton out at Black Rock Falls. Those monsters kept what they referred to as breeders. Although Sheriff Alton claims to have closed down the main players. They were getting their girls from foster care. The girls were reported as runaways. Their babies went through an adoption agency, which I assumed was investigated."

"That doesn't mean another wouldn't spring up, would it?" Cash turned his coffee cup around in his fingertips, moving the small residue around the cup. "If the organization is as big as you say and sent mercenaries to kill you, anything is possible." He rocked back in his chair. "We are three people. We have a snowflake's chance in hell of taking them down alone."

Styles stood. "We can only try, and we have the FBI hunting down the names of the girls on the DVDs. They'll isolate clues from the videos and locate them. They aren't our problem right now. Finding and destroying the pedophile ring is our objective."

The door opened and Amber walked in and stared at them, her expression etched in concern.

"What's happened?" Cash stared at her.

"A girl went missing on her way home from school out at

Bison Ridge sometime after three yesterday. There's no sign of her and the townsfolk have been searching all over."

"Okay thanks." Cash took the report from her trembling fingers. He waited for her to leave and looked at Styles. "Do you figure Shoebridge is out at Bison Ridge?"

Styles shook his head. "Nope, he'd be long gone by now. I'd say he's heading for his new hideaway. He could be anywhere."

"Hmm, I'm not so sure. Like you said, Shoebridge wouldn't wait long before he took another girl." Cash gave him a long look. "I'll make sure to notify all the local counties and ask them to keep on the lookout for him and the girl. It's a big state, but if she's not found in the next twenty-four hours, we can assume Shoebridge has taken her."

Anger that another child had been taken slid over Styles like a bucket of ice water. "We'll find him."

"You should leave it to the local boys. It's way too dangerous for just the two of you. You know these organizations have the resources to hire killers to take you out. They're not going to risk exposure by attacking a complete sheriff's department. It will be subtle, like a mugging or a gas explosion—even a car wreck. That's not the type of confrontation you're used to handling." Cash frowned. "You know if you keep digging, you'll be painting targets on your backs."

After facing worse in his lifetime nothing fazed Styles, and Beth had just proved she could hold her own. He turned toward the door and glanced at him over one shoulder. "That's what I'm counting on."

# TWENTY-ONE

Inches from her head, cold water dripped through slats of wooden boards darkened with age and covered in lichen and moss. Shiloh moved her head in an attempt to avoid the freezing droplets. She pulled the quilt tighter around her, but a chill seeped through the floral material, raising goosebumps on her flesh. Determined not to give in to the horrible man who had taken her, she stared at the cobweb in the corner of the small enclosure. The breeze coming through the holes in the top of the box made the water droplets sparkle to resemble a fine diamond necklace. Her mother had always said she had a stubborn streak and that it would get her into trouble one day. It certainly had this time, as trouble had come in the shape of being thrown inside a wooden cage attached to the eaves of an old shed.

The cop had told her his name was Evan, and as no one had come forward to claim her, she belonged to him now. Her mother had died and no one else in the family wanted her. He'd forced her to sit with him and watch movies. Horrified, she'd tried to shut her eyes, but he'd threatened her and then held her firmly on his lap, so tight she could barely breathe.

She had no recollection of her first night in the cabin or of the videos he had taken of her. She had sobbed and tried to run out of the door. There was no escape. Evan was so strong he could just pick her up in one arm and restrain her without a problem. When he sat her down and told her the rules he expected her to obey, she had shaken her head and refused. He had locked her in a closet for hours. When he had taken her out, he'd asked her again if she would obey the rules. She'd screamed and run for the door throwing it open and running out into the wilderness. Behind her, he'd followed slowly, laughing.

After running around for what seemed like hours, he'd caught her, dragged her back to the cabin by her hair, and then thrown her into the small cage. The quilt had been his only concession, to avoid her freezing to death. The time alone in the tiny space had given her the opportunity to think straight. She had very few options. He'd explained she would never leave the cabin until someone else had made an offer for her. She would need to work for her food and do everything he said willingly or she would spend most of her life inside the cage.

Footsteps and the sound of men's voices came from outside the shed. She had no room to turn around to look at the door, but as the rusty hinges creaked, a blast of freezing air smelling of snow hit her cheeks.

"Get her down, so I can get a better look at her." Another man, carrying a small bag, walked around her cage peering at her.

"She'll fight, scratch, and bite." Evan grinned at her. "She's a little wildcat. Aren't you, Shiloh?"

"There are some who'd like that in a girl." The man smiled. "I might have taken her myself, but my place isn't set up for company just now. I'm staying above the practice, but I do have a nice secluded cabin not far from here. It will be ready in a day or so. I have the men working on it for me as we speak."

"You found a practice already?" Surprise crossed Evan's face. "How did you manage that?"

"These mining towns always need another doctor." The doctor smiled. "I emailed them my credentials and Dr. Clint Brewer got the position. They provided the office in town and a receptionist—an old biddy, been in the town for centuries." He lifted his chin. "They're looking for security guards and I can vouch for you. Our stories are that we came all the way from Dawson, met up in town just yesterday. I've brought all the documents you need to get the job with me. They're in my truck."

"That's great! This place is perfect." Evan rubbed his hands together. "Easy access by chopper or road most times. People on the move back and forth with the mines. No chance of any suspicion."

Trembling, Shiloh tried to pull away as Evan dragged her from the cage. Her numb legs crumpled under her and she fell at his feet. She looked up at the two men. The second man, Brewer, was nodding at her. She looked up at him. "Can you help me?"

"I sure can." Brewer placed his bag on a bench and pulled out a syringe. He filled it from a small bottle and bent toward her. "This will help."

Trying to scramble away, Shiloh gasped when Evan's fingers dug into her shoulders. A sharp prick slammed into her thigh and warmth flooded through her. Lightheaded, she fell forward and lay on the ground, her cheek pressed into the dirt. Moments later, Evan lifted her up and carried her out into the cold and headed to the cabin. He tossed her onto the bed and stared down at her. Lightheaded and dizzy, Shiloh fought the drug rushing through her veins. "I want to go home."

"This is your home." Evan's eyes bore into her like knives. "Get used to it. You know now you can't run and I can make you obey me." He waved a hand at her. "We can give you a little or a lot of the drug as we see fit. Do you want to be like this? It's much easier if you cooperate."

Shaking her head, Shiloh glared at him as he moved in and out of focus. "I hate you. Lock me up, I don't care. I'll never do what you want, not ever." She tried to control the tears spilling down her cheeks.

"Is this how it's going to be?" Evan shook his head. "It makes no difference to me. You think on it for a time. The doctor will be back to see you real soon." He smiled, showing yellow uneven teeth. "I'll make sure he leaves a ton of those shots here just for you. Now, I gotta go. Doc brought another girl for me to check out. Catch you later."

The key in the lock turned, and Shiloh tried to make her eyes focus but the room swam. She couldn't lift her arms and trying to sit up was hopeless. Terror gripped her. She'd never been so terribly alone. Nobody had told her about men like Evan. He frightened her and the doctor was no better. Treating her so bad was like some horrible game to them. She had no chance to escape and now they'd trapped another poor girl. She moved her tongue around her dry mouth and tried to call out. She desperately needed a drink but only a whisper escaped her parched throat. She lay there unable to move for some time before the key in the lock turned again and the doctor walked inside. "Please, can I have a drink of water?"

Brewer said nothing and the smell of cigars drifted inside the room with him. After removing his coat and laying it neatly over the back of a chair, he turned to stare at her. "Evan told you, you must earn your living, didn't he? I'm sure he explained the rules." His gaze moved over her. "This is the easiest way to earn points. All you have to do is smile. You'll get points for every time you smile. Points add up to food and water." He pointed to a red light in the corner. "Why don't you smile for the camera and we'll see about the water?"

Shaking her head as best she could, she turned her head away. "No."

"Have it your own way." Dr. Brewer moved around out of her vision. "I don't really care. I have girls in foster care eager to take your place. You, my dear, are disposable."

She trembled all over. *Disposable?* What was going to happen to her now?

# TWENTY-TWO

*Rattlesnake Creek*

Beth's mind was moving in a thousand directions at once. She ran both hands through her hair and stood, needing to step away from the computer screen for five minutes. She'd been following threads of information on the dark web since arriving at the office, and the moment she believed she had a lead it vanished. The work was time-consuming and frustrating. More so was the death in custody of the man who had been arrested at the motel. He had been found in the exercise yard at County with a shank in his heart. The information had come as a shock to her. She understood the pedophile ring was widespread, with more people involved than she could possibly imagine, but for them to have acted so swiftly in removing a possible threat astonished her.

She filled a cup with coffee, added the fixings, and walked over to the window. From here she could see down Main and wondered where Styles had gotten to. He'd been gone for over an hour and usually when he took Bear for a walk he was back in fifteen minutes or so. He'd impressed her in the way he'd supported her after the incident at the motel. Her conscience was completely clear. She'd discharged her weapon in the course of duty and by the rules: the first and second being the immediate threat to life, and she'd followed procedure by aiming at central mass, and the third, she had no choice but to incapacitate with a head shot. Although, the sheriff had believed her to be incompetent by risking Styles' life by making that shot, Carter and Jo Wells had commended her. Her accuracy with firearms was on the record. She believed their reports and Wolfe's would go well with the director. Her only worry was that the assessment she'd expected earlier regarding her competence to continue in the FBI had never eventuated. Mainly because Styles had made favorable reports about her and made no secret that he appreciated her working with him.

She caught sight of Styles walking along the sidewalk carrying a heavy bag. Bear loped along beside him, tail wagging. That dog was always happy. He had accepted her into his family without reservation and made it his duty to guard and protect her. She'd had absolutely nothing to do with a Belgian Malinois before and had listened to Styles' intriguing account of how they'd been thrown together. The dogs being loyal to their owners, Bear was found clinging to life, beside his fatally wounded handler during a mission. Styles had carried Bear miles to get him treatment and retired from service soon after. His request to allow Bear to retire with him had been accepted and they'd been inseparable ever since. She recalled Styles telling her about his marriage breakdown. Going through what he endured, at least he had Bear. She straightened and turned away from the window. She wished she'd had a Bear in her life as a child—maybe she'd be normal.

Beth went back to her desk and continued to dig deep into Shoebridge's files. He'd been proficient in his file cleanup but not perfect, and it was the imperfections she could exploit. She pulled a line of data from the stream and followed it. To her surprise, it opened up a page of data. She swallowed hard. She'd stumbled into a fraction of the kingpin's files. There were lists of auction dates, activities that came close to troop movements. She'd no idea how far-reaching this organization had spread. She checked the data again, following tiny fragments. Everything she found screamed out it was centered in the US. It spread across the globe, but the main players were in every state. She downloaded the data to her thumb drive and went back to make sure no one could trace her movements and leaned back in her chair. Her heart pounded. No wonder they wanted her dead. They'd discovered her name and by now they'd know her capabilities in cybercrime. For them, she'd just become enemy number one.

The door opened and Bear bounded inside and nudged her leg. "Hello, Bear. Where have you been? Your nose is like ice."

"We went to see Cash and his new assistant by the name of Amber Lane. Just out of college but as smart as a whip." Styles held up the bag. "I dropped by TJ's and picked up some take-out. As you've had your head stuck in the computer all day, I figured you'd appreciate a bite to eat."

Smiling, Beth picked up her coffee cup and followed him to the kitchenette. "I would, thank you. One thing before we start rehashing the case again: have you heard anything on the grapevine about me? I mean, there was supposed to be another review of my competence and now I'm involved in a shooting. Should I be packing my bags?"

"Heavens no." Styles dropped the bag on the counter and stared at her. "I spoke to the director when we got to the hotel. I gave him a verbal report and he'd received reports on our debriefing. I explained the situation and I commended you on your action under extreme stress. He was very impressed. I also told him I need you here on this case."

Swallowing hard, Beth looked at him. "What did he say?"

"Well, actually he said I could keep you here as long as I

wanted and that you'd obviously found your niche in life."
Styles unpacked the bag, spreading the food along the counter.
He glanced at her. "I hope that's what you wanted?"

Inhaling the aroma of hot food, Beth smiled. "I've never
been happier than working with you and Bear."

"That's good because I love having you around, Beth."
Styles flashed her a white grin. "I've forgotten what it's like to
be lonely."

Contented, Beth returned his smile. "Me too." She sighed,
wanting to continue the conversation on how much he loved
having her around, but that would have to wait for another time.
Over a long dinner at TJ's maybe? She flicked him a glance.
"Now, what other news do you have? You've been gone forever,
so something must be brewing in town."

When he explained about the missing girl, Beth's heart
missed a beat. "So I gather they have a full search underway?
Do you know when she was last seen?"

"Yeah, when she left school. It's been twenty-four hours."
Styles frowned. "There's no sign of her anywhere. She's
vanished without a trace."

# TWENTY-THREE

After removing his coat, hat, and gloves, Styles chose a bowl of chili and a bag of crackers from the selection on the counter. He carried them to his desk with a cup of coffee that Beth had poured for him. He dropped into his chair, and Beth sat opposite. As he removed the lid from his bowl of chili, he looked up at her. "I'm not expecting Cash to get any hits on the APB he issued across the state. I believe if our suspects followed the normal bugging-out protocol, they'd have a different vehicle and identification papers ready to go."

"Yeah, they could have swapped out the vehicles and left their current one in a garage anywhere across the county." Beth sipped a cup of pumpkin soup and dabbed at her lips with a napkin. "Our chances of finding them would be zip." She looked up at him over the rim of her cup. "Kids that are victims of opportunistic thrill kills are usually murdered within the first few hours of their abduction. The bodies are dumped and the victims usually discovered within the first twenty-four hours unless the perpetrator buries them somewhere, which in the case of opportunistic thrill kills is an unnecessary waste of his time. He would be long gone by now, but the missing girl isn't our priority if she's dead." Beth sipped the soup and placed the to-go cup on the desk. "Her going missing would fit perfectly into our case. It is too much of a coincidence to believe that this girl went missing within twelve hours of Shoebridge vanishing. From what you've told me about your sister's disappearance, it fits his MO."

Styles sprinkled crackers over his chili, his mind going back to the day when his sister was abducted. It had happened so fast. One minute she was there and the next minute she had vanished. "If Shoebridge did take this girl, how did he know that she'd be walking home alone at that time?"

"She was already a target." Beth nibbled on crackers between sips of soup. "This is exactly how a pedophile ring works. Think of it like a baseball club. They have scouts out hunting down possible players. These people are well paid for information on vulnerable kids and protected by the organization." She finished her soup and reached for a pink donut from a box she'd carried to the table. "I have no doubt that Shoebridge was whisked away to a safe house in another county and collected the girl along the way. Ginny told you she went with him willingly because she believed he was a cop. He'd be using the same ploy every time." She held the donut in one hand as she sipped her coffee. "His security guard uniform could easily confuse a kid."

Allowing her speculations to percolate through his mind, Styles swallowed his last spoonful of chili and leaned back in his chair. "If you're correct, then we know which direction he's heading. We could narrow down our search to heavily forested counties. Somewhere where he could have an isolated cabin in the woods, but not a small hunting cabin, something more substantial."

"He'd also need to work. He'd establish himself in the town as a nice guy so nobody suspects anything." Beth licked sugar from her fingers. "Agreed. Some pedophiles would hide in the forest off the grid, but we've already established that Shoe-bridge's involvement goes a lot deeper than just abducting kids. If he weren't deeply involved in this organization, we would have found him on the side of the road with a bullet in his head. The same with the doctor. What we've stumbled over by accident when we hunted down your sister is two of the key players."

Styles brought up files on his computer and scrolled through them. He turned the screen to show her. "I'm just looking at the file of the incident that happened in Black Rock Falls last year. Sheriff Alton discovered a missing girl by accident which led her to three men living off the grid in Cottonwood Forest. These men purchased suitable girls from foster care. The girls were reported as runaways. They were kept as slaves for years and their babies sold to an adoption agency. It says in the files that although the foster parents were charged, the adoption agency and the judge who signed over the children escaped justice. The adoption agency was working through a doctor who brought them unwanted babies with paperwork signed by the mothers giving up the babies for adoption." He raised both eyebrows. "They had the paperwork from a doctor, and the judge put through the adoptions. The parents no doubt paid a fortune for the babies, but they went through the normal screening process. The hope is they went to loving, rich parents."

"A doctor?" Beth rubbed her forehead and stared at him. "Ginny mentioned a doctor who came and took away her babies. Do you figure our Dr. Paul Benson is the same man?"

Styles had mulled over this case all night and nodded. "It makes sense that it's him. He had a practice in Blackwater, which is driving distance to Cottonwood in Black Rock Falls. It's a central town with good access roads to surrounding counties. If we could discover the doctor's name on the paperwork, we'll know for sure."

"What about the girls taken from foster care?" Beth rested her hands on the table peering at his screen. "What did Sheriff Alton discover about them?"

Scrolling through the files, Styles frowned. "It wasn't in her jurisdiction. The foster parents claimed the girls ran away but were charged with endangering the welfare of children. So we don't know how many people are actually involved. Seems to me there are three separate things going on here: the abductions, the selling of foster kids, and the baby adoption racket."

"Reading these files, we can add murder from our own files, and sex slavery." Beth shuddered. "It can start in foster care. Kids are abused, passed around, and then vanish. I ran away, but I figure if I'd become compliant, I'd have been sold. I believe Shoebridge is running a halfway house. He prepares the girls so they can be sold at a higher price. Either by using drugs or locking them in small spaces until they obey him." She rubbed both hands down her face. "This is just one side of the coin. We're assuming Shoebridge and Benson deal exclusively in young girls, which leads me to the question of who in the organization is dealing in young boys?"

# TWENTY-FOUR

Information gathering at this time was paramount, and Beth searched online maps for Bison Ridge. After studying the small communities in the area, she turned in her seat to look at Styles. "Bison Ridge is a small mining town between Black Rock Falls and here. It's ten miles from Louan, so we can assume Shoe-bridge is heading in our direction."

"He'd easily have driven here by now, but why come to a town with an FBI field office? That's flying too close to the fire." Styles stood and walked over to her desk to peer over her shoulder at the maps. "I figure if he's heading this way, he'll be at one of the outlying mining towns. There are a ton of them all over this part of the state." He ran his finger over the screen. "At least three, including our town, have the require-ments he would need. See here, where the mining areas are surrounded by forests? He'd have seclusion if he had a cabin there and a job just across the river where the mines are oper-ating in all of these places. They'd be far enough away from Louan that it's unlikely anyone would know him." He glanced at her. "If he decides on security work, the smaller towns are screaming out for workers of all trades. He'd walk right into a job, but it will be difficult to find him if he's changed his name."

Agreeing with his suggestions, Beth stared at the map. "I figure that's a given. Look here. These are places we've visited: Serenity, Rainbow, and Spring Grove. He wouldn't be stupid enough to come here."

"But does he know we're still alive?" Styles stood and refilled his coffee cup. He returned to his desk. "He'd have been on the road when we were attacked. We have no idea what the communications are like between him, the doctor, and the organization."

Turning her head, Beth shrugged. "Likely they do. I'd imagine they'd have burner phones. If they arranged for Shoebridge to abduct Shiloh along the way, it proves they're in constant communication." She frowned at the screen. "I'm coming around to believing Shoebridge and the doctor are a team."

"If so, do you figure the doctor would set up a practice in the same town this time?" Styles leaned back in his chair and rested his boots on his desk.

The possibility had entered Beth's mind. "Hmm, I was concerned about how he'd do that... move around the state or go interstate using a new name, but he'd only need to go through the Interstate Medical Licensure Compact to be licensed between states, but that's the legal way to obtain a license. They'd need to hack the database and insert new credentials under the assumed name. I've been attempting to unravel their activity on the dark web, and if you're questioning if they could create phony IDs and credentials to fool anyone checking them, yes, they can. This is a sophisticated organization. They're using cyber techniques to insert people into a life that didn't exist five minutes ago. I'm assuming they are using AI technology to do it so fast."

"So they can also cover their tracks in a few seconds?"

Styles dropped his boots to the floor and straightened. "How are we going to find them?"

Beth smiled at him. "Anything they can do I can do better."

Having a fortune in Bitcoin and offshore bank accounts, Beth didn't need to rely on the income from the FBI. As the Tarot Killer, she had amassed a fortune by taking down all types of schemes and the men running them. The life insurance on her mother and the sale of the family home meant by the time she turned twenty-one, she had more than enough to start a new life. Having a fortune behind her also meant she purchased the best computer hardware and software available. Through other means, she had obtained as-yet-unreleased AI software and could use it to track down criminals.

"You do know that when they discover we're alive and well, they'll likely send more goons?" Styles rubbed his chin. "You can't track their communications, can you? It would be nice to know when they're coming."

Shaking her head, Beth looked at him. "If I could, I'd pinpoint where they are right now and we could haul them in." She met his gaze. "Maybe we should do what we discussed before? I could leave a few crumbs for them to follow and set up a trap?"

"They didn't need a few crumbs last time, did they? The moment we pulled the files on missing kids they were on us. They have a watchdog online or something in place that triggers when anyone gets close." Styles' eyes flashed with anger. "I figure we head out first thing and do a recon of the towns on our list. Poke around some and see what we can find. Maybe stay over and see if anyone crawls out of the woodwork to murder us in our sleep." He gave her a long look. "I figure we need to find this little girl before she's moved into the system and lost forever. We need to stop these men from doing any more damage to people's lives."

Seeing a flash of controlled rage move across Styles'

features, Beth needed to probe deeper into his emotions. What was he really thinking? She leaned forward in her chair. "Can I trust you to bring in Shoebridge alive? We need to find out what happened to all his victims."

"I'm aware, but I have a score to settle with Shoebridge." He dropped his gaze and lifted it back to hers. "My daddy wasn't a serial killer, so I have no excuse to feel this way, but for what he did to my sister and those other kids, I want to tear him apart with my bare hands."

# TWENTY-FIVE

Unaccustomed to the tangled feelings rushing through him, Styles stood and walked to the window. He took a few deep breaths staring into the coming evening but not really seeing anything. During his time in the military police, he was a leader and a role model. The director had sent Beth to his office for him to be a good influence over her. Sure, he took the law into his own hands some of the time, but rather than having men doing jail time for a stupid mistake, they were working and going back to their families. He earned their respect most of the time, but voicing his innermost feelings to Beth had been a mistake. He needed to regroup and move forward. His sister was safe and he had a handsome nephew. He should be happy —but he wasn't.

"Do you want to hear something funny?" Beth walked to his side and inclined her head to look at him. "Last week when I was in TJ's, Wez came to chat with me. TJ was doing something or other. Well, Wez figured we don't act or speak like FBI agents."

Styles kept his eyes fixed on the mountains in the distance. A line of clouds had gathered on the horizon, and he wondered if winter was really over. Although the trees were showing the first burst of spring, the temperature still plummeted every night. "We don't dress like city FBI agents. It wouldn't be practical in this weather or terrain." The idea of speaking like one of the FBI agents on TV made him smile. They'd never been permitted to use technical jargon when speaking to the public. "How exactly are FBI agents meant to speak? We're trained to communicate effectively and professionally when dealing with the public. We're human like everyone else and can tell corny jokes to each other here in the office, but I figure we act with due respect to people in the street."

"I told him he was watching too much TV." She grinned at him. "I also mentioned that he sees us in our downtime. If we haul him in for questioning, he might see a different side to us."

Nodding, Styles turned to look at her. She was very good at deflecting problems away from their working relationship by making inane conversation to break the tension. Or with antidotes about crazy times in her life to lessen the stress of horrific crime scenes. It was these little side conversations that prevented them from becoming robotic, heartless investigators. He met her gaze. "That's true. Can you imagine the complaints if they depicted real crime scenes and investigations in TV shows. Even the true crime shows give a clinical version of the truth. The true horror of what we must endure is never depicted."

"Which brings me around to your comments earlier." Beth sat on the windowsill in front of him. "I'm sure that's not the first time you felt like doing violence to a criminal after seeing what they've done. Heck, I feel like that most times. I've come to the conclusion it's quite normal to be angry against someone who has perpetrated a vicious crime against a child. The fact it was your sister only makes it worse." She searched his face as if trying to see inside him. "There are many people involved in this case and we need to channel our anger into stopping them."

Styles nodded. "Yeah, I will. Thanks, Beth."

Without thinking, he squeezed her shoulder and then dropped his hand. He understood Beth had a problem with anyone touching her. He had battled against office protocol when she'd been in desperate need of a shoulder to cry on after they'd been arrested. It had been playing on his mind all night. He'd be fooling himself if he refused to believe he didn't find Beth attractive. Foolish and blind. In truth, he craved a little compassion from someone as well. He frowned at her. "I'm really sorry, Beth. I shouldn't have touched you. It was inappropriate."

"Do you know how long it's been since someone gave me a hug when I was upset?" She looked at him and her eyes filled with tears. "My mom." She squeezed his arm. "I was so alone in that interrogation room. My mind was replaying everything that happened like grotesque reruns. When you gave me a hug, the world stopped rushing by on fast-forward." She blinked and one fat tear ran down her cheek. "You've been kind and nonjudgmental since I arrived and accepted my quirky behavior. I appreciate you more than you know." She smiled at him. "You don't have an inappropriate bone in your body. Trust me, if you crossed the line, you'd end up on your backside."

Relieved, Styles chuckled. "That's good to know." He glanced at his watch. "We'll be leaving at eight in the morning. I think I'll call it a day. I'll take Bear for a walk and then head to my apartment. Unless you need me for anything."

"I've gone just about as far as I can for now." Beth slipped from the windowsill. "I need a fresh start. It's intense work and I'm way too tired. I'll rinse our cups and then head up for a nice hot shower." She looked at him. "If Cash calls with an update, let me know, but I'll be in bed by ten."

Styles whistled to Bear and, grabbing his coat and hat, headed for the door. He needed a walk to digest everything Beth had told him. Since she'd arrived her lack of emotion had concerned him. He understood she'd been through a bad time and had ghosts from her past, but it had taken over a year for her to drop her guard around him. The lack of empathy that had concerned the director must have been a wall she'd built around herself to prevent getting hurt. He walked out of the building and pushed his hat onto his head as an arctic blast hit his warm flesh, sending goosebumps running up his arms. He quickened his pace along Main with Bear running ahead, sniffing the grass alongside the sidewalk. Having Beth trust him at last was an incredible step forward. He wouldn't let her down.

As he headed into the park, Bear was used to having the freedom to run and disappeared into the half-light. Styles followed him through the shadows with the grass squelching underfoot. The daytime sun had been too weak to dry out the sodden soil. Along the perimeter of the park, piles of gray melting snow filled with dead leaves, sticks, and candy wrappers was all that remained from the deep snowdrifts of winter. He'd walked about one hundred yards, when the crack of a rifle rang out. Beside him, splinters exploded from a tree, showering him with small pieces of bark. Survival instinct dropped into place, and he ducked into the line of trees surrounding the park as another bullet stripped the branches from the tree beside him. There was no mistake. A sniper had him pinned down.

Images of the town flashed through his mind as he considered the shooter's position. He could almost picture the rifle fitted with a suppressor resting on the windowsill of one of the redbrick two stories across the road, or maybe the roof. Not the bank but maybe the library. It would be easily accessible with a lockpick. More shots peppered the trees around him, and he pressed his back against a broad pine. So he'd been right. They had sent more goons to silence them or warn them off.

How had they located him? They couldn't have been waiting all day. Realization hit him and he cursed under his breath. He'd made a classic mistake. Each night, when he was at home, he took Bear for a walk in the park around eight before settling down for the night. He recalled TJ once saying that he could set his clock by him as he would often drop by the bar and grill on his way home. He shook his head, trying to get to terms with the idea that other people had been watching his movements. It had been only a couple of days since he went looking for Ginny. It made no sense. They'd need to follow his movements, unless Beth had triggered an alarm on the dark web when she was hunting down Ginny's whereabouts. It seemed impossible as she was so fastidious about covering her tracks, but right now he had no other explanation. As bullets whizzed past him, he pulled out his phone and called Cash to explain the situation. He needed a distraction to get away. "I haven't seen a muzzle flash. From the angle, maybe he's shooting from a window in the library or from the roof."

*"I'll roll down Main, lights and sirens. That will get his attention so you can move. When you get clear, head down toward the river. I'll meet you there and give you a ride back to the office."*

Styles duckwalked to the next tree and then into deeper cover behind bushes. "Nah, take me to the library. It should be closed at this time of night. I'd like to know who's trying to kill me."

Two more rounds hit close by, showering him with pine needles, and heart pounding, Styles changed direction. "Best you make it fast. The sniper must have a night vision scope. That was a little too close."

*"Copy that."* Cash disconnected.

*Pfft, pfft, pfft.* The rifle discharged. The rounds stripping the tree trunks around Styles' position, pinning him down. He heard the unmistakable sound of Bear running toward him through the thick vegetation and groaned. Charging under fire was what Bear had done many times before. He had no fear of gunfire or bombs going off around him. His priority was keeping his owner safe. A sense of dread washed over Styles. "Bear. Down. Stay. I'm okay. Stay."

A whine came from his far right and he breathed a sigh of relief. "Good boy. Down. Stay." In the distance the sound of sirens wailed in the night and blue and red lights strobed across the park as Cash headed toward the library. In his pocket, Styles' phone vibrated against his chest. He pulled it out. "I'm kinda busy right now, Beth."

*"The sirens, is that to do with you?"* Beth's footsteps echoed on tile. *"What's happening? Where are you?"*

Shaking his head, Styles pushed in an earbud and attempted to crawl away. "I'm pinned down by a sniper. Cash is distracting him, so hopefully I'll be out of danger soon. I can't talk now. I'm moving deeper into the forest." He disconnected, stood, and ran, weaving between the trees. "Bear, come on boy."

When they reached the river, he kept low and ran along the sandy bank, coming out of the forest near the parking lot where Cash was waiting with the back door of his cruiser thrown open. Styles heaved Bear inside and dived in behind him. "Am I glad to see you."

"Stay down, I drove slow and searched the windows but didn't make out the muzzle of a rifle." Cash headed down a backstreet and parked in an alleyway. "If the shooter is on the move, he'll be using the back entrance. We'll be able to catch him if he came this way." He climbed out of the vehicle drawing his Glock.

Styles followed, his hand resting on the .357 Magnum strapped to his thigh. He could draw it fast if need be. "I'll be surprised if it's only one sniper. They sent four men to attack us last time."

"Seems to me you've gotten yourself into a mess of trouble." Cash eased around the corner and then froze. "The back door to the library is wide open."

Being in similar situations many a time, Styles pulled his

weapon. "It might be a trap. Stay low and stick to the wall. I'll cover you. Go!" He aimed at the doorway, but nothing moved in the shadows.

He dashed across the courtyard and pressed his back to the wall on the opposite side of the door to Cash. "Go low." He aimed his revolver around the doorframe and then eased inside.

No sound, nothing came from inside the library. He walked up the stairs, watching for any movement. The first door they came to was locked. "There's no sign this was picked. We'll try the roof."

As they turned onto the next flight of stairs, a whine and a creak came from above. A cool breeze rushed toward them, and Styles turned to Cash. "They've gone." He holstered his weapon and used the flashlight on his phone to illuminate the roof. It was empty, as they suspected, but as they walked along the perimeter, Styles picked up a glint in the dark. He bent to examine the casings spilling across the ground. He pulled out an examination glove from his pocket and collected them, folding the glove around them before dropping them into his jacket. "I'll check them for fingerprints, but I doubt it will be any help. The guys who attacked us before didn't exist."

"Like I said"—Cash shook his head slowly—"you've gotten yourselves in a mess of trouble this time. When are they sending in the cavalry?"

Styles shrugged. "As far as I know, we're on our own."

# TWENTY-SIX

*Rainbow*

"Just remember your new name is Evan Slone." The doctor looked at Shoebridge and shook his head. "If you make a mistake with your name or mine, a small town like this will have tongues wagging. I'm Dr. Clint Brewer."

Evan smiled. "It's not the first time I've transferred to a different location." He slapped the doctor on the back. "You worry too much. Now, you brought two fresh girls with you. Which is the rare beauty you told me about?" He finished his bottle of beer and stood. "Get them out of the van. I'm over waiting."

"Here's the deal: you get Bonnie as a replacement for Ginny, but Bonnie is only sixteen, so she has a few more years before you'll need to trade her for something better. Luna has done her job talking to Shiloh and will be returned."

Frowning, Evan stared at him. "It was nice having Luna waiting here for me when I arrived. Must she go?"

"She's great for settling the new ones and that's her job. We need her elsewhere. Bonnie is very compliant; she'll suit your needs." The doctor emptied a glass of bourbon and poured another. "I'll need you to care for Callie for me until I get my practice settled. I have a place not far from here, but I'll need to be in town for a time, so I'll visit until I can establish a cover."

Heading for the door, Evan shrugged. "Sure, whatever works. The barn is big enough to keep four girls while I'm working if needs be."

"This is why this place was chosen." The doc pulled out his keys and headed down the front steps to his van. "It has easy access from the highway, discreet and unnoticeable. It's perfect. Mine is much the same but your house is bigger."

Excited, Evan stood to one side as the doc fumbled with his keys. "Why didn't you bring your girl with you? You seemed taken with her."

"I wanted to start fresh, so I dropped by one of our foster care homes and left her with them and picked up Callie. Don't worry, she can't tell anyone about our business who cares. She'll be well supervised and then away to a new place before she can take a breath." The doctor swung open the back doors of the van. In fact, she is in an auction next weekend." He smiled at him. "The cash just keeps rolling in." He climbed into the van and unchained the two girls in the back. He pushed one toward Evan. "This one is yours. She can cook and I'm starved. Set her to work right away." He gave him a sideways glance. "Seems to me, you'll be glad I got Bonnie out of the house before I reported the death of her owner. Shiloh is going to be trouble. Keep her for a couple of weeks and see if she settles. If not, I'll move her on."

Nodding, Evan pulled the gaffer tape from Bonnie's mouth and stared at her in the moonlight. The girl dropped her gaze to the ground. Just as the doctor had said, she was a rare beauty. He led her up the steps and into the kitchen. "I'm Evan. You belong to me now. There are supplies in the cartons on the counter. The refrigerator is stocked. Make us all supper."

"How many meals?" Bonnie hadn't made eye contact with him.

"Five." The doctor pulled the tape from Callie's mouth and glared at her. "Go and help her. Remember the options I gave you. Do everything we say or I'll lock you in a dark closet. Run away and I'll chain you. Life can be easy. It's all up to you."

Very happy with his new girls, Evan watched Bonnie searching through the cartons. "When do I start my new job?"

"Not until late Thursday afternoon." The doctor gave him a side eye. "Time enough to get settled in here."

Evan nodded. "That's good, and have you fixed the problem with the FBI snooping around?"

"I hope by now they're a bad memory." The doctor paused in the doorway to look at him. "I have a team on it. They make a move and we countermove. We no longer exist. There are no tracks leading here. Same as always, we and all our fellow enthusiasts are invisible."

Laughing, Evan followed him inside. "That's good to know."

# TWENTY-SEVEN

*Rattlesnake Creek*

Concerned for Styles' safety, Beth bolted along the sidewalk, scanning the buildings opposite the park, but saw nothing. The freezing cold bit into her cheeks and hurt her lungs, but she needed to back up Styles. She'd heard sirens and now it was quiet, but as she ran past the sheriff's office, Cash's cruiser was missing. What was happening and why hadn't Styles called her to tell her if he was okay? A chill ran through her at the thought of him lying injured in the forest. She slowed and slid into the shadows, pulled out her phone, and called him again. The call went to voicemail and she stared at the screen in disbelief. Only minutes had passed since she'd pulled on a liquid Kevlar vest and headed out of the FBI building to lend assistance, and now nothing stirred in town. What was happening?

Ahead, a sound came from one of the alleyways as if someone had knocked off the lid of a garbage can. Heart pounding, Beth kept her back to the wall, and moved along the empty sidewalk. At this time of night, the only lights came from TJ's.

Everyone else had headed home to avoid the bitterly cold night. As Beth moved forward, street lights glistened on patches of ice and from the river the mist was rising and spilling through town. Styles was usually back before nine, even when he dropped by TJ's on his way home. Not that she kept tabs on him, but the elevator clunked and ground when it opened on their floor, and she could clearly hear Styles' footsteps on the tile as he made his way to his apartment. Beth rarely watched TV, preferring to work on her laptop in the quiet.

The noise came again, and not taking any chances of meeting a hostile or a bear, Beth unzipped her jacket and pulled out her Glock. Holding her weapon out before her in two hands, she stepped from the shadows and headed toward the alleyway. If this was the person who'd shot at Styles, a professional hit man was heading her way, and she wouldn't see him until he decided to show himself.

The space between two stores was cloaked in shadows. Beth took a deep breath and, pushing down concerns, moved forward. She'd taken two steps into the dark when something hard smashed down on her wrists. Pain shot up her arms and her pistol slipped from her grasp and slid across the sidewalk and into the curb. She spun around, raising numb hands to defend herself against the threat. A dark shadow came at her, not a bear, a man. She ducked a punch to the side of her head and twirled away, to bring down the heel of her boot on what she hoped was the man's shin. Her boot hit a solid wall of muscle, but apart from a grunt, the threat remained big and solid in the dark. "What do you want? Money? If so, you sure need lessons on mugging people."

The attacker said nothing but moved in and out of the shadows like two people, stalking her. His silence sent shivers of uncertainty up Beth's spine. She could deal with serial killers. They always had a point to prove or a fantasy to play out, but this man was on a mission. Her heart sank. This was another hired killer hellbent on taking her out. She glanced both ways, hoping to see someone walking along the street she could call to, but only the swirling mist was her witness. She moved around, keeping away from the swishing weapon he wielded. One blow struck her shoulder and she staggered, gasping in agony, but when he came again, she danced away. Pain was her friend and she'd use it to pump adrenaline through her veins and keep her one step ahead of him.

Running away wasn't an option. He could throw a knife or shoot her in the back, but she doubted he wanted to call attention to his crime. Mercenaries either went in all guns blazing or murdered with stealth, and from what she'd witnessed so far, he was the latter. She danced away, trying to get closer to her Glock, but the man had her measure, swishing what she believed to be a nightstick like a samurai sword to keep her where he wanted her.

In the past year, her workouts with Styles had honed her fighting skills. He'd taught her the no-rules way of fighting. The true combat of life or death used on the battlefield. When she'd faced serial killers, the extra training and tricks Styles had taught her had saved her life. The attack in the motel had awakened her dark side, and she'd dealt with the problem, using her skills without a second thought. A swish followed by an agonizing strike across her back snapped her into action. She fell hard onto the sidewalk but rolled away just as a large boot smashed down so close to her face the patch of ice beside her shattered and sprayed her cheek with shards.

Her attacker was using the nightstick or similar, with skilled efficiency. As the shadow moved, she could make him out. He wasn't a big man, maybe five-eight, but broad and muscular. He could pick her up and toss her around with ease—if he could catch her. Pushing the pain to the back of her mind, she rolled her hips and smashed both boots into his knees. The man staggered back, giving Beth precious seconds to pull the KA-BAR knife from her belt. It had been a gift from Styles. He had two and had given her one, saying she should never leave home without it. It slipped into her hand as if it belonged. Getting her feet under her, she crouched. The nightstick swished over her head, taking her hat with it. Without a second's hesitation, Beth surged up, knife in hand. Before she could stab him, his giant fist grasped her by the throat and lifted her off her feet. Fighting for her life, and eyesight fading around the edges as he squeezed the life from her, Beth used her last ounce of strength to plunge the sharp blade up under the man's sternum. She could see the path of the blade in her mind's eye slicing through his heart. As his fist slackened, she twisted the knife and then pulled it free, ready to attack again.

The man made a gurgling sound, grabbed her arms, and then toppled over, crashing to the ground on top of her. Unable to break her fall, Beth hit the sidewalk hard, the heavy weight of him forcing the air from her lungs. Intense pain gripped her and she fought to breathe. Sure he'd broken her ribs, a wave of sheer terror gripped her. Would she die here pinned beneath him? The metallic scent of his blood crawled up her nostrils as it flowed over her, soaking her jeans and warming her flesh, followed by the acrid scent of voided bowels. Beth coughed painfully as nausea roiled her stomach. Terror gripped her as she scanned the sidewalk. There could be more of them. Trapped and helpless, she must get out from under him and find help. In the dark, his surprised wide eyes stared at her in death. She pushed with her knees and bucked but couldn't move him. *I'm trapped.*

Forcing herself to remain calm, she wiggled one hand into her pocket and found her phone. It took so long to maneuver it from her pocket, and all the while the pool of blood surrounding her was growing. An awful thought slipped into her mind. Was this man really dead? Dead men don't bleed. If he wasn't dead, she would be at his mercy. With her other hand she searched around the ground for the knife and sighed with relief when her fingers closed around the handle. If he moved, she'd stab him again. Sweat coated her brow by the time she finally got the phone to her ear and used her thumbprint to unlock it. She thought for a beat and then made a decision. "Call Cash."

# TWENTY-EIGHT

Styles stared out of the window of Cash's cruiser as they completed a second lap of the backstreets, checking on motel and saloon parking lots for any signs of the shooter. Mist was billowing across the blacktop from the river. It dampened sound, and if the shooter had driven away without using his headlights until he reached the highway, they wouldn't have seen him. "Seems to me, this guy had a pickup point. He made the shots and then left."

"Maybe it was a warning?" Cash turned back onto Main. "Seems to me, if he was a professional, he'd have hit you."

Shaking his head, Styles frowned. "It wasn't a warning in Louan the other night. That was a hit squad and they wanted us dead."

"That's my phone." Cash's dash screen lit up and he pressed a button on his steering wheel. "Hey, Beth, what's up?"

*"What's up? I'm pinned under a dead man on Main near the post office."* Beth coughed and wheezed.

"I'm coming along Main now." Cash accelerated. "What happened?"

*"Later. Where the heck is Styles? Is he alive?"*

Grimacing, Styles pulled out his phone and switched it on. "I'm fine. Shooter got away."

*"No excuse."* Beth gasped for breath. *"I need you here now."*

Staring along Main, Styles made out a shadowy lump on the sidewalk. "Two minutes. Sorry, Beth, my phone wasn't on. I figured if it rang again, it would give away my position."

When she didn't reply, Styles glanced at Cash as he pulled to the curb. "Call Nate. We'll need a doctor on scene." He leapt from the vehicle and ran onto the sidewalk.

The scene that his phone light lit up made his stomach clench. A bearlike man had her pinned to the ground. Beth's face was hardly visible under his massive shoulder. A pool of congealing blood spread out around them, black in the moonlight. He bent down and peered at Beth. "Beth, look at me. Are you injured? Will moving the body cause a problem? Cash has called for Nate. He'll be along soon."

"I'm banged up some and I can't breathe with his weight on me." Her eyes flashed with anger. "Get that light out of my eyes and pull him off me."

Pocketing his phone, Styles pulled examination gloves from his pocket and snapped them on. Taking two handfuls of the man's coat, he wrenched the man up. He weighed a ton, but the moment he'd lifted him a few inches, Beth wiggled out from under him, a KA-BAR knife in one hand and her phone in the other. He dropped the body and went to crouch beside her, but seeing her blood-soaked clothes, put his hands under both arms and lifted her onto the steps of the post office. "Wait there. I'll grab a blanket out of Cash's truck."

"No!" Beth placed the knife on the steps beside her and took some deep breaths. "Check for a pulse. I want to be sure he's dead. Look at the blood, Styles. Dead men don't bleed."

Styles pressed two fingers under the man's chin and felt for the carotid artery. "He's dead. He bled out, is all, and pressed against you, it took a time to spill out. He blinked as Cash drove closer and his headlights spilled over the scene. Without saying a word, Cash climbed from the vehicle, pulled out his phone, photographed the scene, and then walked to stand beside him. Styles looked at him. "Keep out your phone and record what Beth has to say."

"Copy that." Cash walked over to Beth. "I'm going to record a statement, okay?"

"Do what you must." Beth didn't meet his gaze; her eyes were locked on Styles.

Taking in Beth's angry posture, Styles went to her side and sat on the steps. "Okay, what happened here?"

As Beth explained, Styles noticed the tremor in the hand still gripping the phone. "I should get the blanket. You're going into shock. You were in a fight for your life. There's no crime to answer here. This was self-defense. That guy is three times your size."

"I'm not going into shock. I'm angry." She gave him a look that would have most people running for the hills. "This was a setup. They didn't want to kill *you*, Styles. They wanted to get me out of the building alone and I walked right into their trap. Can't you see, this was never about you. I'm the target. They want to close down the investigation. I'm starting to believe they seeded the information on the dark web to see just how good I am. When I found it and followed it, they were watching me. I'm a threat to them and they know it."

Styles stared at her as the pieces fell into place. The director had told him that as a cybercrime expert she was at the top of her profession, but this was something else. The world of crime had recognized her signature on the dark web even with all the fancy gadgets she had acquired to make her a ghost. "Are you saying that there's no one else capable of breaking their code or whatever in the FBI?"

"I doubt it. I've been doing this since I was a kid. I can move around without being seen—or so I believed." Beth stared into space. "I'm getting close and that's why they want to kill me. They've likely set up traps now, to send me nowhere. Maybe I need to pick someone else's brains."

Uncertain, Styles leaned back, the step digging into his spine. "You mean, we ask the director if he can bring another team into the case? He is already spreading out the information on the missing kids we supplied to other teams. I'm not sure he'll agree to more boots on the ground here. He figures this is a near impossible case to solve as there are so many players with billions of dollars financing them." He let out a long sigh. "He said they move around like pieces on a chess board. The problem is we can never anticipate their next move. Right now, his focus is finding the kids. Once they're located, they might be able to backtrack and find the source."

"All the while more kids are caught up in their net." Cash's mouth turned down in the corners. "They're like mushrooms. You pick off a few and by morning another whole crop springs up."

"Yeah, it sure seems that way, but I'm sure I tripped over a lead to the organizer or kingpin, whatever you want to call him. This is what triggered the attacks on us. We came too close and they want us eliminated." Beth looked from one to the other. "I need help to work a few angles. Not here, we can work remotely and disguise the files as routine uploads. There's too much going through the FBI server for them to pick up one thread. The kid who works with Agent Carter and Wells, his name is Bobby Kalo. He impressed me with his talent for finding the invisible. I'll work with him and see if we can get in deeper without being noticed."

Styles rubbed the scar on his chin. "Is that possible?"

"Nothing's impossible, Styles." Beth picked blood from her nails. "If there's a door, we can open it."

# TWENTY-NINE

"Well, you two sure have me working overtime." Agent Ty Carter grinned at Beth around his toothpick. He indicated to Dr. Nate Mace and lowered his voice. "You didn't allow him to touch you, did you, Beth?"

Indignant, Beth stared at him. "He is my local doctor, but when we discovered Wolfe was on his way, we waited."

"We followed protocol to the letter." Styles stood beside her chair and his fists flexed. "Or she wouldn't be still sitting here soaked in blood and urine."

"I did allow him to call the time of death." Cash moved into the circle and looked at Carter. "He was on scene no more than ten minutes after the attack on Beth."

"Okay. I'll record our interview. It makes life easier." Carter pulled out his phone. He dragged a chair closer to Beth and sat down. "What happened? Start with why you were on the streets and where you were heading."

Beth went through the attack, giving a precise and clear statement. "Then I called Cash and they came running. Nate came along a short time after."

"Why call Sheriff Ryder and not Styles?" Carter frowned.

Beth shot Styles a look and then turned back to Carter. "He had his phone switched off. He didn't want it giving away his position when he was under fire. Check my phone logs. I did call him, and the call went to voicemail, so I called Cash."

"Can you pull up your sleeves?" Carter raised both eyebrows. "I'd like to see the bruising from the nightstick. It was a telescopic nightstick as you surmised, and he was carrying a Glock and a knife. Why do you figure he used a nightstick? If he'd wanted to kill you, why not shoot and run? The streets were empty as you mentioned. It seems a risky way to attack an FBI agent."

"What are you implying?" Styles glared at him.

"Nothing, but these are the questions the director will expect me to ask." Carter moved his attention back to Beth. "You know that right? After three takedowns, another person killed by an FBI agent doesn't look so good."

Exhausted and hurting all over, Beth pulled up her sleeves to display the angry blackening welts across both wrists. "Satisfied? I'm sure Wolfe will provide all the necessary images of the injuries I sustained." She lifted her chin and sucked in a steadying breath. She needed to cool her temper. Carter was only doing his job. He wasn't her enemy. "He followed this with a punch to the temple, but he missed and it grazed my shoulder. I figure it was a lethal punch. He was skilled and brutal. He wanted a clean and silent kill just like the others."

"I happen to agree with you, but you know the deal." Carter gave her a long look. "The director sent me to question you by the book. Don't kill the messenger. Give me the facts, is all. Why do you figure he was trying to kill you?"

Trying hard to ignore the blood drying on her clothes and the stink rising from her body, Beth explained her theory. "I could dig deeper with Kalo's help. He is a smart kid. He might see something I've overlooked."

"Using Kalo isn't a problem." Carter smiled. "He'll love the challenge." He stopped the recording. "I found your weapon." He met her gaze. "It was just where you said it would be. From your statement and my observance of the crime scene and the fact the guy who attacked you has no fingerprints, my report will say it was a righteous kill. I'm sure Wolfe will back it up with a forensic report." He glanced at the door behind her and smiled. "Here he is now."

Relieved, Beth turned in her chair to see Wolfe come through the sheriff's office doorway, and then her heart sank. Right on his heels was the FBI authority on serial killers, Agent Jo Wells. Not that she had a problem with the behavioral analyst personally. In fact, Jo had always treated her with a friendly attitude, but the underlying professionalism was always there. "So my state of mind is going to be the hot topic around the office again this week?"

"We all go through it after discharging our weapons." Carter smiled at her. "Don't take it personal."

"How are you, Beth?" Wolfe looked down at her, his gray eyes missing nothing as they moved over her. "I'll need your clothes." He looked down. "You can keep your boots. They look clean and I don't want you walking home barefoot." He looked at Styles. "Did you get her a change of clothes?"

"Yeah." Styles indicated with his chin toward the bathroom. "I left them outside the shower."

"Okay." Wolfe placed his forensic kit on Cash's desk and pulled out a large evidence bag. "Strip down to your underwear and bag them. I'll be along to take swabs and photograph the injuries."

Glancing at Nate, Beth swallowed hard. "I'd like Dr. Mace to be there. I'm hurting all over and might need ongoing care."

"Sure." Wolfe nodded to Nate. "When we're done, you can take a shower and Jo will have a chat with you. I know you're anxious to get back to your current case, but we need to clear you fit for duty." He met her gaze, his eyes filled with concern. "You've had a tough week."

Not used to sympathy, Beth swallowed hard. "It's going to get tougher if we don't catch this guy. You are aware I'm the only one capable of following the trail he's left on the dark web? It would take me months to bring someone up to speed with where I am on this investigation so far. If I'm taken off this case for medical reasons, when I might be banged up but my mind is working just fine, more children are going to be put in danger. There are times when we must put our own welfare to one side and look at the bigger picture." She waved a hand toward Carter. "How many times has Carter been injured and fought on, or Styles? I'm no different. I can cope with the physical stuff and my head is clear."

"You can see she's exhausted." Styles looked at Jo. "Can't this wait until the morning?"

"I wish it could." Jo frowned at him. "While we're waiting, I'll have a chat with you. Have you been under fire by a sniper before?" She led him away.

Beth struggled to her feet. "Okay let's get this over with. I can't stand the stink much longer."

# THIRTY

## THURSDAY

A slow rhythmic thumping dragged Beth out of a deep sleep. The room was dark but heavy drapes covered the windows. It could be any time between dusk and dawn. She sucked in a deep breath and winced at the pain in her throat. The memory of the attack flooded her mind and she rolled onto one side to stare at her bedside clock. The thumping got faster and something cold touched her arm. She sat up and grasped her aching head, one hand flailing for the touch light on her bedside table. A bark almost split her eardrums, and she stared into Bear's big brown eyes. His paws were on the edge of her bed and his face and doggy breath a few inches away. The dog always had this loving expression on its face and seemed to smile at her. She stretched out one hand and smoothed the fur on his head. "What are you doing in here?"

"Waiting for you to wake up, I imagine." Styles filled the doorway and the smell of coffee drifted toward her. "Wolfe's orders were to check you every two hours overnight. He was concerned about the bump on the back of your head from where you fell. That guy must have weighed three hundred pounds, I'm surprised he didn't break every bone in your body."

Beth searched around for her alarm clock. "My clock seems to have gone missing. What time is it?"

"Almost noon. I didn't want you getting up at six and heading to the gym." Styles handed her a cup of coffee, dragged a chair from in front of her dressing table, and sat down beside the bed. "Wolfe was reluctant to give you a shot to make you sleep, but as both he and Nate couldn't determine any signs of concussion, they both decided that making sure you had a long sleep would be more beneficial than leaving you to toss and turn around in pain all night."

Trying frantically to recall everything that had happened during the examination and the hours she'd spent at the local hospital having X-rays and an MRI on her skull, Beth did recall drifting off for a time on a hospital cot. In fact, that was the last thing she remembered. They had left Wolfe to deal with the transportation of the body to his office in Black Rock Falls, and Nate, Styles, Jo, and Carter had accompanied her to the hospital. She'd had her little chat with Jo as she waited for the hospital to get organized. She recalled Wolfe coming to see her after the MRI, and explaining everything was okay but she would be sore and sorry for herself for a few days. She recalled him giving her a shot and then nothing. She sipped the coffee. Styles had made it ready to drink, and she appreciated it greatly. "How did I get here? Last thing I remember is being in the hospital."

"Carter carried you, and I opened doors." Styles smiled at her. "He's asleep in my apartment. We took turns watching you all night. Jo stayed over in the apartment upstairs. We'll need to keep it ready for them in the future. I had plenty of spare bed linens and rustled them up some coffee and fixings for the night. TJ sent breakfast along, so everyone is good for now." He pointed to a bottle on the nightstand. "Nate prescribed some pain meds for you and something to take down the swelling. Your neck and ribs are badly bruised."

Everything hurt and Beth nodded. "Tell me about it. I feel like I've been hit by a train." She allowed the warm coffee to bathe her sore throat and leaned back against the pillows. "So I guess visiting the neighboring towns to look for Shoebridge is out of the question today?"

"Yeah, well it is for now and it might be a waste of time." Styles sipped his coffee and eyed her over the rim of his cup. "It seems that Amber, Cash's new receptionist, is more efficient than we gave her credit for. She has already contacted the sheriffs of the towns and asked them to watch out for anyone fitting the description of Shoebridge or the doctor. She has contacted all the local mines and left Shoebridge's name with them just in case he does try to take a job in his current name. She mentioned that people come and go on a daily basis in the mines, so it would be very difficult for them to pinpoint if he was one of the new men that they'd hired over the last week or so. Security guards were a dime a dozen. They didn't last long because the workers find them invasive, which leads to resentment and trouble in town at times, so usually the security guys don't last too long in the position."

Beth placed her cup on the bedside table. "What about a new doctor? He'd be easier to find."

"Apparently not. Unless he opens a new practice in town, he would hardly get a passing glance." Styles shrugged. "Many of the doctors who visit these outlying towns are on a rotation basis or they just fill in at some of the local hospitals, so rarely the townsfolk get to know them. They're just glad to have one available when they need them. I believe Nate is the only doctor in these parts who has a practice in the middle of town. The mines have their own medics, and if it's anything serious, they can go to the local hospital. It seems to be the way of things of late. It seems that doctors are in short supply."

Beth pushed both hands through her hair and then threw back the blankets. She still wore the clothes that Styles had taken to the sheriff's office for her, apart from her coat and woolen cap. "I need to take a shower and then get something to eat."

"We'll head over to TJ's for lunch." Styles pushed to his feet and collected the cups. "Carter has already been in contact with Kalo. He mentioned a few ideas he wanted to toss around with you when you're feeling better."

Clearheaded, Beth headed for the bathroom. "I'm okay. Go and wake Carter. I'll be ready to leave in fifteen." She stopped with one hand on the door handle and turned to face him. He was always there, like a rock she could depend on. She needed to thank him, say something, and she chose her words with care. "Thanks for watching out for me. I appreciate you more than you know. Bear too. He is one special dog."

# THIRTY-ONE

Styles insisted on driving to TJ's Bar and Grill. He gave the excuse that the weather was cold and miserable. Insisting that Beth take the ride rather than walk to the bar in her condition would never have worked. Admitting to being unable to do her job was never an option for Beth. They left the dogs in the office, although Carter's Doberman, Zorro, gave the best impression of sulking he'd ever seen. Beth had insisted she was fine, but the bruises on her neck were getting blacker by the second, likewise the very painful marks across the backs of her wrists. She moved slower than normal, indicating that her ribs were more painful than she would admit. They took a quiet booth at one end of the bar and ordered their meals. He added fixings to his cup of coffee and looked at Carter. "Did Kalo get back to you?"

"Yeah, but not about the abductions. All the info on those is on the server." Carter removed his hat and pushed a hand through his shaggy blond hair. "He has a theory about the missing babies, but not the girls taken from foster care. He figures because the girls are taken from foster care and reported as runaways, they're never followed up on. He said it was impossible to distinguish which girls had actually run away from those who had been sold into slavery. In the majority of cases, neither have ever been found. So he concentrated on running the DNA profiles of the men who are known to be the fathers of some of the babies through some popular databases. He started his search when Jenna and Dave exposed the baby-selling racket in Cottonwood Creek."

"Yeah, I know about those sites." Beth leaned forward in her chair resting her hands on the table. "Many adopted kids are using it to find their real parents. Did he find anything interesting?"

"Oh, yeah." Carter added cream to his coffee and smiled. "The three men involved in Jenna's case had sired five children listed on the database. So this goes way back." He stirred slowly and raised both eyebrows. "Five we know about. All old enough to be seeking their parents. This was only one of the databases. Since that hit, Kalo has expanded his search." He narrowed his gaze. "This is Jenna's case, but she handed over the hunt for the missing babies and the location of the foster carers to the FBI. The foster parents of the three missing girls they found were doing jail time but the investigations died there. No one would talk about any involvement with a pedophile ring and all took the blame for the scheme."

Styles shook his head. "I'm not surprised. They'd be aware whoever is masterminding the organization would have murdered them before they opened their mouths."

"So it would seem." Carter leaned back in his chair and blew out a long sigh. "Thing is, they all died in jail within a month of being sentenced. Same with the daddies of the babies. They're all dead. Someone cleaned up real well."

"So, the kids' searches would have met a brick wall." Beth lifted her gaze from her cup. "But Kalo would have their names and contacts. That's how these sites work: kids and parents leave contact details. If we have names, we can discover who adopted them. The judge involved in the case would be on file as well. The parents are the people we target. We'll discover which agency they went through and which judge signed the adoption papers." She shook her head and raised both eyebrows at Styles. "I told you a door would open. I'll contact Kalo and get right onto this today. I'd bet dollars to dimes the parents had no idea of the circumstances that led to them adopting their kids. They likely paid a huge amount to push the adoption through and believed them to be legit. If they hadn't, they'd have never allowed their kids to be DNA tested, but when we explain, I'm sure these respectable families will give us the information we require to bring down the organization behind the illegal adoptions."

"It's gonna be dangerous." Carter rubbed his chin. "I figure you're going about this the wrong way."

"How so?" Beth stared at him.

"Maybe hunt down one family but keep well away from them." Carter's brow creased into a frown. "If they're innocent, we don't want them murdered. Maybe call them and say you're the mother of a friend of one of the kids. Ask if she can recommend an adoption agency."

Styles stared at him. "What good will that do? They'd cover their tracks or make it all look legal."

"You have one of the best undercover agents, sitting right there." Carter indicated to Beth. "She can create a backstory, an entire new life that no one will question. Don't forget to add your ability to pay any amount to obtain a baby or two. Wherever this agency is, make an appointment. Maybe to add another level of security we'll swap partners. I'll go with Beth looking for a baby. We need to know who is involved. We'll need to see a birth certificate or insist we meet the doctor who will be delivering the baby. We'll offer double what they want for a newborn and see if money talks."

"I can manipulate Bitcoin accounts over the dark web."

Beth nodded slowly. "Once they give me their wallet details, I'll be able to track the money. What we use won't actually exist, and I'll be able to drain their accounts dry in seconds."

"What exactly do you mean, Beth?" Jo turned her concerned expression on her. "You're not planning on stealing from this organization, are you?"

"Not stealing, removing." Beth's eyes flashed but she smiled. "They need a currency to pay everyone along the way. Removing their funds will cripple them." She shrugged. "It will appear to vanish into cyberspace. In truth, I'll make sure charities get a boost." She looked around the table. "Think about it. Who would ever know outside of this room? I didn't need to tell you, did I? My way means people in need get it. Kids needing lifesaving operations, the cancer foundations. I can donate to them anonymously and everyone who really needs the money benefits."

"It's against our code." Jo blinked a few times and then shrugged. "It's Bitcoin, right? So only you really know how much we're talking about, am I right?"

"Yeah. Well, Kalo might as well." Beth rubbed the end of her nose. "I guess I could hand it in, but it seems such a waste and it will only go to pay politicians."

"I don't want to know the value." Carter blew out a long sigh. "Hand it in and sleep well at night."

"I always sleep well at night." Beth met his gaze. "My heart tells me to give it to people who need it." She suddenly frowned. "The thought of it going to buy weapons, when it was made on the suffering of children, hurts my soul." She let out a long sigh. "Okay, Mister Incorruptible, I'll make sure Uncle Sam gets the loot."

Not believing that for a second, Styles gave her a long hard look, recalling another time she'd taken money from crime and dropped it into a local homeless shelter. She met his gaze and shrugged. He'd talk to her later. He rubbed the scar on his chin.

"Okay, that covers the baby racket, but what about the kidnapped girls? We can't prevent that happening and then there's the girls missing from foster care."

"That's a tough one, but I figure they're all tangled together. We have opportunistic abductions and the foster care racket, but from what we know from the past cases, both must be involved in the same scheme. If I work with Kalo, we might find an auction site." Beth refilled her coffee cup from the pot on the table. "They're not watching Kalo, and if he tracks them down, he might be able to put in an order. I can arrange the Bitcoin payment. That will appear legit. Then we wait." She looked around the table. "We need to go big to bring the players out of the woodwork. I'm thinking we ask for six girls between ten and twelve. We can offer a massive amount, make it appear we have an ongoing business of some type, an exclusive brothel or similar. When they deliver, we'll insist on a meet to transfer the rest of the payment and to establish an ongoing agreement for supply. They'll want the big bucks and the easy sales. We'll have them."

"If the person who abducted the missing girl Shiloh Weeks is a player, it could be a way to find her abductor." Jo nodded. "I can't think of another way to locate her if she's been taken out of her county. It might be worthwhile speaking to Sheriff Alton to see if she was able to get any information from Styles' sister, Ginny. I know she planned to speak with her."

"I figure taking the soft approach is a mistake." Carter shrugged. "By all means go along that route, but you're relying on the abductor to talk and I doubt he will. Beth has a valid point. It would be dangerous but could offer the shortcut we need."

Considering the implications, Styles looked at Carter and raised both eyebrows. "The director will never agree to taking a risk like this. If we do it, we'll need to do it alone and play our cards close to the vest. One wrong word, one mistake, and I figure we'll be setting ourselves up for a quick and violent death."

"Amen to that." Carter shook his head slowly. "So are we giving it a try?"

The rush of the hunt shivered through Styles and he smiled at Beth. "Absolutely."

# THIRTY-TWO

After swallowing a couple of the pills Nate had insisted she take for the swelling around her ribs, Beth spent some FaceTime with Kalo. The teenage black hat hacker, who'd joined the FBI after hacking the Pentagon, had what Beth would call ongoing genius. He wasn't a one-hit wonder. His skills expanded at a rapid rate and she realized just how fast young minds adapted to technology. She'd noticed toddlers picking up phones and playing games, and kids as young as twelve could create innovative software using advanced skills she would never have thought possible. It was as if something remarkable had been switched on in their brains. It had been unusual for her as a child to be in tune with programing, her instant understanding had been looked upon as peculiar. She craved information and found her skills expanded rapidly. Like Kalo, her brain processed data at an increasing rate. It was as if they were all becoming super cyborgs.

After explaining what she needed, she found Kalo enthusiastic and with a few angles of his own to explore. She smiled at him. "That's a great idea. Find some back doors and we'll see if we can pinpoint their communication network."

"Sure." Kalo wrinkled his nose and shook his head. "This part of the work gives me nightmares. If I find any sites, I'll pass them on to you if you don't mind. I'm trying to link all the names we have of the siblings from the DNA profile matches to adoption agencies. The problem I'm having is these places are much like their owners. They are there for a time and then vanish. I'm looking for a pattern. All these people have a pattern of behavior but don't know it. I figure they wait as long as twelve months between vanishing and setting up somewhere else. They arrive in town with all their paperwork in order and appear legit. They actually arrange for a few legal adoptions to avoid suspicion, but for the illegal ones they have a judge waiting to move them through the system real fast. They use the judge's discretion to avoid the normal checks usually required for an adoption agency. The judges are the constants and this is their downfall."

Excited, Beth leaned forward in her chair. "All of the judges are involved in the ring but only handling a few adoptions to make them look clean?"

"My thoughts exactly." Kalo grinned. "I figure if we can find them... well, their identities on the dark web, we'll be able to use what we find for leverage. This is my realm of expertise. It's like gaming. They'll all have their online identities, and believe it or not, most of them are so overconfident they keep the same name. They don't realize people like us are lurking in the dark waiting to pounce on them."

Nodding, Beth smiled at him. "Okay, I'll let you get back to work. Call me if you find anything interesting."

"Oh, I'll find something. With the both of us online, we'll catch these big fish in our net."

As Beth got to work, behind her she made out the soft chatter between the others. They had split the workload: Jo was in contact with the people searching for Shiloh and would follow up her theory with Sheriff Alton from Black Rock Falls. Styles and Carter were searching the internet for exclusive adoption agencies, ones that charged high fees and promised the earth. She'd suggested they look for any that serviced towns over a wide area, worked mainly via a website, and had satellite offices. While they were busy, she gathered all the strands of information she'd collected and went to work. It was dark outside by the time she'd discovered a tiny thread with a recurring word: *Rotcod*.

She stared at it and then followed lines of data finding Rotcod was like a big fat spider in the middle of a web. Data flowed in and out of the web constantly. She'd found the king-pin. Wanting to yell out and tell the others, she stared at the screen and swallowed hard. She'd vowed to make sure the kingpin of this despicable organization would pay for the lives he'd destroyed and taken. He was the king of the monsters and now she knew his code name. The name seemed to light up in her mind as it slowly reversed. Rotcod... Doctor.

Heart pounding, she scanned the screen. The incoming data streams were encrypted and indicated a sophisticated network of many players. Could this person known as Doctor be the same doctor Ginny mentioned had delivered her babies? The one who practiced in Blackwater and then conveniently vanished? She switched computers and hunted down Dr. Paul Benson. His credentials looked impressive and typical of a local GP. She delved back, hunting for his practices and found two of the same name in the US but dismissed them as impossible. Two others were possibilities: one in France and one in Spain. Using a satellite map, she located the buildings and found a small restaurant at one location and a beauty parlor at the second. Her suspicions grew stronger when only one of the hospitals where Benson had supposedly gained his qualifications had a listing of his name. She leaned back in her chair. He must be a qualified doctor, a fake would soon be recognized by a local pharmacist or there'd be complaints made against him. She found no reports on Dr. Paul Benson in Blackwater or the surrounding towns.

This man was smart, but Beth understood human nature and no one would erase their original qualifications. Having them would act as a safety net and the rope that would eventually hang him. Beth smiled. At last she could pull the noose tighter and all she needed was an image of him to run it through the facial recognition software. Soon, she'd discover the real person behind the fake name and the spider in the web. She opened the database for the Montana Motor Vehicle Division and ran the name. Drumming her fingers on the desk, she waited frowning when no results appeared on the screen. Next, she went state by state running the name and found a few, but none of them fit the age or race. In desperation, she went back to the listings of doctors in France. Maybe she could search the local areas for images, but when she scanned the page again, Dr. Paul Benson's name had been erased. She went back to the Blackwater listing and slapped the desk in frustration. In the short time she'd been searching the MVD, the efficient machine behind the pedophile ring had deleted Dr. Paul Benson from existence.

# THIRTY-THREE

Panic gripped Beth as she turned back to her other computer. The data moved across the screen in a rapid flow. She stared transfixed watching for any anomaly, but it was business as usual. No one had detected her intrusion. Relieved she hadn't triggered a mass exodus, she stared at the data stream for some time just to be sure, and then copied a few pages as they slid down the screen. She'd have no trouble removing the encryption, and when she had, she'd apply the software to the incoming data stream and be able to read it. It wouldn't be easy tracking down everyone involved, but with Kalo's help they'd do it. Her stomach clenched. *At last.* The doctor was in her sights, and she had an overpowering desire to bring this monster to justice. Right now, she needed an image of the doctor, but as that was impossible, a description of him would have to do.

*So close I can almost touch him.* Beth smothered her exhilaration, turned in her chair, and stood. For now, she must withhold her revelations from the others. One slip and he would escape justice. This man was as slippery as an eel. She walked casually over to where Jo was sharing a desk with Carter. "Can you get back to Sheriff Alton and ask her if she can talk Ginny into giving a description of the doctor who delivered her babies?"

"Have you found something?" Styles looked up at her.

Avoiding his gaze, Beth shrugged. "It occurred to me that when we arrange a meet with an adoption agency and insist on meeting the attending physician, it would be good to know if it turns out to be the same man."

"There's something else you need to consider." Carter stared at her. "We know the doctor is a pedophile, so ask Jenna to find out if he could possibly be Billy's father." He looked from Jo to Beth. "We know it's not Shoebridge. Seems to me the only other man Ginny mentioned was Dr. Benson. If he is Billy's father, we'll have his DNA."

Confused, Beth stared at him. "What good would that do when we meet him? I need an idea of what this guy looks like."

"If he is the father of Ginny's son, you can obtain an image of him." Jo looked up at her. "I'll call Wolfe. He'll have Billy's DNA. If he removes the mitochondrial DNA and runs the father's through the Snapshot DNA analysis program, you'll get a photograph. It's been used for a time now. Haven't you heard about it?"

The program was familiar to her and she smiled. "Yes, I'm aware of it, but I didn't know it was that accurate. By all means, if Wolfe recommends it, I'm on board."

"Good. I've seen some amazing results, but it takes time. Weeks usually." Jo reached for her phone.

Beth shook her head. "Then it's a waste of Wolfe's time. We don't have weeks to stop this monster."

"Okay, then in the meantime, I'll try and convince Jenna to ask Ginny some delicate questions." Jo smiled. "I'm sure she'll at least be able to give a description of him."

Nodding, Beth frowned. "Okay, stress how important it is that we get the information."

"Jenna is very good at her job." Jo frowned. "She'll get the information."

Beth pulled her hair into a ponytail and secured it with a band from her wrist. "That's good to know. When you speak to Wolfe, ask him to send the father's DNA profile to Kalo. He's exploring DNA databases for siblings from Shoebridge and when and where they were adopted."

"We are on the edge of a breakthrough." Carter grinned. "We make a great team. I'm looking forward to trapping this monster."

"He likely won't talk if you corner him." Jo pushed hair from her face and sighed. "He's smart. You'll need to find another way."

"If he shows to the adoption meeting, then we can follow him." Styles nodded slowly. "We're planning on breaking the rules, so placing a tracker on his vehicle won't make a whole lot of difference." He leaned back in his chair and yawned. "I guess we'll all go down together?"

"Maybe." Carter tossed a toothpick into his mouth and grinned like a wolf. "If we do, a team like us would make a mighty fine detective agency. I figure we'd head for the big city and charge the big bucks."

Astonished, Beth looked from one to the other. "I figure if we crack this case, the director will be so happy he'll overlook everything. We'll make him look good." Suddenly exhausted, she rested one hip on the edge of Styles' desk. "I'm beat. I've gone as far as I can right now. Once Jo has called Sheriff Alton, can we call it a day?"

"Fine by me." Styles stood and collected the coffee cups. He took them to the sink and rinsed them.

Beth went back to her computer and backed out of the system, not leaving a trace of her presence. She pushed the thumb drive into her purse. She'd work on the encrypted files in her apartment later. In the background she could hear Jo speaking on the phone. She turned and looked at her. "How did it go?"

"Good. Jenna will go and see Ginny now and Wolfe will run the tests." Jo stood and stretched. "Now we can do nothing but wait."

"Okay, so let's eat. I hear TJ's does a fine rib eye." Carter stood and reached for his jacket.

"He sure does." Styles wiped his hands dry and strolled back to his desk. He pushed his hat on his head and whistled for Bear. He looked at Beth. "We'll walk to TJ's with the dogs. Why don't you drive with Jo? It's freezing outside."

Beth looked from one to the other. "If you're planning on walking anywhere, there may be a sniper out there. Wear your liquid Kevlar vests just in case."

"Sure." Styles smiled. "But I figure they won't try that in town again." He patted his pockets for his keys. "You can take my truck if you want."

Keeping a pleasant expression on her face, Beth met his gaze. Getting close up and personal with Jo concerned her. Although a very nice woman, Jo always gave Beth the impression she was dissecting her. It unnerved her and she needed to always be on her guard around her. Keeping her distance and not becoming BFFs with her had worked fine so far. "We'll take my truck." She looked at Jo. "Are you ready to leave or do you want time to freshen up?"

"I'm fine." Jo smiled at her. "It will be good to have time for some girl talk."

Heart sinking, Beth took her coat from the peg by the door and pulled it on, followed by her hat and gloves. The last thing she wanted was her mind probed by Jo. She'd need to keep the conversation on Jo and not her. Taking a deep breath, Beth turned to her. "I'd love to know more about your little girl. Jaime, isn't it?"

"Yes, she's doing well at school." Jo smiled. "But I want to know more about you, Beth. I'm interested in how you cope with having a serial killer as a father. I get to interview the perpetrators but never the families. How it affects your relationships would be a fascinating subject."

Beth looked away, trying to smother the rising panic and forced a smile. "When I have a relationship, you'll be the first to know."

"You seem to get on well with Styles." Jo wasn't giving up.

A cold shiver of trepidation crawled up Beth's spine as she took the keys from her desk drawer and straightened. "He's my superior, so that's a given." She gave Styles a wave. "See you in ten."

# THIRTY-FOUR

*Rainbow*

Footsteps came from outside along with the sound of someone crying. Terrified, Shiloh slid from the sofa and backed into the corner of the room staring at the doorknob as the lock turned and the door creaked open. Evan filled the doorframe, but a cold breeze still leaked in from around his body. The smell of mountain air and pine trees filled the room with an icy chill. She stared at him too afraid to speak and peered at the girl he was holding by the neck.

"This is Callie Davidson. She'll be sharing your room for a time." Evan grinned at her. "Doc has brought along another box of clothes for y'all." He pushed the girl into the bedroom. "I've explained how to use the washer and dryer down here, I want to see clean sheets on the bed. If you walk around in dirty clothes with your hair filthy, you will be punished. Do you understand, Shiloh?"

Nodding, Shiloh dropped her gaze to the floor. Speaking and following directions was part of the rules if she planned on eating and drinking. She raised her chin and looked at him. "I understand. Thank you for the clothes. I'll change the sheets on the bed right away."

"Don't forget to take a shower and make sure Callie takes one too." Evan gave Callie a push toward her. "Explain the rules. Callie is having a hard time understanding what we expect from her. Doc has left, so she'll be here until he gets back. Luna has gone, and a new girl, called Bonnie, will be bringing your supper tonight. Don't talk to her. I'm going to work but I'll be by to check on you when I get home." He looked from one to the other and nodded slowly and then went to the front door and collected a cardboard carton. He dropped it inside the door with clothes spilling from the top. "See you later."

A key turned in the lock and Shiloh let out a long breath. "I'm Shiloh. Where have you come from?"

"Foster care, a long way away." Callie rubbed at her eyes and looked around. "This is better than the place I was living in before, but I had no idea what was going to happen when I arrived. That man they called Doc took me to a motel on the way here and told me to call him Daddy. I tried to run away but he carried me inside. I started to cry and he dug me with a needle." Callie, sniffled. "I woke in the truck just before we arrived here yesterday and I hurt all over. What's happening here? It isn't a foster home, is it?"

Keeping her voice low, Shiloh explained. "I escaped but there's nothing but trees out there. The dirt road goes for miles. They put me into a cage when they caught me. If we want to eat, we must do as they say. They hate it when we cry, but if we smile, they give us candy." She pointed to the pulsing red dot in the ceiling. "Luna said they are cameras. Everything we say or do Evan knows about."

"That's horrible but I know that was happening to one of the girls in the foster home too. I told the foster mom and she said it was to be expected. I was hoping Doc was adopting me and he had a wife at home, but he doesn't." She walked around picking up things and putting them down. "Do we ever leave this place?" Callie stared at the door. "I hate being inside all the time."

Shaking her head, Shiloh touched her arm. "Not so far but I've only been here a few days."

"Is Bonnie free?" Callie wiped away tears on her sleeve.

Taking a box of tissues from beside the sofa, Shiloh handed them to her. "I'm not sure how free she is. If she's the same as Luna, maybe. I didn't see her often. Food is delivered through that small hole in the wall over there." She went to the door and pointed to a hole above a small shelf. "I guess Bonnie will access it by a sliding panel from the outside. If we can't talk to her, we won't know what's happening outside."

"It's boring here." Callie dropped down on the bed and sighed. "Do you figure if we do as they say, they'll give us a TV?"

Unable to believe her ears, Shiloh shook her head. "I don't know. There are plenty of things to do before Evan gets back. If you're bored, help me change the sheets. We can check out the box of clothes and then we'll take a shower." She thought for a beat. "Then I'll show you how to use the washer and dryer."

"I have an idea." Callie moved close to her and cupped her mouth against Shiloh's ear. "How about we make secret plans to escape? I know how to pick a lock." She moved away. "How long will Evan be away?"

Shiloh shrugged. "I don't know. He hasn't left before now."

"Time enough, I hope." Callie winked at her. "For us to get all this work done, I mean."

Excited by the idea of escaping but terrified of being alone in the forest overnight in the freezing temperatures, Shiloh shook her head. She moved closer and cupped her mouth. "We'd freeze to death."

"If he's working nights, he has to sleep sometime." Callie's voice was just above a whisper as she dragged sheets from the bed and bundled them in her arms. "Show me the washer."

It seemed that Callie was older than her years. Shiloh guessed that being in foster care for as long as she could remember did that to a person. They dumped the linen into the washer and were heading for the sitting room when Callie beckoned her into the bathroom. She followed. "I'm not taking a shower with you."

"I don't want you to." Callie ran the shower and closed the door behind them. "When we wanted to talk at my last place we went to the bathroom. In here the steam fogs up the cameras and the noise of the water covers our voices. We can speak in here without them knowing." Callie grinned at her.

Nodding, Shiloh stared at her. "So what are your plans?"

"We'll know by tonight how long he's going to be away. I know he works security at one of the mines, so he'll be doing the same shift each day. When we're ready, we'll wait for him to come home. When he heads for bed, we'll wait for half an hour and then we'll put on as many clothes as we can. We'll go to the house and raid the kitchen for supplies and then we escape. He'll be asleep for hours and so will Bonnie. They won't discover we're missing until breakfast." She grinned at her. "I'll take a shower now. We'll act like good little girls for the next couple of days and he'll believe he has nothing to worry about and sleep like the dead."

Shiloh frowned. "When is the doctor coming back for you?"

"Not for ages. He has workers at his house." Callie smiled. "Maybe as long as a week. I heard him talking to Evan. We have time to make plans and escape. They'll never find us. I know the forest. We just find the river and follow it. They always lead to a town. Then we'll be safe."

A shiver raised goosebumps on Shiloh's flesh. "I hope you're right and we get away, because if they find us, we might not survive the punishment. I near froze to death in that cage and that was just the beginning. They're monsters."

"Well then, we must make sure we're not caught. We'll need to start making plans and collecting things we'll need. Trust me, if you figure he'll kill us, our chances are better in the forest." Callie stared into space thinking. "Have you been inside the house?"

Shiloh nodded. "Yeah, only once. Why?"

"I helped Bonnie make supper last night. I know where everything in the kitchen is. We'll take knives and anything else we need." Callie frowned. "Maybe we'll be lucky and find a flashlight."

In spite of her misgivings, Shiloh nodded. "I'll go and find you some clothes."

She left the bathroom and dragged the box of clothes from a charity store to the sofa and peered inside. The thought of running again and what would happen if Evan caught her again frightened her. She chewed on her bottom lip. *What have I gotten myself into this time?*

# THIRTY-FIVE

## FRIDAY

*Rattlesnake Creek*

After working out with Styles and Carter, Beth staggered into the shower. Man, those two were intense. The testosterone in the gym was overpowering, each man wanting to show her new moves. The last thing her bruised ribs needed was two overenthusiastic instructors. Anyway, the workout had actually helped her stiff muscles and the hot shower soon made her feel ready for the day. It had surprised her how easily she'd slipped into the workout routine with Styles. Keeping in shape was essential in her job and she'd always trained alone, enjoying long runs with time to think, but the runs during the cold months just weren't practical. They hurt her lungs way too much. She'd dressed and finished drying her hair when her phone buzzed. It was Kalo and she accepted the video call. "You're up early. I assume you don't work out?"

*"When Carter's not around, I let it slide."* Kalo grinned. *"He treats me like I'm a Navy recruit. I get seasick going on a ferry."* He chuckled. *"The reason I called is that I've located a family that used one of the agencies to adopt one of Shoebridge's kids. As*

*luck would have it, I followed up on a kid my age on an adoption DNA site and we chatted. I asked where he came from as I was trying to find other siblings. He asked his mom and she told him. She mentioned it wasn't around anymore, but she had the bank account numbers for the transfer of funds and wondered if I could trace the Company owners from there."*

Heart racing with anticipation, Beth gripped the phone. "Don't keep me in suspense. What did you find?"

*"I found them. Well, I found the group."* Kalo's chair squeaked as he moved around. *"Man, when they started this racket, they were green. I followed the money. They left a trace when they moved funds offshore. It was a stupid mistake to use an intermediary bank. I used the account number and traced it all over the world. It led to a Bitcoin wallet, sitting out as plain as day. And... it's active and is part of a distribution network. So I followed the money again. Funds were provided for a setup for a company."* He grinned at her through the phone. *"Long story short, they opened an agency in Helena six months ago. The Big Hearts Adoption Agency. It's by appointment only. I'll send you their details."*

Grinning, Beth looked at him. "You are a genius. I'll get onto this right away. I'm thinking money talks, so I'll offer them double just to get an appointment. We'll see how we go." She looked at him. "Send me everything you have on the Bitcoin folder. I'll fake a deposit. I'll need it set up ahead of time."

*"You got it."* He gave her a long look. *"We can't risk encrypted files. I'll forward you invoices for office consumables. I'll add all the info you need to the barcode on the end of the page. It will read using your fingerprint scanner. I adapted them for just this use a few months ago."*

Astonished, Beth shook her head. "You never cease to amaze me. I'll give you a heads-up when I make the deposit."

*"I'll follow the money trail. It's all on the dark web. It looks legit until you get into the webpage and pull it apart."* Kalo's

expression turned serious. *"This is a massive organization. I know you have Jo and Carter with you, but take care out there now. I don't want to end up running the Snakeskin field office alone."*

Beth shook her head. "Don't worry about me. I have Styles to watch my back as well. Thanks for the info. Catch you later." She disconnected and grabbing her jacket headed to the elevator to the office.

Of course Styles was there. He'd already been to TJ's to collect breakfast. They'd decided the night before to grab takeout and eat in the office while they planned the next steps. She went to peer into the bags and grabbed a pastry. Beside her, Styles filled a cup with coffee and slid it toward her. She looked at him. "Thanks. Kalo called just before. We have a lead to an adoption agency out at Helena. This is really happening. We're going to break this ring. Our plans are finally falling into place."

"Whoa." Styles turned to look at her cup in hand. "Not so fast." His brow furrowed. "This is going to take careful planning. First up, we wait for Carter to get here. Being an ex-Navy SEAL, he is very good at strategy. I figure we'll need him to make the call to the adoption agency as well."

Beth folded her arms across her chest and stared at him. "Going undercover is my specialty and I won't have Carter telling me what to do in the field. We're equals here."

"Do I hear my name being spoken in vain?" Carter pushed through the door to the office and looked from one to the other, eyebrows raised. "I have no intention of telling you what to do."

Trying to keep her temper under control, Beth glared at him. "Styles was implying that I wouldn't be able to organize an undercover mission."

"Ah, well I've run a lot of missions in my day. Being a SEAL it comes with the territory." Carter smiled but Zorro's attention was on Beth. The dog lifted his gums, showing his sharp canines, and a low growl rumbled from his chest. Carter didn't move to instruct his dog. His green eyes had fixed on Beth with an interested expression. "Maybe we should discuss some details of this mission you need to deploy, before we fight over who has the best skills?"

To Beth's surprise, Bear, as calm as you like, just walked in front of her and sat down. His large body leaned against her knees with a "you have to get through me first" attitude. She put a hand on his head. Both dogs had felt her aggression and had taken different stances. She turned back to the counter and retrieved her breakfast items. "I guess we can discuss this over breakfast." She sat down at the table Carter and Jo had been using for a desk. Beside her, Bear rested his head on her lap and his big brown eyes searched her face. "It's okay, boy. I'm fine."

"I'm sorry if I gave you the impression that I believed Carter to be more knowledgeable than you when it came to undercover missions." Styles placed his coffee cup on the table and regarded her closely before sitting down. He opened a large box of donuts and selected one with pink frosting. "Do you like donuts, Jo?"

"I like them just fine, but I think a croissant would be better." Jo placed one on a plate and spread it with butter and strawberry jelly. "Now what's got you two so hot under the collar?"

Beth explained the call from Kalo. "I'm not planning on jumping in boots and all. I do know we have to discuss the plans on how to catch these guys in the act. We literally have nothing on paper. Ava is our only real witness and at twelve years old, her testimony is hardly going to stand up in court. Ginny refuses to say one bad word against Shoebridge. If that's his name. At this point in time we have no idea. This organization is better than witness protection. I've been scouring the internet, and once they leave a town they vanish forever. Seems the only thing they leave behind is the DNA in their progeny and we have no idea how many men or young people are involved in the baby rackets. We assume it must be hundreds, but it could be thousands as we know they've been doing this for years." She took a deep breath and looked around at the table at the faces staring at her. "We have no idea how many murders have been committed to keep their secret. We're dealing with not only the biggest pedophile ring in the country, but it's run by a serial killer of the highest degree. We don't know if he is actually killing the people personally or he's paying people to do the deed. Whatever, he is equally responsible for the deaths of people who came a little too close to discovering the truth."

"Okay, I can understand why you're concerned that Styles and I might be a little bit heavy-handed when it comes to dealing with adoption agencies." Carter opened his hands. "The thing is, we've both had a lot of experience in extremely delicate situations. Going into enemy territory to take out a target or to rescue a friendly takes a lot of skill and this isn't really much different. It all comes down to meticulous planning."

"When you went undercover, Beth, you had an entire team planning your every move." Styles gave her a compassionate stare. "Months of planning would have gone in before they risked your life. This is no different. The only thing is we haven't got months to plan if we intend to locate Shiloh before anything happens to her."

"So we split the workload and come to an agreeable mission plan." Carter reached for a donut and took a bite. He looked at her. "There isn't another option, Beth."

# THIRTY-SIX

After dealing with monsters in her own way for so long, working with a team gave Beth the impression of moving in slow motion. With them, she had to explain every move. She had no choice but to give them the doctor's name as a key player, but she'd keep the fact she suspected him to be the kingpin to herself until she'd removed him from the game. She took her time considering everything they'd said and then nodded. "Okay, as I see it, we have four different avenues to consider at the same time." She stood and went to the whiteboard and pushed it toward the table. It squealed and screeched on its little wheels as she moved it into place. "We need to establish fake identities for us as the intended parents of the child we're planning to adopt. This will take specialist skills. These people will spot a phony in seconds. I can work with Kalo on this, and we can create backgrounds, bank accounts, real estate, everything that you can think of but what we need is a base to work from out at Helena."

"There are safe houses all over owned by the FBI we can use." Styles shrugged. "They're owned by paper companies. You could easily manipulate the paperwork for one of those to make it look legit if you need a place for the happy couple to be living."

"Once that is in place, then I suggest you contact the adoption agency." Jo looked at Carter. "You have the charm to convince anyone how important it is for your wife to adopt a baby."

Beth nodded and added the suggestion to the list. "You're going to need to be able to discuss how you made your fortune. What do you want as your field of expertise?"

"I spent many of my summer vacations on my uncle's cattle ranch before I joined the Navy." Carter smiled at her. "I know the basics and I'll make sure I know the local price of beef just in case it comes up in general conversation. I still remember all the breeds and how to run a cattle ranch." He grinned and then took a bite of his donut. "There's no denying I'm a cowboy. Dressing like a rich cowboy will be easy enough. I'll buy myself a nice new shirt when we get to Helena." He gave Beth a long look. "The thing is, how are you going to act like the wife of a cattle baron?"

Trying without much effort to hide a smile, Beth looked at him. "If I can pass as a pole dancer in a strip club, being the wife of a cattle baron is going to be a breeze." She added Carter's career choice to the list. "Once I've created our backgrounds, you make the call. Offer them any amount to make the deal. The figure doesn't matter. I can make it appear that money is being transferred into their account."

"You can do that?" Carter winked at her. "There's a new truck I've been hankering over. Maybe we need to visit a dealership when we get to Helena. We'll buy a new truck to make it appear as if we're filthy rich."

Beth shook her head. "Ah, no, as tempting as it might be to use other people's money to buy things, I only do this to criminals." She shot Styles a look. "Even though I know you all disagree. I figure anything on the dark web is fair game and better placed with people who need it to help others."

"Oh..." Carter nodded slowly. "I really need a new truck to help others. Does that count?"

"Let it go, Ty." Styles shot him a warning glance. "You wouldn't like Beth when she's angry."

Beth cleared her throat. "We have to assume the same agency is handling the foster kids. This is going to be your angle, Styles. You and Jo will have to go there and try to convince them that you are prepared to take a number of girls and boys under your guardianship for an exclusive school. Say six for a start, with the option for more." She swung her gaze to Jo. "You can handle this any way you like, as a religious cult or whatever. Your intention is to take the children out of foster care to give them a better education and start in life. Anything you can come up with. If these people are honest, they would be questioning why you want so many young children. If they are more interested in the money, then we will be opening up another area of this business that we need to shut down." She glanced at Styles. "I know this is a ton of information, but this is what we do."

"This going undercover and discovering the players will only scratch the surface." Carter shrugged. "What's your endgame here?"

Beth nodded. "First, finding Shiloh because we know she's been sucked into their world. Finding her will get us to Shoebridge or whatever his name is this week. He is a key player." She sucked in a breath. "Getting eyes on the doctor is the key because I know he's a main player. We know he is linked to Shoebridge. I figure from what Ginny said they work together, and the doctor probably has many teams. He travels around when needed and delivers and collects the babies. We must track the doctor to his current home base. I'm convinced he'll lead us to Shoebridge."

"The request for six kids will raise eyebrows." Styles leaned forward, his gaze intent on her. "If we find them acceptable to the idea, I could ask to speak to the person in charge to make an ongoing deal. If this guy is the doctor, as Beth believes, we'll know he is involved with both parts of the business." He looked at her. "The problem is, I figure that asking for that many kids will make them wary of us. On the surface they look legit and we're asking them to break the law. What I need is the name of someone who I can use as a reference to open doors."

"We have names." Jo looked at Carter. "The men Jenna arrested were involved in the baby racket and had girls from foster care. We'll use one of their names and no one can check on them because they're dead." She turned her attention to Styles. "I'll brief you about the case. You can say you go way back. We know the names of his friends too and they were all involved."

"That works for me." Styles reached for another donut. "Okay, Beth. When we track the doctor and locate where Shoebridge is holding Shiloh, we'll need to go in and arrest them without getting anyone killed. The thing is, how do you plan to find everyone in this ring? Two men won't make a dent."

Having the end in sight, Beth leaned back in her chair. "If the doctor is a main player as I suspect, all I need is his laptop. He must have a list of customers or suppliers at hand. They run auctions as well, so anyone invited would be scrutinized before they'd be allowed to participate." She smiled. "I'm good at what I do and so is Kalo. You can trust me to break this wide open, but before they trip any alarms, I'll strip them of operating funds. This will prevent them from retaliating. I can keep the ring in a holding pattern while the FBI moves in to arrest everyone involved. It will look like business as usual because I'll be running the ring via the doctor's laptop. We'll be dealing with Interpol as well for those outside the US." She stood and made more notes on the whiteboard and then turned to look at them. "When it comes to the raiding of their houses and rescuing the kids, I'll leave that part of the mission to our very capable agents." She smiled at Styles. "That is out of my field of expertise."

"Not a problem." Styles brushed sugar from his hands and stood. "Time to get to work."

# THIRTY-SEVEN

## SATURDAY

Invigorated by her work the previous day, Beth stared out of the window just as the sun peeked over the top of the mountains. Although still cold, a deep blue sky spread out forever and she had a longing to get outside and breathe in the cool mountain air. At this time of the morning Styles would usually walk Bear to the park so that he could have a run before being cooped up in the office all day. She grabbed her coat and headed to the door. This morning they would have company. As she headed along the passageway toward his apartment, the elevator grinded to a halt and the door slid open. She stopped mid-stride as Carter and Zorro stepped into the passageway. "Morning, are you going for a walk?"

"Yeah." Carter ran a hand through his blond-streaked hair and pushed on his Stetson. "I was just dropping by to collect Styles along the way." He gave her a long considering stare as they walked toward Styles' apartment. "I figured you'd be snuggled up in bed for at least another hour."

Beth flicked him a glance as she knocked on the door. "You don't know me at all, do you? If the weather were a little warmer, I'd be out running by now. It loosens me up some before I go down to the gym to work out with Styles." She turned to look at him. "It looks like a beautiful spring day and I just couldn't resist a walk in the park before work."

The door to the apartment opened and Bear bounced out and did the doggy walk-around with Zorro, who totally ignored him. She looked up as Styles came out pulling on his gloves. "Hi, Beth." He smiled. "The moment I saw the blue sky, I just knew you'd be waiting out here for me." He nodded at Carter. "We might as well drop by TJ's for breakfast. He opens at six and we'll be through by then."

"Sure." Carter turned back to the elevator and punched the button. "I'll grab takeout for Jo. She likes her sleep and I know she'll want to speak to her daughter before she heads out for work this morning."

Steam escaped from their lips as they headed along Main toward the park, and underfoot, ice still crunched on small patches of water on the sidewalk. The wind had died down this morning and only a light but cool breeze brushed Beth's cheeks as she walked beside them. The men beside her strode along, their long legs eating up the distance with ease, and Beth pulled on Styles' sleeve. "If I'd wanted a run, I'd have dressed different-ly." She coughed as an icy breath seared her heated lungs in a bolt of pain.

"Sorry." Styles shortened his stride. "I like to keep moving when it's cold in the mornings and the dogs are anxious to get into the park. I gather you would have worked on your laptop all night, so I'm surprised to see you up so early." He walked back-ward to look at her. "Did you manage to create our fake identities?"

Frowning, Beth stared at him. "You'll end up walking into a street light or falling down a ditch if you don't turn around." She waited for him to fall into step beside her. "Yeah, I've created some absolutely foolproof documentation and backgrounds for the four of us. In case we make a mistake writing our names, I've stuck as close to our normal names as possible without being obvious. Carter and I are Betty and Tim Carson. You and Jo are Steve and June Simons. I followed Carter's suggestion about being a cattle baron. That worked well, as one of the safe houses you suggested is a large ranch that currently runs cattle."

"I like it." Carter grinned and swung open the gate to the park, standing to one side to allow the dogs to pass into the massive area.

"And what story do you have for me?" Styles followed them through the gate and closed it behind him.

Beth had enjoyed creating Styles' background and tried hard not to smile as she stared at the dogs tearing around like lunatics. "You're a businessman on the wrong side of the law." She turned to smile at him. "I made you the owner of a few seedy establishments, since closed. I'll give you a rundown before you do your thing." She looked at Carter. "Same with you, but as I'll be with you, I can cover for you if anything goes wrong."

"I'm still not clear why you prefer to do this with Carter and not with me, your partner." Styles tipped back his Stetson and peered at her. "Do I really look as if I would be involved in a pedophile ring?"

Seeing a flash of anger cross his eyes, Beth shook her head. "No, of course not, but then if we could recognize them by face value, they wouldn't be walking around free, would they? Unfortunately, they come in all shapes and sizes and various occupations, from the lowest paid to the highest." She lifted her chin and held his gaze. "It's nothing personal, it's just that since I've known Carter he has this smooth easy way of talking to people. When we get to the adoption agency, he has to come over as extremely rich and very sincere in wanting a baby, particularly a newborn. I honestly think he's the best person for the job and that's no reflection on your skills."

"Makes sense, I guess." Styles frowned and shook his head slowly. "I've faced greater challenges."

They followed the dogs down toward a wooded area and watched them disappear into the trees. As they reached the perimeter of the park, a black SUV stopped at the curb and four men dressed in SWAT gear jumped out. Before Beth could register what was happening, they'd leapt over the fence and were on them in seconds. At once, Beth reached for her weapon only to find it missing. In her rush to meet Styles, she'd left it hanging on the back of the chair by the front door. A heavy body rammed into her, and they tumbled to the ground. Pain from her sore ribs shot through her, stealing her breath. She rolled, and bringing up her elbow, smashed it into the man's throat. She lifted her knees and gripped her legs around his waist and squeezed. As he gagged and choked above her, she tried to fend off punches.

It was the same as before, a silent attack, no guns. These men considered themselves to be skilled enough to take them down, but Styles had taught her to fight dirty. Screaming a war cry, she jerked forward, headbutting the man's nose, and heard a satisfying crack. His blood sprayed her face, but she hadn't beaten him. When his hands went to her throat and squeezed, she reacted without a second thought and jammed both thumbs into his eyes. Her attacker let out a long scream, and his hands dropped from her bruised throat to defend his sight. Bunching her fists, she punched him hard under both kidneys. The effect was immediate. He howled in pain and tried to roll away. She unclasped her legs and pushed him from her. Up on her knees, she stared at him curled up in a ball sobbing. He wasn't going anywhere. All around her grunts and thuds broke the quiet morning as Styles and Carter defended themselves.

The men they'd sent this time were lacking skills and more like street brawlers than the martial arts experts who had broken into the motel. They didn't stand a chance. They had expected to take down three FBI agents and ended up facing a serial killer and two ex-military specialists. From the bulges under their coats, Carter and Styles were carrying their sidearms, plus they carried KA-BAR knives on their belts. They didn't need her help; they were handling the three men with less effort than a morning workout. She stood slowly, searching her pocket for a tissue to wipe the blood from her face and keeping one eye on her captor when two streaks flashed from the forest. The two combat-trained K-9s attacked at once. She held her breath as Zorro's open snarling mouth closed around one man's leg and Bear threw himself at the third man, his sharp teeth locked around one arm.

In that second, Styles hit the second man, attacking him with an uppercut that sent him flying backward and sprawling motionless on the grass. Beth gaped in horror as the man in Bear's grasp drew a knife, the sharp blade sparkling in the sunlight. Beth ran toward him. "Knife."

A shot rang out, so loud Beth fell and rolled to the ground. She turned as Bear dragged at the motionless man's arm and gasped. The ground was visible through the hole in his chest, tall pieces of wheatgrass sticking out of the bloody mess as if they belonged there. She turned her head as Carter swept the second leg from his attacker and the man fell on the ground.

"Get that dog off me." The whites of the man's eyes showed in his absolute terror.

Beth's gaze moved to Carter. As if he had all the time in the world, Carter drew his weapon and aimed it at the man.

"Ask me real nice." Carter's mouth twitched up at the corners. "My gun has a hair trigger. It would be a shame if my finger slipped. Look around you. I have two FBI witnesses to say you drew a weapon on me."

"Please call off your dog." The man's face twisted in agony.

"With me." Carter waited for Zorro to come to his side. He flipped out his phone and stared at Beth for a few seconds and then nodded. "Morning, Cash. We have a few men for you to arrest. We'll need Nate too. Someone jumped us in the park. One dead, three injured. Once you've arrested them, I'll call County to come by and get them." He disconnected and stared at their prisoners. "There you go. Duty of care satisfied."

"Who sent you?" Styles had the man who had attacked Beth by the collar and was giving him a shake. The man whimpered. "You figure she can hit hard? You've gotten off easy. If I'd hit you, I'd have driven your nose out the back of your head."

The conscious men said nothing, just looked at each other as if seeking support. Beth moved closer and found Bear at her side, looking from her to Styles. She patted the dog's head. "Good boy."

"It's been a time since either of these dogs have seen action." Styles rubbed Bear's ears. "They never forget."

Head thumping and aching all over, Beth crouched near the man who'd attacked Carter. She'd noticed he'd led the attack and must be the leader. "Look, you might just as well make it easy on yourself and give us information." She leaned in conspiratorially and lowered her voice. "We know Doc is involved. He sent you to take us down, didn't he?"

The man clung to his damaged leg and glared at her. Like the others, he refused to name anyone, but she'd seen a flash of recognition in the man's eyes at the name of the doctor. "Have you ever heard the expression *why come to a gunfight with a knife*? Surely you must have known that we would be armed? Did Doc tell you to do that to make it a nice quiet death for us?"

"If I talk to you, he'll sell my kids into slavery." The man's voice was so low, she almost missed it.

Leaning closer, she met his gaze. "We could've killed you in self-defense, but we spared your lives. If what you say is true, we can put you into witness protection for your testimony against the doctor. Your family will be safe."

"No, they won't." The man shook his head. "We failed. It's already too late." He lifted his dark gaze to her. "You have no idea who you're dealing with, have you? We're dead and you will be soon. Nothing can stop him."

## THIRTY-EIGHT

Styles and Carter assisted Cash with the three men, getting them cuffed and safely into the back seat of the sheriff's vehicle. Dr. Nate Mace had bandaged the eyes of the man who'd attacked Beth and suggested he be taken with the others to County for further treatment. They'd agreed to remain with the dead body with Nate for the ambulance to arrive. The body would be transported to the local hospital morgue. Carter would go with Cash. Styles turned to Carter as he pulled open the passenger door to Cash's vehicle. "Zorro won't fit in there as well."

"He'll wait here until I return." Carter gave him a long look. "Don't try and move him. He only takes orders from me, and occasionally Deputy Dave Kane out of Black Rock Falls. This is why he's a patrol dog. I raised him from a pup, trained him in detecting explosives, and he came with me and passed all the requirements to join the SEALs. Problem is he won't eat or do anything else unless I give him the command. So if by chance I get hit by a meteorite on my way back from the sheriff's office, call Dave Kane, or Zorro will wait here for me until he dies."

Styles frowned. "Okay. Thanks for the heads-up." He

turned and walked to where Beth was standing irritably as Nate checked out her throat. "Are you okay?"

"Yeah, I'm fine." Beth's voice sounded raspy and her neck was a mixture of red and blue patches. Blood splattered her face, but had missed her hair, thanks to her blue woolen cap. She met his gaze. "There's going to be a ton of paperwork again to explain why you discharged your weapon."

Styles took a packet of wipes Nate handed him with a meaningful stare and shrugged. "It's part of the job and this time Carter is going to report the incident to the director. He took a ton of crime scene images. I don't believe we'll have a problem. It was self-defense." He held up the wipes. "Do you mind if I wipe the blood from your face?"

"Thanks." Beth's gaze fixed on his face. "That's very thoughtful of you."

He went to work but Beth had this way of looking at him with a mixture of gratitude alternating with waves of fear. How often had she been offered kindness only to be hurt? He could still see the frightened child inside sometimes. Right now, she was fighting a battle between the frightened child and the grown woman. He must find a way to make her trust him. If it took baby steps, so be it. She was worth it. "It's not so bad. I'll have you good as new in a few seconds."

"I feel so dirty." Beth took a handful of wipes, removed her gloves, and rubbed them all over her hands. "I can smell blood."

With care, Styles removed the blood and then pulled off her hat. "It's gone now. Most of it was caught by your hat." He tossed the wipes and hat into a garbage can alongside the fence and searched his pockets. "Here, wear this." He handed her his black woolen hat. "One thing about these hats: they fit every-one, well, except little kids, I guess."

"Thanks. I feel so much better." Beth pulled the hat down over her ears and her gaze moved past him. "Ah, there's the ambulance."

"I'll follow the ambulance and complete the paperwork." Nate collected his bag and straightened. "The ME will need to be contacted. I'll call Dr. Wolfe. I'll contact you when I know he's coming. No doubt he'll want to speak to all of you."

Styles nodded. "Thanks. I appreciate your help, Nate."

"Seems to me the FBI is similar to delivering babies." Nate chuckled. "I usually get a call at dawn or in the middle of the night." He gave them a wave and went to meet the paramedics.

"So we wait for Carter?" Beth indicated to Zorro. "We can't just walk away and leave him here."

Styles turned to look at the Doberman, sitting straight, ears erect, watching the road. He wore a thick padded coat but every so often he shivered. He looked at Bear. His thick pelt kept him snug under his waterproof FBI jacket. "We'll go and stand with him. He looks freezing." They walked closer, but Zorro was having none of it, and when they got six feet away from him a low growl rumbled from his chest. He might as well have had a warning sign hanging around his neck. Styles flicked a glance at Beth. "Ah, maybe we'll wait here." He looked toward Main. "Here he comes now."

As Carter crossed the road, he let out a piercing whistle and Zorro took off, leaping the fence and tearing along the sidewalk. Styles raised both eyebrows. "I didn't know he could jump. I guess this means we can get breakfast."

"You're not disturbed about blowing a hole in that guy's chest?" Beth stared at him as he wiped his leather gloves with wipes.

Shaking his head, Styles tossed the wipes into the garbage and opened the gate. "Nope, he was going to kill Bear, and Bear was carrying out a legal duty in the manner he was trained to do. He was restraining the man from attacking me. Hurting him was a felony." He shrugged. "I was aiming for the arm with the knife but he moved." He gave her a long look. "I was dealing with two assailants at the same time and could have legally shot both of them for attacking a federal officer." He blew out a long breath. "I figure we all showed restraint in an attempt on our lives."

"Oh, I'm not complaining, not at all." Beth fell into step beside him as they headed toward Carter. "It's that you rarely draw your weapon. I noticed Carter is much the same. He likes to fight." She shrugged. "I stupidly left my weapon behind this morning. I figure there's a first time for everything, but I'd have drawn my weapon."

Styles nodded, wondering if she'd have shot her assailant. She had the right as a federal agent and as a local citizen if she believed her life was in danger, and there was little doubt the man had tried to kill them, but he didn't believe they'd counted on Carter or Beth being with him. He looked at Beth. "That was an attack on me again." He shook his head slowly. "I need to change my routine but it's difficult. When Bear needs to pee, I can't expect him to cross his legs for hours while I play it safe. It's never been a problem before. We must be getting close to the kingpin. The problem is, we don't know who it is, do we? I mean not for sure."

"If we had a name, it would make life easier." Beth blew out a steamy breath.

They met up with Carter and walked to TJ's Bar and Grill. After ordering breakfast of hotcakes, maple syrup, and bacon, they sat in a booth at the back away from everyone. The restaurant was surprisingly busy for breakfast. Truck drivers staying over at the local motel dropped by for a good meal and takeout before they left on their journeys. Miners in for the weekend appeared bleary-eyed from a night out at the saloons. Styles looked at Carter. "After this attack, I figure we're getting close. Beth believes it's the doctor, but we only have circumstantial evidence at best against him. His house was clean, apart from the signs he had a young girl living there."

"Yeah, Jo checked that out and he apparently adopted a kid

some years back, but she'd be older." Carter grimaced. "Unless when he moves around he recycles them. If he is who we believe, it's more than a possibility." He shrugged. "Unless we catch him with a girl, we don't have a case against him strong enough." He looked at Beth. "What do you need to make a case against him stick?"

"His laptop or whatever he's using to access the dark web. It would be the evidence we need to prove he's involved." Beth's brow creased into a frown. "Finding him and Shoebridge is a priority. We go with the plan and see what happens. Once I have the information from the doctor's laptop, finding all the players involved will be easy. It will take careful planning to infiltrate and bring down the entire ring, but the FBI specializes in doing just that and all they need is someone to open the right door."

Anger shimmered under the surface as Styles envisioned someone else taking down Shoebridge. He shot a glance at Beth. "I want Shoebridge. Before you hand over the case, we need to bring him down and the doctor."

"You got it." She gave him a slow smile. "I figure I'm becoming a bad influence on you, Styles."

# THIRTY-NINE

Back at the office, Beth stared out of the window. With the chaos erupting around her, the mountains and river offered her peace. The beauty of the pine forests and majestic snowcapped peaks surrounded her and washed away all her fears and doubts. Ahead, she faced a confronting time, decisions needed to be made on the fly. She needed the chance to take down the doctor and destroy his ring of destruction. With three FBI agents working the case alongside her, opportunity would be in short supply. Failing or being discovered as the Tarot Killer wasn't an option. Victims needed her to find them justice. The eye-for-an-eye, life-for-a-life idea worked for her just fine. She recalled researching that ideal, just to see if her internal justice system was flawed, and discovered, apart from being in the Bible, it went right back to the Mesopotamian Empire in the eighteenth century BC. The idea that it wasn't part of a deluded psychopathic mind, rather a compromise to control her urges, calmed her. Her father's face flashed across her mind, and she thrust it back into the darkness. *I'll never be like you.*

"Beth." Carter walked toward her, a concerned look on his face. "Everything okay?"

Blinking away images, Beth nodded. "Yeah, I'm fine, just taking a few minutes looking at the view to center myself. What do you need?"

"We have an appointment this afternoon at four with the adoption agency. I need you to transfer funds." He held out a piece of paper. "These are the account details."

Concerned, Beth took the note and stared at him. "You made the appointments from here? They'll be able to trace the call."

"No way." Carter smiled around his toothpick. "Kalo did something to our phones, ours and everyone at Black Rock Falls, so they can't be traced. It's all good. Do you want me to get the same protection for you and Styles? He can do an update remotely."

Beth stared at him. "You mean, not even he can trace the caller ID?"

"Nope, he designed the update himself. He's great at things like that and it's passed every type of scrutiny and hackers to date. He keeps it updated as well." Carter shrugged. "He's just a call away."

If no one could trace her calls, she would have no need to use a burner ever again. Wanting to know more, she moved closer. "The FBI can trace our phones for our protection, I mean, using the GPS in the phone, right? If they can, so can a hacker. They might not know your name, but when it comes up you're in the FBI field office in Rattlesnake Creek, it's going to send up a red flag, especially as they've tried twice to kill us in the last two days."

"Ah, yeah." Carter grinned again. "He thought of that, so we can just turn it off and on. It's like an app. Look, I'll switch it off and call you." He pulled out his phone and changed the settings.

Beth answered the call and his caller ID popped up on her screen. She traced his whereabouts, and it gave his location on a map as a red throbbing spot. "Okay, disconnect and activate the app." She waited for him to make the changes and on her screen his call came up as a private number. She frowned and held up a finger. "One second." She tried to find him on the phone and nothing came up, so she went to her computer. "Don't disconnect. I'll see if I can find you." She tried everything she knew but his phone was completely secure. She stood and went back to him. "This is perfect. You sure Kalo will share it with us?"

"I'm sure." Carter disconnected and deactivated the app. "Try and run my number on your computer again. You'll find me now. It works. The kid is a genius." He shrugged. "Just remember to activate the app when you're not undercover. The director would have kittens if he knew we were masking our phones."

The idea intrigued Beth. It was like an incredible gift. No more worrying about being traced or anyone knowing her whereabouts or who she called. No suspicious burners hanging around for her to worry about. She smiled at him. "Call him. I want this app yesterday."

"Yeah, me too." Styles leaned against a filing cabinet, grinning at her. "When I go fishing, I don't want to be disturbed, and Beth likes to disappear so much she leaves her phone behind on her downtime. This way is much safer. Beth, if you get into trouble, deactivate the app and I can come and find you."

"I'll call Kalo and then we need to get organized." Carter looked at Beth. "We'll fly into Helena. We'll leave the choppers at the airport and there's a bird we can use waiting for us."

Beth frowned. "Won't someone notice two FBI choppers arriving? I figure it's too dangerous."

"So did I, but they come and go into Helena all the time." Carter frowned. "I've arranged an unmarked chopper for us to travel to the ranch. No one will see us when we arrive, even if they knew about it being an FBI safe house, which they won't. It's in a remote area and very secure."

"I have a meeting with the adoption agency as well, but ours is tomorrow morning at ten." Jo smiled. "It seems the older kids, as in ten to twelve, are not in such high demand as babies right now. When I explained our mission in life as wanting to educate and find the best placings for our children, she seemed to understand my meaning. The woman transferred me to another person, and she wanted referrals. Those names you gave me worked like a charm. They dropped the legitimate-business act and got straight down to work. I must admit being given a Sunday appointment was unusual, but they seemed very keen to see us." She smiled. "Then she asked for a ten-thousand-dollar deposit just for a meeting to discuss our options." She looked at Beth. "Now where are we getting the ten grand?"

Beth smiled. "Leave that and the clothes to me. I'll need to raid a few closets to get the clothes we'll need for you and Styles. Jo, feel free to take what you need from my closets. I still have a ton of things from when I lived in DC and we're the same size. I'll go and see TJ and Matt. Between them, we should get the look we need."

"Thanks, I appreciate it." Jo smiled. "I just packed the necessities for a week here."

"I'm good." Styles gave her a smile. "I have Sunday go-to meeting clothes in my closet. I'll dress slick and I have a selection of dress boots as well if Carter needs them."

"Great, well, do that first. It will save time if you have clothes for Carter as well." She glanced at her watch. "When will we need to leave, Carter? I assume we're all traveling to the ranch together?"

"Yeah, be ready by noon. We'll fly to the airport in Helena. We'll need both choppers just in case we get split up and anything unexpected happens." Carter indicated toward Styles.

"I'll go with Styles and sort the clothing and then we'll do the preflight checks. Can you arrange supplies, Jo? I don't know how long we'll be away. Two or three days maybe?"

"Sure." Jo nodded. "How do you plan on tracking the doctor if you get to meet him?"

"I have a number of tracking devices we can use." Styles folded his arms across his chest. "Tiny, we could drop one into his coat pocket, into his bag if he has one with him, and I figure most doctors carry bags of one description or another."

Being able to pick pockets went both ways and Beth could place the tracker. She smiled at Styles. "I can do that. I'm very good at sleight of hand." She shrugged. "Just get me in the same room as him, and I'll get the job done."

*Leave me alone long enough with him, and I'll cut his throat.* Beth looked away as her dark side fought its way to the surface. She had seen what the doctor was capable of doing, delved into his darkest secrets. He was a monster and if it meant she risked her own freedom, she'd take him down once and for all. It would be worth it.

"You okay, Beth?" Styles cleared his throat. "I know it will be difficult coming face-to-face with an animal like him."

Trying to act nonchalant, when her heart was hammering in her chest, Beth lifted her gaze, hoping she appeared normal and not like some crazed lunatic. She nodded. "I'm fine. He's just another monster we need to take down. We've faced much worse. This time he's dealing with adults, not defenseless kids."

"Okay." Styles straightened. "Let's get to work."

# FORTY

Beth enjoyed the scenery as they flew to the ranch in Helena. They followed the mountain range for some time and the way the trees seemed to walk up the side of the mountains intrigued her. The sky stretched out in an endless sea of blue with the odd puffy white clouds on the horizon. A multitude of rivers meandered throughout, like shimmering snakes crawling toward each small town along the way. Herds of elk were making their way through the forests to the green pastures on the lowlands. Tall wheatgrass moved in a sea of golden green. The tops moving like waves on the ocean as the chopper went overhead. They spooked a herd of bison and it took off in a brown arrow in the middle of the grass, throwing up a cloud of dust behind them. At the beginning of their journey, she'd walked toward Carter's chopper and received a very strange look from Styles. Unable to interpret his sudden change of mood, she'd turned on her heel and walked back to him, making a joke about heading to the wrong chopper. She'd noticed him relax as he grabbed her bags and placed them in the back of his chopper before he settled Bear. It seemed that Styles took the fact that they were partners very seriously. She believed she should say something and considered her words very seriously. She adjusted her headset. "It's going to be very strange working with Carter." She smiled at Styles. "You're used to my idiosyncrasies. He might just believe I'm batshit crazy."

"I personally figure it's like leaving matches and sticks of dynamite with a child." Styles flicked her a glance. "They call me a maverick because I use my hands rather than shoot people. Carter always appears to be laid-back and easygoing, but in truth he's as sharp as a whip." He turned his attention back to flying the chopper. "He knows you can be a little impulsive at times, but so can he. Having you together facing danger alone isn't something I'd advise."

Concerned, Beth stared at him. "You really believe we're irresponsible? That's a little harsh."

"Carter is with Jo because she's a calming influence on him." Styles shrugged. "It's worked and he's a better agent for working alongside her. You're the opposite. Heck, you even encourage me to take crazy risks." He snorted. "Okay, they've worked fine so far, but you must admit we've come a little too close at times. We've skated round the rules more often than I would like to admit." He flicked her a glance. "Like now. This is an unsanctioned investigation. No one knows we're here. If it all goes to hell, we don't have backup in place. We're literally on our own."

Shaking her head, Beth raised both eyebrows and stared at him. "We've literally been on our own since I arrived in Rattlesnake Creek. This is the first actual mission we've gone on with the Snakeskin Gully team. Loosen up, Styles, it's all good. We'll catch these guys and put them away for a long, long time."

"I hope you're right." Styles landed the chopper at the Helena airport behind Carter's bird. "There's no more time to think it over. It's game on." He looked at a chopper parked a short distance away. "That's our ride to the ranch. Nice and inconspicuous. We'll be able to drop our things and drive into Helena for the meetings."

Beth gathered her things as the chopper propellers slowed to a halt. She climbed out and took her bag from Styles. "Are you two going to argue over who is the pilot?"

"Nope." Styles pushed on his hat and smiled. "I've been to the ranch before, so I was the natural choice. You'll feel safer with me piloting, Carter takes risks."

Beth frowned. "I heard it was the opposite. You're the crazy one."

"Only when I need to be." Styles led Bear to the other chopper. "We'll dump our things and I'll do a preflight while Carter does the paperwork. There's coffee inside. Do you remember where to go?"

Beth nodded. "Yeah, are you taking a break before you leave?"

"Only while our choppers are being refueled." Styles walked away to speak to Carter.

Beth headed toward Jo. "I guess we're on our own."

"Yeah, there's nothing for us to do here." She looked around. "Restrooms?"

Beth led the way inside. "Yeah, over there. I'll get coffee and sandwiches. I figure it's going to be a long afternoon."

---

They arrived at the ranch an hour later. Beth was surprised to see the place deserted. She turned to Styles. "Who cares for the cattle?"

"They'd be here on agistment." Styles stared at the sky for a second. "Ah, I forget you're a city girl. The cattle are turned out here to fend for themselves. There is water in the river and plenty of food and shelter. They don't need daily tending. The owners would ride by to check on them or move them from pasture to pasture over the course of the year. I'd say they're owned by a neighboring ranch and they likely pay for the privilege. I have no idea."

Beth frowned. "You mentioned transport?" She turned to stare at him. "Supplies?"

"We have supplies enough for a week." Styles dragged bags out of the back of the chopper with Carter. "The vehicles are always ready. This is an FBI safe house, so all the essentials are here. We just brought fresh food because we know you'd prefer fresh milk on your cereal rather than powdered and fresh fruit and vegetables, is all."

Beth headed inside, trailing her suitcases behind her, wheels rumbling across the polished wooden floors. The house smelled of stale air, as if it had been locked up for a long time. She walked along the passageway and peered into each bedroom and picked one with a dressing table and mirror. She would need a decent mirror with lighting to complete her disguise before she went to the adoption agency with Carter. After the attempted murder in the park, she'd taken everything she'd need to disguise him as well. If they were recognized by anyone from the pedophile ring, their chances of discovering the identity of the doctor would be over. She'd created their identities, used deepfakes to create the photo IDs and everything they needed to convince anyone who looked that they were legitimate.

The bedroom had two beds, which made life easier for her as she didn't bother unpacking, rather just laying the clothes she needed across the bed and setting up her disguises on the dressing table. Once she was done, she walked into the kitchen to meet the others. "This is a good setup, with plenty of room, and each bedroom has its own bathroom, which makes life a lot easier."

"Yeah, and the refrigerator runs all year round." Carter was packing the shelves with food from a cooler. He handed Styles a bottle of beer with a smile. "Well stocked with beer and wine as well. I wasn't expecting that luxury from the FBI."

"I've stayed here before." Styles filled the coffee pot and ground beans from a packet he'd purchased in town. "We have about an hour before you need to leave." He looked at Beth. "How long do you need to fix your disguises?"

Beth stacked cans into a cabinet. "Not long."

"You should get ready now." Jo took the can from her hand. "You don't know what the roads are like between here and Helena. "You don't want to miss your appointment. We can finish up here." She gave her a long look as if reading her mind. "Have you gotten your story straight? I've been questioning Carter all the way here."

Having played so many parts in her lifetime, Beth had confidence she could convince a horse to drink sand, but Jo might be another matter. The feeling Jo knew something wasn't quite right about her always shimmered on the surface and it made her wary. In times like this, she usually had her psychopath charm to fall back on, but with Jo it might be a red flag. She just shrugged. "Of course I'm a little nervous. I wouldn't be normal if I weren't and that might be a good thing. I believe couples would be nervous going to an adoption agency." She smiled. "Don't worry about me, I spent a good part of my early years with the FBI being an undercover agent. This will be a walk in a park in comparison to some of the roles I've had to play in the past."

"She's good." Styles dropped another box of food on the counter. "In San Francisco she had to dress as an underage sex worker. She knocked on my door at the hotel and I didn't recognize her and sent her away."

"I'd like to have seen that." Carter shut the refrigerator door and grinned at her. "Did he run a mile?"

Beth chuckled. "Something like that. He wouldn't be seen

with me in the hotel." She sniggered. "He has his reputation to uphold."

"Why don't the two of you get ready to leave. Time is a-wasting." Styles waved them away. "And we'll leave the dogs behind. They're a dead giveaway."

"Copy that." Carter headed along the hallway with Zorro at his heels.

# FORTY-ONE

Excitement thrummed through Beth as Carter pulled the white SUV to the curb outside the discreet entrance to the Big Hearts Adoption Agency. She glanced over at him. The blond hair had remained but she'd added a mustache and long sideburns. She'd given him brown contacts to cover his distinctive emerald-green eyes. He looked natural, with the black Stetson, a collared shirt, well-tailored black jeans, a sports jacket, and black boots polished to a high shine. She stuck to the new boots she'd purchased recently, her best jeans, a brand-name shirt, and a fitted leather jacket with a belt. She wore a dark brown short-hair wig, brown contacts, and had enhanced her features with makeup. She'd placed her mother's plain wedding band on her finger, but had added an expensive gold bracelet and earrings.

"Ready?" Carter took a wedding band from his inside pocket and slipped it onto his finger. He shook his head slowly. "This belongs to Styles. I gather he told you about his ex-wife. I'm wondering why he kept it. I'd have tossed it down a drain."

Beth recalled the hurt in Styles' eyes when he told her about his wife. "Maybe deep down he still cares for her?"

"I very much doubt that." Carter turned in his seat to look at her. "I know you don't like people touching you, but if we're going to convince these people we're a loving couple, I'll need to hold your hand. Maybe even hug you." He raised one blond eyebrow. "You're not gonna freak out if I do, are you?"

Wondering what Styles had said about her, Beth shook her head. "No, I'll be fine. I'm not sure what Styles has told you about me."

"Nothing, only that you don't appreciate being touched." Carter held up both hands. "He doesn't gossip about anyone. He's not like that and neither am I."

Gathering her courage, Beth met his gaze. "My father is a serial killer. I guess you already know that, but what you don't know is that I was abused constantly in foster care. This is why I so want to bust this pedophile ring wide open. Personally, I'd like to see all of them dead, but jail will suit me fine."

"Oh, Lord." Carter whistled and shook his head. "I'm so sorry." He gave her a long look. "We'll get them." He thought for a beat. "You know, Jo was a great help to me. I was off the grid suffering from PTSD. I'd lost touch with people and she dragged me back and set me to work. If you ever need to talk to someone, she's great."

A shiver went down Beth's spine at the thought. "No, I'm good. Wolfe has offered to chat with me and I have Nate as well. Both are covered by patient-doctor privilege, so anything I want to say won't get back to the director."

"Trust me." Carter chuckled. "There's nothing you could ever say to me that would get back to the director. Man, I've flown so close to the fire myself I'm surprised I'm still working." He glanced at his watch. "Time to go. We don't want to be tardy."

.  .  .

The Big Hearts Adoption Agency was a clean, almost hospital-like building. After stopping at the front counter, they were escorted to an office. Inside, they were introduced to Marybeth Hadley.

"Betty and Tim Carson." Ms. Hadley waved them to a seat in front of her desk. "It's good to meet you." She tapped away on her computer. "The initial funds have arrived, thank you, and you'll be happy to know your credentials check out."

They went through a grilling and handled it with ease. Carter was as smooth as silk and was winning over Ms. Hadley.

"That's all we need. You are the perfect fit for our babies." She smiled, showing a line of expensive porcelain veneers. "We can't be too careful when young lives are at stake." She looked from one to the other. "I can see you're a special case. We have provisions in place for people like you."

"Maybe you need to explain?" Carter leaned forward.

"There is a way to cut through the red tape, but it's expensive." Ms. Hadley folded her arms on the desk and smiled. "It's our way of getting our babies into the best families."

"How fast can you move things along, for the right price?" Carter smiled. "You can see how anxious my wife is to have a baby."

"I can make it happen before the end of the week." Ms. Hadley beamed at Beth.

A shimmer of rage slid through Beth and she swallowed hard. "That's good to know. Do you have a baby expected in the next week or so?"

"Indeed we do." Ms. Hadley beamed at her. "Twins are due, but we don't mind splitting them up."

"We'll take them." Carter took Beth's hand and squeezed. "You'd like that wouldn't you, darlin'?" He looked at Ms. Hadley. "Price is no option whatsoever, as long as our names are on those babies." He nodded slowly. "We can do a Bitcoin transfer to your wallet today if need be."

"Okay." Ms. Hadley consulted her computer and then wrote a figure on a piece of paper and slid it to Carter. "This is our fee. Everything is included, all the legal paperwork as well. You'll just need to sign the paperwork and the judge will do the rest."

"That's fine." Carter took the note, looked at it, shrugged, and dropped it into his pocket.

Beth leaned forward. "I need to speak to the doctor who will deliver the twins. I want to hear it from his mouth that they'll be fit and healthy." She took a tissue from her purse and dabbed at her eyes. "I lost all my babies, you see. I can't go through that again." She looked at Carter. "Make that part of the deal, Tim. Pay them what they want, but do this for me."

"I'm sure that can be arranged for you. Can you be back in town tomorrow morning? I know it's Sunday, but the doctor is in town right now." Ms. Hadley smiled.

"That's not a problem." Carter nodded. "We need to make this happen as soon as possible."

"As luck would have it, the doctor is due here first thing in the morning for a meeting at ten." Ms. Hadley tapped away on her computer. "I can make an appointment for eleven? His fee will be one hundred thousand in advance. Can you arrange payment by then?"

"That's fine." Carter smiled. "Although, I'm no fool. I'll pay you half the agreed amount for the adoption of the babies tomorrow—if my wife likes what the doctor has to say—and the other half when the papers are signed."

"Agreed." Ms. Hadley stood. "I'll make the arrangements. Drop by again at eleven in the morning and the doctor will see you."

Excitement slithered through Beth and she looked at Ms. Hadley. "What is his name?"

"Dr. Clint Brewer." Ms. Hadley smiled. "Out of Rainbow. It's a small mining town. He just set up practice there, but he's been working with us for years. He's a great doctor. You'll love him."

*Oh, I'll love him to death.* Beth smiled. "Thanks."

# FORTY-TWO

## SUNDAY

*Helena*

Back at the ranch, Beth had worked the previous evening hacking every local hotel and motel's computers for lists of bookings until she'd found Dr. Clint Brewer. He'd booked two nights and was in room number twelve in a hotel right in the center of town. Surprisingly she'd slipped into an easy working relationship with Carter. He guarded his past, which intrigued her because she'd read his file and knew about his PTSD and time off the grid. To her, he appeared laid-back and relaxed most times. He loved his work and was a dedicated agent. Instinct told her he'd report her in a second if he discovered her hidden identity.

At the kitchen table, with Styles one side of her and Carter the other, they discussed tactics. Jo had fixed breakfast and they were lingering over coffee. She turned to Carter. "We know the doctor will be leaving the hotel to go to the Big Hearts Adoption Agency to arrive for his appointment at ten. So if we stake out the hotel, we'll know what vehicle he drives and you can attach one of your trackers."

"How are we gonna know it's him?" Carter raised both eyebrows. "It's a big city."

Beth had considered this and smiled. "Nothing has come back from Wolfe yet, but we do have what Ginny told Sheriff Alton. He's in his fifties, balding, and fat and likely carrying a bag, briefcase, or something similar."

"We should have eyes on him the moment he leaves the hotel. If possible, we'll get photos." Carter added cream and sugar to his cup and stirred slowly. "I'll get a tracker on his vehicle. The moment he goes near it."

"The thing is, we don't know if his vehicle is a rental. He could fly away to parts unknown and we'll lose him again." Styles looked at Beth. "I figure it's essential that you get a tracker into his bag when you go see him."

Mind working overtime, Beth nodded. "I'll do my best." She checked her watch. "You'll need to leave soon to get to your appointment early and can't risk being seen with us."

"You have a point." Styles gave her a long look. "You'll be in disguise as well, and he might notice you too."

Beth shook her head. "No, he won't. I'll wait to put on my wig before our appointment. I'll look different with blonde hair. He won't take a second glance at me."

"Okay, I'll grab my things." Styles stood. "Ready, Jo?"

"Yeah." Jo smiled at Beth. "He won't slip away from us, Beth. I have a tracker with me as well to drop into his bag if I can. Styles can distract him."

"Just don't get caught." Carter frowned. "If he discovers a tracker, he'll shut down everything."

"I won't." Jo followed Styles to the front door, grabbing her coat on the way.

Beth finished her coffee and placed her cup in the dishwasher. All night she'd tossed and turned, making plans and then dismissing them. She must get to the doctor and remove him from the equation. Once he was dead, there'd be no need for search warrants. His property would be open for them to legally peruse. She'd have full access to his files, but not his patients, although she doubted he'd have a list already. She'd make sure their confidentiality was preserved. The rest, his links to the dark web, would lead her to Shoebridge, the one she considered to be his second in command, and hopefully, Shiloh Weeks.

The network of monsters would crumble, each section removed from the ring by the FBI, but first she needed to take out the doctor. Cutting the head off the snake was her only option. Arrest and a long time in custody before trial would see his ring moved into oblivion, and left to continue with another monster in his place. His people would be scrambling to take over the empire. Setting up a plan and making it work would be difficult under the scrutiny of three special agents, but she'd been in worse situations. The false bottom in her FX bag would supply everything she needed for a swift and fatal encounter. Determination strengthened her spine and she straightened with conviction. She'd make it work, whatever the outcome, she must stop this monster.

"It's been good getting to know you, Beth." Carter rinsed his plate and added it to the dishwasher. "When this is all over, we should all go out and let our hair down."

Surprised, Beth looked at him. "Yeah, well letting our hair down in Rattlesnake Creek is dinner and a game of pool at TJ's Bar and Grill." She chuckled. "I hear Snakeskin Gully isn't much better and has tumbleweeds rolling up Main."

"Ah, I forget you're a city girl." Carter grinned. "TJ's is fine dining where I come from and a night drinking beer and playing pool would be my idea of bliss." He closed his eyes and sighed. "Talking Jo into coming would be difficult. She's a mom and, with Jaime at home, she rarely takes any time for herself."

Beth headed for the door and pulled on her coat. She turned to look at Carter. The brown contacts made him look so different. "That's a shame. I'm good to go. My wig is in my bag along with your mustache. Don't forget your other hat."

"It's in the truck." Carter pulled on his coat, pushed on his old brown Stetson, and followed her out the door. "I'll wear my old hat until we go see the doctor."

Beth climbed into the truck. "That sounds like a plan."

After driving for half an hour, they arrived in Helena and easily found the hotel. They parked a ways away, where they could make out people coming and going. The streets were relatively quiet. Still being so cold and kind of between seasons, tourists were fewer at this time of the year. It was two hours before the doctor's appointment with Jo and Styles. Beth yawned and Carter tossed a toothpick in his mouth and slid down in his seat.

Beth waited for ten minutes and then groaned, clutching her belly. At once Carter looked at her and she shrugged apologetically. "Sorry, it's cramps. Just what I need right now and two weeks early." She peered out of the window. "I need to find a convenience store and a restroom."

"There's one down there, same side as the hotel." Carter frowned. "That diner will have a restroom. Do you want to head there, and I'll grab what you need and bring it to you?"

Touched by his consideration, she shook her head. "No, you might miss the doctor and that's our priority right now. I'll be fine."

"Do you figure it was caused by that animal trying to kill you yesterday?" Carter frowned. "Maybe you need to see Nate for a checkup?"

Beth reached for the door handle. "I'm okay but I must go. Now. I'll be back as soon as I'm able." She hurried along the street checking her watch. Time was moving way too fast.

# FORTY-THREE

Once inside the convenience store, Beth purchased a packet of feminine products and a pair of panties. She might need proof she'd actually purchased them. After pushing them into her pocket, she dashed out of the door and into the diner. It was reasonably busy serving breakfast and she slipped through the dining area to the restrooms and then to the back door. She dragged it open and wedged it with one foot to examine the mechanism. It would lock when she left. After searching her pockets for the small roll of tape she always carried for similar situations, she placed a strip over the mechanism. The door now shut but didn't lock. She slipped outside and moved along the alleyway. It serviced the hotel as well and she soon located the open kitchen door. Cigarette butts surrounded the entrance, and the dumpsters filled the space with the stench of rotting food. She peered inside the back door of the hotel, finding a small space with coats, hats, boots, and a large chalkboard with names scribbled against times. Ahead, she could see a pair of swing doors with glass circles giving a view of a busy kitchen. To her right was a passageway with room service carts, piled high with clean linen on the top and on one side a holder for dirty linen.

She checked her watch, Carter would have seen her leave the convenience store with a paper sack, and she doubted he'd be timing her, or mention what had happened to anyone. The front counter was empty and she made out brass signs with numbers written on them. After pulling on latex gloves from a box on the cart, she grabbed the handle and pushed it down the passageway toward room twelve. She needed a fast-acting and silent weapon, and during a recent undercover mission, Nate had given her the idea by supplying her with what looked like an EpiPen but filled with a tranquilizer. Inside her pocket, she'd obtained something incredibly lethal from the dark web. A similar device that delivered a dose of anesthetic drugs combined with enough fentanyl to kill a horse. It was small, effective, and easily dropped down a drain. Her hand closed around it, flipping off the lid. She knocked on the door. "House-keeping."

The door opened and the man who hurt kids stood in front of her in a waft of cigars and sweat. He didn't resemble a monster. He looked like someone's dad. Out of shape, with a greasy combover and a large belly hanging over the belt of his pants. She sucked in a breath waiting for a reaction. He should recognize her if he had her on his hit list, and she hadn't even removed her coat. "I was just heading home and the manager told me to make up your room."

"Are you sure?" The doctor looked at her and frowned. "Can it wait? I'll be leaving soon." He held the door open, with one hand exposing one side of a clean blue shirt, with the cuffs rolled up to the elbows.

Shaking her head, Beth stepped forward. Excitement at facing him at last made her heart race. Time was running out and she needed to act now. Forcing her words to remain calm, she lifted her chin. "No, I need to get home to my kids. I can make up this room now or leave it if you prefer."

It was as if recognition hit him in a flash. He stared at her and took two steps back. In her time in the FBI, she'd come to the conclusion pedophiles were usually cowards. His face drained of color and his eyes flicked to the shoulder holster on the bedside table. The handle of a Glock poked out. She wanted to smile as the psychopath in her rose. Time slowed to the seconds between heartbeats as he telegraphed his next move and turned, diving onto the bed. As one of his pudgy hands reached for the weapon, heart pounding, Beth dived after him, landing heavily on his back. The doctor's hand closed around the gun, and with his superior weight, he tossed her off him like a ragdoll, almost knocking the device from her hand. He was more agile than she'd imagined, and in the next second the gun came up and he straddled her, his huge belly crushing her bruised ribs. One knee pinned her left hand. She couldn't risk losing the dispenser. It was her only escape. Remaining still, she glared at him. "Get off me."

"I'm going to kill you, Agent Katz, and no one will ever know what happened to you." The doctor's lips stretched wide between flushed cheeks, covered in spider veins. "Coming here without backup was a big mistake."

Gasping for air, Beth glared at him. "I'm never alone. You won't be either when you're burning in hell."

"Not me." He chuckled. "My cleanup crew will have you swimming with the fish by tonight. One prick of a needle and you'll be asleep, but I'll make sure they wake you before they toss you into the middle of the lake." He pressed down hard on her, pushing the air from her lungs. "It's dark in that lake and you'll try to hold your breath, but death is inevitable. I wish I could be there to watch you die."

As he reached for a pillow to push over her face, to no doubt use to render her unconscious, Beth pressed the dispenser onto the bare flesh of his arm and pushed her thumb down hard on the plunger.

"What have you done?" He stared at his arm, mouth hanging open and eyes wide in disbelief.

Laughing, Beth watched the anesthetic take effect. "That's for all the forgotten girls, you sick creep."

In seconds, his eyes rolled up in his head and the Glock slipped from his hand as he fell sideways hitting the floor with a thump. Beth scrambled from the bed, and panic gripped her. Her hair or DNA could be all over the bottom sheet. Without a second thought, she dragged the sheet from the bed. Carefully opening the door to check outside, she tossed it in with the other soiled bed linen on the cart. She grabbed a clean sheet and spread it over the bed, and then tossed the rest of the bed linen on top. She considered returning the Glock to the holster and then dismissed the idea. Taking a few precious seconds, she stared down at him. He wasn't breathing. His reign of terror was over. She placed a tarot card on his chest, walked out of the door, and pushed the cart along the empty passageway to join the others. As she turned into the hallway, she heard voices. Someone had heard the doctor hit the floor. She needed to get away right now.

Panting, Beth checked her watch, it had taken longer than expected. Carter could be out searching for her by now. She needed an excuse for taking so long. She ran out the door, tossed her gloves into the dumpster, and dropped the device down a drain before hotfooting it back to the diner. She removed the tape from the door and peered into the eating area expecting to see him waiting for her. She went to the counter and ordered coffee and donuts. The service was fast and, gathering her purchases, she headed for the door just as it opened and Carter walked inside. A wave of unease gripped her as she stopped walking and stared at him. "Is there a problem?"

"Nope, not now." He inclined his head and looked at her. "I

was concerned you'd fainted or something. You look flushed. Anything I can get you? Do you need to sit down?"

*Flushed? That's the look of exhilaration from removing a child predator from existence.* Beth handed him the donuts and they headed for the truck. "Thanks, but no, I'm okay and I've never fainted. I needed to tidy up some and then wait for the coffee. After being out here in the cold it was hot in there and the service in the diner was very slow." Trying to find the appropriate thing to say, she gave him a sideways stare. "I really appreciate you checking up on me. You might be right about speaking to Nate. This hasn't happened before."

"Yeah, go and see Nate. It's not really in my field of expertise." Carter peered into the paper sack, obviously needing to change the subject. "Mmm, my favorite—donuts. No wonder Styles likes having you around. Jo brings me celery sticks and carrots."

# FORTY-FOUR

The feeling something was wrong crawled over Styles as the time for their appointment went over by thirty minutes. Finally, they were waved into an office by someone who introduced herself as Ms. Hadley. Had someone recognized Beth and Carter yesterday? He sat on the straight-back wooden chair and stared at the woman. "Our appointment is with the doctor."

"Yes, I'm aware of your needs, but unfortunately we haven't been able to locate the doctor this morning." Ms. Hadley opened her hands. "He may have been called out on an urgent case. He does deliver babies all over many counties. We had twins due anytime and maybe he got the call." She raised both eyebrows. "Nevertheless, as we mentioned previously, you come highly recommended and we'll be happy to fulfill your needs. I've made a few calls, and as you will imagine, we'll need time to organize the amount you require, but once we've established a line of, let's say, communication, we'll be able to keep up with demand."

Styles nodded. This was getting them no closer to finding the doctor or Shoebridge. "I need four minimum. I'm sure you understand."

"I made a few calls, and obtaining that number will take time. We can possibly have two ready for you in a couple of days." Ms. Hadley frowned. "Our agent will need to collect them and arrange delivery." She looked at him. "If you have a suitable van, we can sedate them for transport and arrange a pickup point? You do understand, this office is our only point of contact for now. We don't occupy the same offices for more than a few months. However, once you are on our books, we'll contact you for delivery."

"If not today, when can we speak to the doctor?" Jo leaned forward in her chair. "We'll need to view them before we take them. Our clients are very particular. I'm sure you understand. The price isn't an option. Can the doctor arrange for us to view a video of at least one of them?"

"Very well." Ms. Hadley nodded. "We'll reschedule the meeting for the morning, same time. I'm sure the doctor will be available."

Styles stood. "Okay, we'll see you tomorrow."

As they left the building, he called Beth. "The doc is a no-show. Have you seen him?"

*"Nope, but I've had time to check the car rental computers and he has a license under the name he's using. We located his rental close by the hotel and it hasn't moved. Carter just received a call rescheduling our appointment, saying the doctor was on a call. As far as we can determine, no one matching his description has left the hotel since we arrived."*

Styles thought for a beat and headed for the truck. "I'll get Jo to call him at the hotel. If he doesn't pick up, I figure we need to do a welfare check on the doctor. He's a person of interest. If something has happened to him or he's slipped the net, we need to know now and stop wasting our time."

*"You'll blow the mission. What if he's holed up with a woman?"* Carter's voice came through the speaker.

*"Maybe ask the local cops?"* Beth cleared her throat. *"Then we won't be compromised."*

Nodding, Styles pulled their FBI creds from the glovebox and handed Jo's to her. "We'll go and speak to the local cops. I'll tell them we're on a case and his name came up. I'll make some excuse for them to do a welfare check."

*"Okay."* Beth blew out a sigh. *"We'll be waiting here, although I might dash across to the diner to use the restroom and grab us some coffee. It's cold sitting here. I just hope the doctor hasn't discovered our plans and skipped town again."*

Styles locked the truck and leaned against it. "Me too. If he has, we're back to square one."

The moment Styles and Jo walked into the police station, they got the "why is the FBI here?" stink eye. It always amused him how when they needed assistance the hostility was minimal, but not every cop appreciated them and this was certainly the case in this instance. He made his request and received puzzled stares as if they'd suddenly grown two heads. "We could go in and bang on his door, but we've had him under surveillance and don't want to blow our cover."

"It's not that." The cop at the counter scratched his graying hair and went to his computer. "That name just came in on a 911 call. The paramedics are on their way. One of the guests heard a loud noise, like someone hitting the floor, and called the manager. They went to check on everyone in the area and Dr. Brewer wasn't answering his door. When the manager went to check on him, he was on the floor unconscious. They called 911 and the paramedics are on their way. That's all I know. I'd say he'll be heading for the hospital anytime now."

Styles nodded and slapped the desk. "Thanks." He looked at Jo. "We need to get there now."

The moment they stepped outside, he called Carter. "The doctor is down, paramedics on their way. You'll need to get there now. We're right behind you."

*"The paramedics are heading into the hotel."* A door slammed and Carter's boots tapped on the sidewalk. *"We're on our way."*

Styles disconnected and he followed Jo to the truck. They jumped inside and in five minutes they were outside the hotel. "If he's had a coronary or worse, there goes our lead to Shoebridge."

"Maybe not." Jo ran along beside him. "If he has his laptop with him, we can take it if he's dead. It will cut through a ton of red tape."

Styles ran up the steps and into the hotel. "I love your optimism." He moved into the foyer and went to the counter. "FBI. What room is Dr. Brewer in?" He held up his cred pack.

"Room twelve." The woman pointed. "The paramedics have just arrived and so have two other agents." She frowned. "Is Dr. Brewer someone important?"

"No." Jo glanced at Styles. "Just a friend."

Walking fast, Styles headed along the passageway, to find Beth just inside the door to a spacious room. Beside her, Carter was holding his badge out to the paramedics and raising his voice.

"Okay, you've established the man is dead, now step back." Carter glared at them. "This is a crime scene. Go and wait outside or you'll destroy evidence."

"How do you know it's a crime scene?" One of the paramedics stood hands on hips, nose to nose with him. "There's no evidence of injury."

Styles shouldered his way into the room. "If Agent Carter says it's a homicide, you better believe him." He held up his creds. "Agent Styles. Now please wait outside. As soon as we've taken photographs and called this in, we'll speak to you again."

The paramedics walked out, mumbling to each other, and Jo came inside.

"I grabbed these from a housekeeping cart." She held out gloves. "What happened here?"

"I'm not sure but he's dead—and look here." Carter pointed to the floor bedside the body. "If I'm not mistaken, that's a tarot card." He looked at Styles. "The thing is, no one went in or came out of the hotel since we arrived. People walked past and someone came out to pick up a pile of newspapers from the steps. That's all. If the Tarot Killer is here, he's still in the building."

Shaking his head, Styles stared at the card and then took out his phone and took photographs. "I very much doubt it. I'm assuming this place has a back door and a fire escape. He'll be long gone." He looked at Beth. "Glove up and we'll search the room for evidence."

"Chances are if the Tarot Killer murdered him, he took his laptop." Beth pulled on gloves with a snap. "I hear he strips Bitcoins from his victims. He'd need the laptop to find the wallets." She went to the bed and tossed around the sheets and then bent to look under it. "Touchdown." She dragged out a laptop and smiled. "Now we can find Shoebridge. He'll have all his contacts hidden right here."

"What else do you need?" Carter smiled at her.

"Any personal property he has with him." Beth dropped the laptop on the bed and opened it. "Oh good, fingerprint protected." She picked it up and went to the body placing it beside him. "Right index finger, for sure."

Always amazed by her businesslike attitude around corpses, Styles watched as she pressed Brewer's finger to the reader and the laptop opened. "Good, now move away. I need shots of the room."

"I'll remove the password protection." Beth went to work. "Done. Okay, did anyone find anything else we can use?"

"Yeah, wallet and keys to the rental on the bedside table." Jo opened drawers. "Ah good, plastic laundry bags. We can use them for evidence." She dropped the keys and wallet inside.

"It looks like he tried to shoot the Tarot Killer." Carter bent to pick up a Glock. "This might have the killer's prints on it." He examined the gun. "Interesting. He didn't rack the slide." He dropped it into the bag Jo held out for him.

Styles looked around the room and frowned. "It looks to me as if they struggled on the bed. It was a mess when we arrived. Brewer tried to fight back but was overpowered. He didn't get the chance to shoot." He bent to look at the body. "There's no signs of injury. Maybe he had a heart attack."

"The Tarot Killer must be a big guy to take him on. He must weigh three hundred pounds and then some." Beth bent to look at Brewer. "I wonder how many lives he ruined or ended. Serial rapist and killer."

Styles looked at her. "You'll need to prove it, Beth." He looked at Carter. "Who do you want in on this?"

"Right now, I figure this is so sensitive we play our cards close to the vest." Carter turned away from the closet and looked at him. "This man is a respected doctor who might have had a heart attack, but we need a forensic sweep done on this room. There is only one person we can trust and that's Wolfe."

The Black Rock Falls medical examiner was licensed to practice across the entire state, and he'd be the one to call. "Okay, call him and explain what we need." He thought for a beat. "Without elaborating, I'll call the director and inform him we have a suspected Tarot Killer murder in Helena and we're on the case. It will cover us for any problems down the line."

"What reason will you give him for why we're all here?" Beth straightened from bending over the laptop.

Shrugging, Styles met her gaze. "We're following up a lead Ginny gave me." He indicated toward Jo and Carter with his chin. "Jo and Carter were needed for surveillance, and it was too sensitive to bring in the local cops."

"Yeah." Carter grinned. "That works for me. I'll call Wolfe now. He headed into the bathroom and closed the door.

After making the calls, Styles spoke to the manager about opening the vacant room next door. "We'll need a place to wait for the medical examiner."

"Okay, that's fine." She handed him a key. "I'll keep everyone away from the rooms."

Styles tossed the key to Beth. "Get started on the laptop. We'll go and grab some takeout from the diner. It will be hours before Wolfe arrives."

"Okay." Beth moved to his side. "I'm not sorry he's dead. That man was pure evil."

Nodding, Styles looked into her brown eyes and blinked. "I wish you'd both remove those contacts. They're darn-right scary." He looked at Carter. "You both look so weird it's like I'm talking to strangers."

"I don't like wearing them, and I'll be happy to oblige." Carter grinned at him as they headed for the door.

As they waited for the takeout, Styles pulled Carter to one side. "How did you cope with Beth? She can be a little over the top at times."

"Fine." Carter frowned. "Don't be too hard on her today. I don't figure she's feeling well."

Rubbing the scar on his chin, Styles frowned. "She looks fine to me, a little flushed maybe, but as normal as Beth can be."

"Well, you need to make sure she sees Nate." Carter removed his hat and ran a hand through his hair. "She was squashed by that guy and it might have done some damage. The thing is, Beth is too stubborn to seek help. Has she always been like that?"

Nodding, Styles walked up to the counter to collect the bags. "Yeah, she's independent."

"So I see." Carter picked up the tray of to-go cups of coffee and followed him to the door. "Maybe it's because she'd never had anyone to care about her before now." He gave him a sideways glance. "She needs to know she's a valuable part of a team and we all have each other's backs. In case you've missed it, Beth is lonely and has trust issues. You could make that go away. I figure she's been hurt bad at one time. Like the rest of us, she's damaged goods. We need to bring her closer and make her fit, so she's got a group of friends around her."

Blowing out a sigh, Styles turned to him. "Trust me, that's easier said than done."

## FORTY-FIVE

As they waited for Wolfe to arrive to complete a forensic sweep of the scene and remove the body, Beth went to work. Carter had retrieved her laptop from the truck and she'd set up a video link to Kalo. She sent him links to anything interesting and they worked at searching the thousands of pathways the doctor had created on the dark web. With his laptop and her skill to open backdoors, she had one objective and that was to find Shoebridge. She had a hunch he'd have a code name, but which one? There were so many chat rooms, all created for the clients of a monster or the suppliers who moved children and young women around as commodities. In these chat rooms, they discussed topics that made her want to spew. She hurried past, running ideas to link the doctor to the second in command.

"*I have something.*" Kalo's voice made her start. "*A recurring codename in six different chat rooms, along with Rotcod, or the doctor: T-A-K-A.*"

"That sounds like 'take her.'" Styles stopped pacing and sat down beside her at the small table.

Beth punched the air and moved her fingers swiftly over the keyboard. Excitement thrummed through her as another chat room opened up before her eyes. "I've found their private chat room. I just needed that thread." She grinned at Kalo through the screen. "Man, you are a legend."

She cracked her knuckles and wiggled her fingers. After reading the messages, she could easily word her message to Shoebridge so he'd never know it wasn't from the doctor. She looked up from her screen and smiled. "They were going to sell Shoebridge's new girl, who we believe is Shiloh, and the doctor's new girl, but I'll convince him the doctor is sending two replacements. Here we go." She typed a message. "*My phone is out. I forgot to bring the darn charger. I have a delivery. I won't need your girl after all, or mine. Unless you want either of the new ones I'm sending. Your choice. The problem is I tried to explain where you live but the guy refuses to drive into the forest at night without a GPS coordinate. I'm stuck in Helena doing a deal. I know how to get to your place, but I need an address. You don't need to worry. He's one of us. They'll be delivered first thing Monday morning, but I'll need the address right away to set things up. We struck gold today. I've sold the twins for a fortune and we have an ongoing customer for the foster kids or any others we can obtain. I'll have the entire crew out searching for potential sales. Message me ASAP.*"

She turned to look at the others. "Now we wait. It might take him a time to get back online."

Twenty minutes dragged by. A knock came on the door. It was Wolfe. Beth stood to stretch her legs and hoped he hadn't found any of her DNA in the room. "Did you find anything interesting?"

"I'd say he died of a drug overdose." Wolfe's gray eyes moved over her face as if searching her mind. "Typical Tarot Killer MO. Small mark on left forearm, likely a needle stick injury. I'll need to determine what was used to kill him." He pulled a small bag from his pocket. "I found blonde hairs on the bed. Did you happen to go near the bed at all?"

Beth placed a hand to her mouth. "Oh, I'm sorry. I did toss the bed. I was searching for a laptop and lifted the mattress. I touched the bedding. It was in a mess all twisted up and the laptop was under the bed."

"Okay." Wolfe smiled. "I'll need a couple of your hairs for comparison. We don't want you blamed for murdering the doctor, do we?"

"It wouldn't stick anyway." Carter shrugged. "She wasn't out of my sight all day and with the three of us, miles from here, before that."

"That's good to know." Wolfe nodded. "But I still need those hairs." He reached a gloved hand toward her and plucked out a few strands. "Okay, I'm done here. I'll keep everything under wraps until you hunt down the other suspect. I don't file my reports until the autopsy and the drug tests are completed, so you'll have plenty of time to keep it legal."

Beth walked him to the door. "Thanks. We'll get this guy soon. I've already baited the hook."

"Good." Wolfe nodded. "Parents will sleep better knowing predators like Brewer are off the streets."

A shiver went down Beth's spine. "This one, yes indeed, but unfortunately, they're like cockroaches: You'll never kill them all at once and there's never just one. Search long enough and you'll always find a nest."

# FORTY-SIX

*Rainbow*

Heart pounding, Shiloh followed Callie from the cabin. It was a trial run. They couldn't risk leaving now in daylight. If Evan hunted them down, the underbrush hadn't regenerated enough regrowth to hide them. At night would be their best chance, regardless of the risk of wildlife. They'd worried about the cameras seeing them and spent hours searching each room for the tiny peepholes. They'd found them, opposite the bed and in the bathroom. It seemed Evan wasn't interested in what they did in other parts of the house. This made it easier for them to plan their escape and they'd waited until they heard the sound of a vehicle moving away. Without a clock they had no idea of the time and went on the intervals between meals. Each took turns listening with one ear pressed against the food hatch. The lock on the door had opened without a problem. It seemed that Callie was as experienced in cracking locks as she'd insisted and managed it easily with a bent fork.

Cold wind smacked at Shiloh's face and flashed across her eyes like needles the moment she stepped outside. The building where Evan kept them was at least warm, as long as they kept the fire going and he left a good supply of wood for them. "Why don't we offer to take Bonnie with us? She's trapped here just like we are and it won't be long before the doctor takes you away. You really don't want that. He's a horrible man. I can't imagine living with him. He stinks of cigars."

"They both do." Callie pressed her back to a tree and scanned ahead. "Do you figure Bonnie will tell on us if she sees us?"

Shrugging, Shiloh looked at her. "I don't know. She doesn't talk to us at all does she? I don't know what Evan does to her. Maybe he beats her? She acts like a frightened mouse."

"Hmm." Callie headed for the house, moving from one tree to the other. "All the reason to be running away with us." She turned as Shiloh moved to her side. "She must want to escape and she'd be able to find us supplies. If we plan to survive even one night, we'll need food and coats. He must have our coats inside the house. She'd know where everything is kept."

Stomach flip-flopping, Shiloh crept toward the back door and pressed against the wall. The cold from the logs seeped through her clothes and raised goosebumps on her arms. They'd only been outside for a few minutes and her teeth chattered like castanets. She placed one hand on the doorknob. The ice-cold metal bit into her flesh as she turned the knob. The door opened and she peered inside. The house smelled of boiled cabbage and cigars. One thing for sure, Bonnie wasn't a good cook. She boiled everything and created a meal they called a forever stew. From the taste, she kept the pot boiling day and night and just added things to it.

"Go inside, we need to grab a few things we can use." Callie moved through the door. "We need to speak to Bonnie. If she won't come with us, we'll leave right away, or she'll tell on us when Evan comes home."

Following her, Shiloh spotted her coat hanging on a peg in

the mudroom. She grabbed it and shrugged into it. "That's better. Is that your coat?" She pointed to a pink hoodie.

"Yeah, but I'll take the brown one." Bonnie took it down from the peg. "It will hide me better. It fits just fine." She pulled up the zipper. "Oh good, there are gloves in the pocket. "Now we need food and water. Maybe a backpack or something similar. Look around."

They found what they needed and filled two old and stained backpacks with anything useful but not too heavy. Shiloh heard footsteps and gripped Callie's arm. "Someone's coming."

They hid beside the washer as Bonnie walked into the kitchen and Shiloh gasped. To her dismay, Bonnie was carrying a chain that led to ankle manacles. Evan had chained her legs to prevent her from escaping when he was at work. Poor Bonnie needed to walk bent over to lift the chain so it didn't drag on the floor. Throwing caution to the wind, she stepped into the kitchen and startled Bonnie, who dropped the chain and one hand went to her mouth. Shiloh took a step toward her, hands outstretched. "Bonnie, don't be afraid. We need to get away from here, from Evan. He's evil. We're going to escape when Evan goes to sleep tonight. Come with us."

"You need to go now." Bonnie's eyes widened. "He's coming back before he goes to work. He's probably on his way. He only went to the doctor's cabin. He said he would be twenty minutes. He's angry. The doctor made him go to collect more beds. He's getting two more girls first thing in the morning. They'll be sharing with you."

Terrified, Shiloh gaped at her. "Okay, but we're leaving tonight and we'll need supplies. We need you to get them—and water and a first aid kit. Wear warm clothes. It's going to be freezing overnight."

"I'll get the supplies, but I'll stay here. I can't run in the chains and I'll slow you down." Bonnie pointed at her bruised ankles. "You go and get help. Send the cops."

"I can pick that lock, no worries." Callie smiled at her. "Just be ready to leave the moment Evan is asleep."

They headed for the door and in the distance Shiloh made out the sound of an engine. Panic twisted her stomach and she swallowed hard. "Run, we need to get back before he knows we're missing."

"One second." Callie was sifting through a tool kit open on the counter. She selected a few items and then smiled. "This will make things easier for picking locks and there's a pocketknife as well. We might need it."

Terrified, Shiloh grabbed her arm and dragged her out of the door. "We haven't got a second."

They took off, running back through the forest. Shiloh slowed to look behind her just as Evan's truck turned the corner. She ducked down and rolled in the grass. "He's coming."

# FORTY-SEVEN

Grinning, Beth punched the air when a response came into the chat room from Shoebridge. "He took the bait."

They'd been waiting patiently for over an hour, and she'd been on the brink of giving up. She scanned the page and then looked at Styles. "He's complaining that he's doing all the work. He mentions organizing auctions and distributing photographs to members as well as working night shift. He also says that he doesn't have any beds to take to the cabin where he's keeping the girls and will need more but he doesn't want to attract attention to himself by going into town to buy them. He suggests collecting them from the doctor's cabin." Beth looked away from the screen. "I assume it's closer to him than town."

"I figure you tell him that's fine. Go ahead pick up the extra beds he needs from the cabin." Styles met her gaze. "Maybe add how pleased he'll be with the new delivery and see what he says?"

Beth typed a suitable reply and they sat back and waited for Shoebridge to answer. She smiled. "He's going to get that done before work and he also mentioned that the auction that they had planned for the first of next month is going to be a money spinner. They have overseas and out-of-state interest. He suggests increasing the minimum bid as the demand is increasing by the day."

"Maybe tell him that they can discuss that when he sees him tomorrow." Jo leaned on the desk and looked at her. "Mention that he's late for his appointment so he has to go. You need to keep this conversation as short as possible before he discovers that you are not the doctor."

Nodding, Beth cut the conversation short. "I've added for him not to forget to send me the address for the delivery." She chuckled. "Here it is. We have the address. Kalo, can you give us a location, please?"

*"Yeah, I've got it."* Kalo smiled at them and a satellite map popped up on Beth's screen. *"It's in Rainbow, not far from Rattlesnake Creek. You could drive from there. If he works nights, maybe you'd have a better chance of checking out his place when he's out."*

As Styles and Carter wrote down the coordinates, Beth's mind moved into planning mode. She turned to Styles. "We need to move on this right away. How long will it take us to get home?"

"Some time." Styles pushed a notebook inside his jacket pocket. "We'll leave now for the ranch. Fly back to the Helena airport. Preflight checks will take time. Once we're back home, we'll change into tactical gear, night-vision goggles, and then drive to Rainbow and try and locate this guy's cabin." He looked at Carter. "I figure we'd get there around ten—if we can find his place in the dark."

"Yeah, it will take that long to get there." Carter chewed on a toothpick, frowning. "It would be faster if we took one of the choppers to Rainbow but then we'd announce our arrival."

"We'll drive." Styles rubbed the scar on his chin. "If we find any kids, we'll need to transport them back to town or

Rattlesnake Creek. We'll also need a suitable vehicle to transport Shoebridge or whatever his name is this week."

Beth had closed down her computer and thanked Kalo
during the discussion. She went to Styles' side. "You'll need
Cash and maybe bring Nate along as well in case anyone needs
medical attention."

"I don't figure we should risk Nate in a raid. If Shoebridge is
at home, things could get nasty." Styles frowned. "TJ would be
better and Cash can deputize him. Maybe have them as
backup? I'd really prefer if they watched the road in case Shoebridge slips past us."

Agreeing Beth nodded. "Yeah, that would work."

"We can discuss all this on the way." Carter pulled on his
coat and gloves and whistled to Zorro. "We'll meet you back at
the ranch." He looked at Beth. "I'll make sure the bag you left in
my truck is on the chopper."

Beth smiled at him. "Thanks." She turned to Styles. "I'm
good to go."

From the moment they stepped from the hotel, Beth noticed
a distinct change in Styles' demeanor. His shoulders had stiff-
ened and his mouth formed a straight line, as if he was trying to
prevent saying something to her. He drove like a man possessed,
weaving in and out of traffic and taking the narrow backroads to
the ranch at high speed. Agreed, Carter was nowhere in sight,
but Bear needed a potty break before they left and they had
fallen a little behind. "Is there a problem?"

"Nope." Styles didn't look at her and they slid around a
corner on a dirt road in a cloud of dust and loose gravel.

Gripping the side of her chair, Beth turned to look at him.
"Well, if you keep driving like a maniac, we'll never live to arrest
Shoebridge. I'm sure you want to see him brought to justice."

"I'd like to see him dead." Styles laughed but it wasn't
meant to be funny. "I'm having this inner turmoil. It's FBI agent
versus brother. One part of me wants to see him locked up for

life; the other part of me wants to beat him to death with my bare hands."

Relieved that he wasn't going to question her about the death of the doctor and why she had been so careless searching the room, she puffed out a sigh. It wasn't as if she could tell him. It had been her only chance to make an excuse for any latent DNA that Wolfe discovered after she'd killed the doctor. She turned in her seat to look at him. "If it helps any, I feel the same way, but Ginny isn't my sister. After seeing the images he had in his possession, there's no saving a man like that. There's no way he can be rehabilitated or whatever the do-gooders believe, and from the files I pulled from the doctor's laptop, the pair of them orchestrated an entire selection of horrific uses of a child. He should get the death penalty and so should a great deal of the men connected with them. They all have code names, but we can lay traps for them."

"How so?" Styles' shoulders relaxed as they headed into the ranch.

Beth smiled. "They would travel across the country to get to a kid. Many of them have been trapped by cops pretending to be kids online. If they believe they can get to them—the kids, I mean—they'll go to any lengths. Trapping them by, say, holding a live auction where they get to actually see the kids, which is something they do. We could round up fifty of them at one time. It all takes careful planning and held at a place they believe is safe. I'm sure we have people in the FBI capable of taking the entire ring down, piece by piece. The trick is making everyone believe that it's business as usual."

"Will you help coordinate that? I'm sure it will take a ton of people to keep something like this running." Styles stopped outside the ranch house and looked at her. "We'd need to involve all the countries this network has infiltrated. I know they have task forces for this type of thing." He shrugged. "I'm so glad you're an expert in cybercrime. This is way over my field of expertise."

Beth gathered her things. "You just concentrate on finding Shoebridge and saving Shiloh. Leave the tech part of it to me and Kalo."

"You got it." Styles slid from behind the wheel and opened the door for Bear. "I just hope he resists arrest."

# FORTY-EIGHT

Shiloh barely had time to stuff her coat behind the sofa before the door flew open and Evan filled the entrance. They'd made it to the door only minutes before he arrived. Trembling, she made herself look busy by adding more wood to the fire, but she could feel his eyes boring into her. She turned to look at him. He was looking at her strangely as if assessing her. With trembling legs, she straightened.

"Move the bookcase into the corner." Evan stared at her and then scanned the room. "Callie, get in here and move the bookcase. I need to set up two camp beds. You're getting roommates in the morning."

They rushed to do as he asked and heaved the bookcase along the wall. The moment they'd made a space, Evan dragged in two camp beds and dropped them onto the floor. He went outside and came back with a plastic bag. When he motioned her closer, Shiloh winced but, not wanting to cause trouble, went to stand before him. "That will be nice." She forced her lips to curl into a smile.

"You learn fast." Evan cupped her chin and turned her face

back and forth. "I like that about you. I might keep you. Although if the other girls are prettier, you'll be auctioned."

Shiloh frowned. "Auctioned? What is that?"

"That"—Evan dropped his hand—"is another word for money." He righted the cots and tossed the bag on them. "Sleeping bags. The girls won't be here for long. Callie will be leaving soon and then it's just you and me." He tousled her hair and then went to the door. "I'm late for work. I'll be by later. I only work a couple of hours tonight. Seeing as it's Saturday, most of the miners are in town letting their hair down." He chuckled. "Maybe I should bring a few home to meet you?"

Terrified, Shiloh backed away shaking her head.

"No? Okay." He walked out and locked the door, his laughter echoing behind him.

After he'd left, Shiloh stared at Callie. "Maybe we should leave when he goes to work? It will be easier in the forest now it's not full dark yet."

"How far do you figure we'll get in a couple of hours?" Callie frowned. "We don't know the forest or which way to go. He'll come by when he gets home and see we're missing. It's better to wait until he's asleep, then we'll have eight hours at least before we're missed."

Shiloh nodded. "Okay, but we'll get everything ready before we escape. We'll go to the house when he leaves for work and collect what we need. We can leave it in the forest and collect it along the way."

"Good idea." Callie smiled. "The moment we hear him leave I'll start on the lock."

They had everything set and waited for the sound of Evan's truck arriving home. He came to the door, unlocked it, and walked in. Shiloh could smell beer on his breath, and she took a step back when he came toward her. She gathered her wits and lifted her chin, frowning. She needed to say something to make him go back to the house. "You look so tired. Did they work you really hard today?"

"Yeah, I am tired, but not because of work, because Doc expects me to do all his chores as well." Evan ran a hand down his face. His nails were dirty and unkempt, his skin grubby. "I hope Bonnie has something nice for supper. I'll see you in the morning." He turned to go and neglected to lock the door behind him.

"He's been drinking." As usual, Callie's voice was just above a whisper. "He'll sleep well tonight."

Time dragged by and then they heard the familiar sound of Bonnie coming toward the cabin. The swish of her chained feet made a strange noise. They'd eaten supper. Why had she left the house? The key in the door turned and the door opened a crack. Keeping her voice low, Shiloh stepped away from the door. "What are you doing here?"

"He's asleep. Get these chains off me so we can get out of here." Bonnie waved them outside. "Hurry, just in case he wakes up." She waved a flashlight. "It's only small, but I found a new battery for it and I have a spare in my pocket."

"Okay." Callie bent and fiddled with the manacles and then held them up in triumph. "We'll get our coats."

Soon they were running along a dirt road into the dark forest, the small flashlight bobbing ahead of them. They'd been moving for a few minutes when they heard a roar from behind them. Evan had discovered them missing and was as mad as hell. His voice boomed through the forest, making wildlife scatter. The sound of a shotgun blasted, followed by more cursing. Terrified, Shiloh turned to the others. "He's going to kill us. We need to find a place to hide."

"There's not many thick bushes but follow me." Callie turned into the forest, winding through tree trunks, her tiny flashlight hardly visible in the tangle of trees.

A door slammed and an engine roared. Headlights lit up the

darkness as Evan's truck headed along the road straight for them. Panic gripped Shiloh. "He's coming."

Running after Callie with Bonnie close behind, terror had Shiloh by the throat and she gasped in each breath. Frightened of the dark, and with spiderwebs hanging down all over, created her worst nightmare. Underfoot, roots and dead vines littered the underbrush. She tripped and ran into trees. She could hardly make out Callie running ahead of her. Dead bushes reached out like long witch's nails to claw at her clothes and legs. Branches whipped across her face and tangled in her hair. Behind her she could hear Bonnie's labored breath and staggering footsteps. Powerful beams lit up the forest as Evan turned the corner and they were trapped in the headlights like deer. The truck screeched to a stop, a door slammed, and he ran toward them. His flashlight lighting up the forest with every step. Panting, Shiloh kept running, but Evan was faster and fitter than she'd believed possible. He came crashing through the forest like a bull elephant screaming his arrival.

Shiloh increased her pace, catching up to Callie. "Run faster."

"I see the river." Callie veered off to the left. "Come on, it will be easier to run along the sand."

Legs aching, Shiloh grasped the back of Callie's coat, as the terrain sloped down toward the glistening river not far ahead. Behind her, Evan was still yelling obscenities at them. A scream pierced the darkness. Evan had caught Bonnie and she was fighting for her life. Evan's flashlight beam moved erratically up and down. As Bonnie screamed, thuds echoed through the forest. "He's beating her with the flashlight. Change direction and run."

Nausea swam over Shiloh and she tugged at Callie's coat as they reached the river. "Turn off your flashlight. He won't be able to see us down here. There's enough moonlight for us to find our way in the dark along the riverbank. Head upstream.

That's the direction of the road. It must lead to a town eventually. Most towns out this way are by rivers."

"Okay." Callie slipped down the riverbank, climbing over boulders, and turned right.

Following, Shiloh tripped and fell, rolling down almost into the river. From the forest, the sound of Evan's bellowing was getting closer. She scrambled to her feet. Ahead, she made out Callie hiding behind a boulder and ran to her side. A wide bright beam hit the river and Shiloh made herself as small as possible. She cupped her hand to Callie's ear. "Don't make a sound. He's right above us."

# FORTY-NINE

After leaving Cash and TJ parked on the road to prevent Shoebridge from escaping, Beth followed behind Styles, Carter, and Jo on foot along a dirt road. The house where they expected to find the man they knew as Shoebridge was two hundred yards or so ahead. A scream echoed through the forest, sending an icy chill walking up her spine. She tapped her comm. "That must be one of the girls. Something is going down."

Beth's night-vision goggles made the forest glow an eerie green and her team resembled aliens from outer space with big green eyes. Styles and Carter dived into the forest with the dogs, and she followed with Jo close behind. When Styles' hand came up, they stopped running and went to his side. A lump lying between the trees looked like a body. In her earbud she could hear Styles' voice.

*"Keep to the trees. I'm going to see what that is across the trail."* Styles moved toward the lump and dropped to his knees. *"Female, approximately sixteen, head injuries but alive."*

The sound of someone yelling obscenities came on the wind. Beth tapped her comm. "There's someone up ahead running through the forest and yelling."

"*Yeah, I can hear him.*" Carter moved to her side, his voice loud in her comm. "*Stay here with the girl. We'll go after Shoebridge. It has to be him.*"

Shaking her head, Beth went to Styles' side. She bent and felt for a pulse. "Take off her backpack and roll her into the recovery position." She grabbed the backpack and placed it under the girl's head.

Beside her, Jo had removed her backpack and was kneeling beside her, pulling out a first aid kit. She turned to her. "Can you stay with her? Listen to that maniac. He's hunting someone. I bet it's Shiloh. We need to stop him. Will you call Cash? He'll get the paramedics rolling. They'll be a while."

"*Yeah, I'm fine and armed.*" Jo covered the girl with a foil blanket. "*Anyone who comes through that forest who isn't wearing an FBI jacket is going down.*"

Relieved, Beth stood and tugged at Styles' arm. "He's getting away. Let's get this SOB."

With a nod, Styles pushed his way through the forest, cutting a path. The pace of the men was frantic and Beth's ribs still ached. Sucking in freezing air didn't help, but she kept running and jumping over obstacles along the way. To her surprise, Bear ran along beside her as if he sensed her injuries and was watching out for her. Ahead, she made out a bright LED flashlight and Styles' voice came through her comm.

"*Carter, the missing girl must be ahead. The river is through those trees. Go around and see if you can come in upstream. She'll see your FBI jacket and know you're a friendly. We'll take down Shoebridge. The girl's safety is our priority.*"

"*Copy that.*" Carter ran parallel to the river, weaving in and out of trees.

Beth turned off her comm and pulled on Styles' arm. His big green luminous eyes turned slowly to look down at her. She lifted her chin. "Don't throw your life away on this scum, Styles."

Why she'd become Mother Teresa, she had no idea. She wanted the monster dead, but she figured Styles was a better person than she'd ever be. He needed to be on the right side of the law. If anyone was going to kill Shoebridge, it would be her. When he shrugged and took off running toward the screams of a madman, Beth ran after him. It was difficult to see the way ahead behind Styles' large frame, but the sound of the angry man was getting closer. Suddenly without warning, Styles took off running so fast Beth had no chance of keeping up with him.

As the river came into view, Styles flew through the air, tackling the man with the flashlight. They rolled across the ground. Bear's barks echoed through the forest along with thumps and punches. Tree branches cracked as both men struggled on the forest floor. She arrived and gasped as Shoebridge swung the flashlight down hard on Styles' head. The man rose slowly and came straight for Beth. Her hand went to her weapon.

*"Don't shoot him."* Styles' voice came through her comm as he staggered to his feet. *"I haven't finished with him yet."* He was on his feet running toward him.

The man was bigger than Beth had expected and she ducked behind a tree. As he ran past, she stuck out her boot and he crashed to the floor, the flashlight spilling from his hands. Styles was on him in seconds, dragging him up and tossing him into a tree. Beth ran toward him. "That's enough."

"Do you forget what he did to my sister?" Styles waited for the man to stagger to his feet and punched him in the stomach. "Men like you don't deserve to exist in our world."

"Sweet girl, your sister. She'll never tell you about me or my friends." Shoebridge grinned through bloody teeth. "You can't kill me, Mister FBI. I'm home free. You have nothing on me." He laughed. "You wanna fight me for her? I might be older than you, but I took you down. How you gonna live that down, Mister FBI?"

Shocked when Styles removed his jacket and unbuckled his holster, tossing them to one side, she stared at him.

"Hold these for me." Styles removed his goggles and handed them to her. "Keep out of the way. Don't draw down on him. Give me your word he's mine. I'm taking him in." He turned to Bear. "Stay."

Beth swallowed hard at the sight of his grim expression. She wished Carter was close by and the need to call him over was eating at her. She wanted to say something but stepped back beside Bear and placed the goggles next to a tree. In the dark, the men danced around each other trading blows. Styles had Shoebridge's measure and could have hurt him, but reason was slowly taking hold. His anger was ebbing, and he grabbed Shoebridge's arm, ready to cuff him, when the man pulled a knife. Styles twisted out of the way, lunged forward to grab Shoebridge's wrist, but tripped over an exposed tree root. She gasped in horror as he staggered back, smacking his head hard against a pine tree before sliding to the ground. Panic gripped her. Styles wasn't getting up and Shoebridge was advancing, knife raised. In a split-second decision, rather than draw her weapon, Beth bent and picked up a broken branch and ran into the fray. "Hey, you."

As Shoebridge turned to look at her, she swung the log like a baseball bat, striking him across the front of his skull. The impact shot up Beth's arms and she dropped the log. Suddenly afraid, she stared at him, one hand going to her weapon. Shoebridge stood very still and then fell straight back like a felled tree, crashing into the dead underbrush and not moving. Bear whined and shot past her to lick his owner's face and Beth ran to Styles. Her partner was staring straight ahead into the darkness. She sighed with relief when he moaned and pushed Bear away. "Are you okay?" She indicated to Shoebridge. "He's down."

"Just a lump. I tripped when I avoided the knife and hit my

head. I figure I blacked out for a time." He staggered to his feet, rubbing the back of his head, and went with her to look at Shoe-bridge. The front of the man's head was embedded with bark fragments. He felt for a pulse and then turned slowly to her. "He's dead." He shook his head and found the log she'd used. It had been torn from a tree during the fight. "It looks like he broke this branch clean off the tree when he ran into it."

Trembling, Beth stared at him. Could the incorruptible Styles be covering for her or had he really blacked out? Either was possible and she sure as heck wouldn't be confessing. She shrugged. "Best get your weapon and jacket before Carter gets back. He doesn't need to know, you two got into a fight." She gave him a long look. "I witnessed him resisting arrest and threatening you with a knife before he ran into that branch."

They both stopped talking when Carter's voice came through their comms.

*"Do you copy? I've found two very terrified girls. Have you found Shoebridge?"* Carter sounded annoyed.

Beth tapped her comm. "Yeah, we've been kind of busy. We tried to take him down alive, but he fought like a bear."

*"You've been offline for a time. Is he dead?"*

"Yeah." Styles rubbed his head and looked at a smear of blood on his hand. "He knocked me into a tree, took off, and then ran into a low branch. Killed him outright."

Beth looked at him. Not one trace of guile showed on his face. She stared at the ground, unable to believe her luck. Maybe Styles had blacked out, maybe not. She guessed she'd never know.

# EPILOGUE

## FRIDAY, WEEK TWO

*Rattlesnake Creek*

Sunshine spilled into the office forming a patch on the floor where Bear lay, legs up and belly exposed, enjoying the rays. Beth smiled at him. It was strange how much he had become part of her surrogate family. She yawned and stretched. It had been a very long and hard week poring over all the evidence they discovered. After a couple of days in the hospital in Black Rock Falls, Shiloh had been returned to her family. After treatment, Callie and Bonnie had joined Ava and Ginny at the Her Broken Wings Foundation women's refuge in Black Rock Falls. There they would receive extensive counseling. Likely, Bonnie would stay there until she was eighteen. In that time she would be rehabilitated and offered various opportunities to allow her to enter the world. Ginny continued to be in self-denial about everything that had happened, and although she had been deemed a fit mother, she would be under supervision for some time. It was hoped that with special care and training she would be able to rejoin society. It was difficult for Styles as he wanted to be there for her, but it would take time for her to accept him in her life again. The hunt for the whereabouts of Ginny's lost babies and all the other children involved could take years to complete as very few records had been discovered. For the FBI it would be an ongoing investigation. The news hadn't been welcomed by Styles, and it had taken Beth some time to explain the slow process of checking adoptions across the US within the vague timeframes Ginny had offered and by cross-matching DNA samples.

After the chase through the forest, Beth had dragged a reluctant Styles to see Nate, and the doctor had put three stitches into the cut in his head. During the debriefing, the fight and Beth's attack on Shoebridge hadn't been mentioned. She'd been free to get back to work and had joined forces with Kalo. After cross-referencing all the dark web information obtained from the laptops belonging to the doctor and Shoebridge, they'd discovered they'd caught the two men in the center of the pedophile ring. The men known as Shoebridge and Dr. Brewer had a cache of identities, all backed up with life stories and credentials. Beth had figured her stash of identities were second to none, but she'd been mistaken. A ton of work unraveling the pedophile ring lay ahead. It covered so many states and countries that the FBI needed to move like ghosts on the dark web to maintain the appearance that everything was business as usual. All the while moving in and dismantling various groups. It was going to be a long and arduous task, but in the last week forty members had been arrested and over seventy children rescued. Not one hint of the massive undertaking had leaked, and with Interpol involved as well, Beth was confident that not one of the doctor's members would walk free to hurt kids again.

She pushed both hands through her hair. If only child abuse ended with the doctor's demise, but it would spring up again somewhere else before too long like a deadly mold.

Although the dismantling of the doctor's organization was in the safe hands of many departments in the FBI, it still bothered her sleep at nights. She stood and went to Styles' desk. It was too early for lunch, but restlessness crawled over her. She needed a new case to clear her head, but nothing had come into the office. "I'm going down to the gym to hit a few balls, and then I might have an appetite for lunch."

"Good idea." Styles flipped a pen in his fingers, catching it and flipping it again. "The debriefing was tough, wasn't it? At one point I figured they'd be taking me away in handcuffs. After the autopsy report on Shoebridge, who by the way was wanted in three states under the name Charley Dodds, Wolfe's conclusion that it wasn't only the head injury that killed him, but internal bleeding from either a fall or the fight, almost had me suspended. The fact I'd sustained so many injuries trying to take him in alive was my saving grace."

Beth nodded. "I told the director you ordered me not to shoot as you wanted him alive to answer questions and that you both fought like dogs. I didn't mention anything about giving up your weapon to fight him man-to-man." She slid one hip onto the desk. "He questioned me about the Tarot Killer and how he'd slipped past me and Carter during our surveillance."

"What did you say?" Styles stood, removed his jacket, and hung it on the back of his chair.

Beth straightened. "I told him we watched a few people come and go but our main focus was trailing the doctor. The Tarot Killer is ambiguous. We had no positive ID of him, so how could we have recognized him going in and out of the hotel?" She shrugged. "I did mention that because the doctor was dead we were able to move faster on the trail of Shoebridge. When he died, it cut through the red tape, and later with Shoebridge's laptop we were able to infiltrate the entire network." She smiled at him. "He said we worked well together and got results. I figure he was pleased."

"So he should be." Styles led the way out of the office and

down the elevator to the gym. "I'll watch you and then we'll swap. I'll feed in the balls."

The baseball baffle net and pitching machine took up a good part of the footprint of the building. The other half was dedicated to a fully equipped gym. It had been part of the deal for Styles to work in the field office alone. Beth had discovered hitting balls calmed her dark side, and the joy of swinging the bat had become a passion of late. It kept her fit in body and mind.

After Styles loaded the machine and switched it on before standing outside to watch, she picked up a bat. It didn't take long to get into the swing and she missed very few balls. Sweat ran down her back and her mind relaxed. Beth had found her niche in life, and Snakeskin Gully was the home she'd been searching for. She craved to get back out to her cabin for a time, just to do nothing, or to plan her next revenge. The last ball came out of the machine and she smashed it with all her strength. The ball hit the bat and shimmering energy vibrated up her arms, bringing back vivid images of hitting Shoebridge. Outside the cage, Styles gave her a slow clap.

"Wow! Your timing and follow-through are powerful." Styles opened the cage and grinned at her. "I'm glad you're on my team. With a bat in your hand, you're darn-right dangerous."

# A LETTER FROM D.K. HOOD

Dear Readers,

Thank you so much for choosing *Forgotten Girls* and coming with me on another chilling Beth Katz crime thriller. If you'd like to keep up to date with all my latest releases, just sign up at the website link below. Your details will never be shared and you can unsubscribe at any time.

*www.bookouture.com/d-k-hood*

Here we are, on book four already and what an adventure it has been. Beth Katz is certainly a different type of special agent and it's been a pleasure giving you a deeper insight into what makes her tick.

I really appreciate all the wonderful comments and messages you've sent me during the writing of this novel. Writing can be an isolating business and I really enjoy hearing from readers, so feel free to ask me questions at any time. You can get in touch through social media or my webpage. I'll always reply. If you enjoyed my book, I would be very grateful if you could leave a review and recommend my book to your friends and family.

Thank you so much for your support.

D.K. Hood

# KEEP IN TOUCH WITH D.K. HOOD

www.dkhood.com

 facebook.com/dkhoodauthor
x.com/DKHood_Author

# ACKNOWLEDGMENTS

For my editor, Helen Jenner, for always being there when I need her. To the team behind every book I write. Those dedicated people who make sure the books are edited and presented in the best possible way are all listed at the end of the book under 'Publishing Team'. I really appreciate everything you all do for me.

Many thanks to my readers for their support and wonderful reviews, especially those who share promotional posts. It means so much to me when I see a post for one of my books shared by a reader.

A special mention to the bloggers who take the time to include reviews of my books on their blogs. Thank you.

## PUBLISHING TEAM

**Turning a manuscript into a book requires the efforts of many people. The publishing team at Bookouture would like to acknowledge everyone who contributed to this publication.**

### Audio
Alba Proko
Sinead O'Connor
Melissa Tran

### Commercial
Lauren Morrissette
Hannah Richmond
Imogen Allport

### Cover design
The Brewster Project

### Data and analysis
Mark Alder
Mohamed Bussuri

### Editorial
Helen Jenner
Ria Clare

Made in United States
Orlando, FL
26 July 2024

49573179R00161